# The Villain's Dance

BY THE SAME AUTHOR

*Tram 83*, 2015

Prix SGDL du premier roman, 2014

Etisalat Prize for Debut African Fiction, 2015

Nominated for the Man Booker International Prize, 2016

Internationaler Literaturpreis, 2017

Peter Rosegger Prize, 2018

*The River in the Belly*, 2021

# THE VILLAIN'S DANCE

Fiston Mwanza Mujila

Translated from the French
by Roland Glasser

DEEP VELLUM PUBLISHING
DALLAS, TEXAS

Deep Vellum Publishing
3000 Commerce St., Dallas, Texas 75226
deepvellum.org · @deepvellum

Deep Vellum is a 501c3 nonprofit literary arts organization
founded in 2013 with the mission to bring
the world into conversation through literature.

The publishers thank J.-P. Métailié and the Géode lab at the
University of Toulouse-Le Mirail for the map.
Originally published as *La danse du vilain* by Éditions Métailié in Paris, France, in 2020


FIRST EDITION, 2024

Support for this publication was provided in part by grants from the National Endowment for the Arts, the Texas Commission on the Arts, the City of Dallas Office of Arts & Culture, the Communities Foundation of Texas, and the George & Fay Young Foundation.

This work received support from the Cultural Services of the French Embassy in the United States through their publishing assistance program. This work received support for excellence in publication and translation from Albertine Translation, formerly Hemingway Grants, a program created by Villa Albertine.

LIBRARY OF CONGRESS CATALOGING-IN-PUBLICATION DATA

Names: Mwanza Mujila, Fiston, 1981- author. | Glasser, Roland, translator.
Title: The villain's dance / Fiston Mwanza Mujila ; translated from the French by Roland Glasser.
Other titles: Danse du vilain. English
Description: First edition. | Dallas, Texas : Deep Vellum Publishing, 2024.
Identifiers: LCCN 2023043598 (print) | LCCN 2023043599 (ebook) | ISBN 9781646051274 (trade paperback) | ISBN 9781646051281 (ebook)
Subjects: LCSH: Street children--Congo (Democratic Republic)--Lubumbashi--Fiction. | Congo (Democratic Republic)--Fiction. | LCGFT: Social problem fiction. | Novels.
Classification: LCC PQ3989.3.M94 D3613 2024 (print) | LCC PQ3989.3.M94 (ebook) | DDC 843/.92--dc23/eng/20230920
LC record available at https://lccn.loc.gov/2023043598
LC ebook record available at https://lccn.loc.gov/2023043599

ISBN (paperback) 978-1-64605-127-4 | ISBN (Ebook) 978-1-64605-128-1

Cover design by Jack Smyth

Interior layout and typesetting by KGT

PRINTED IN THE UNITED STATES OF AMERICA

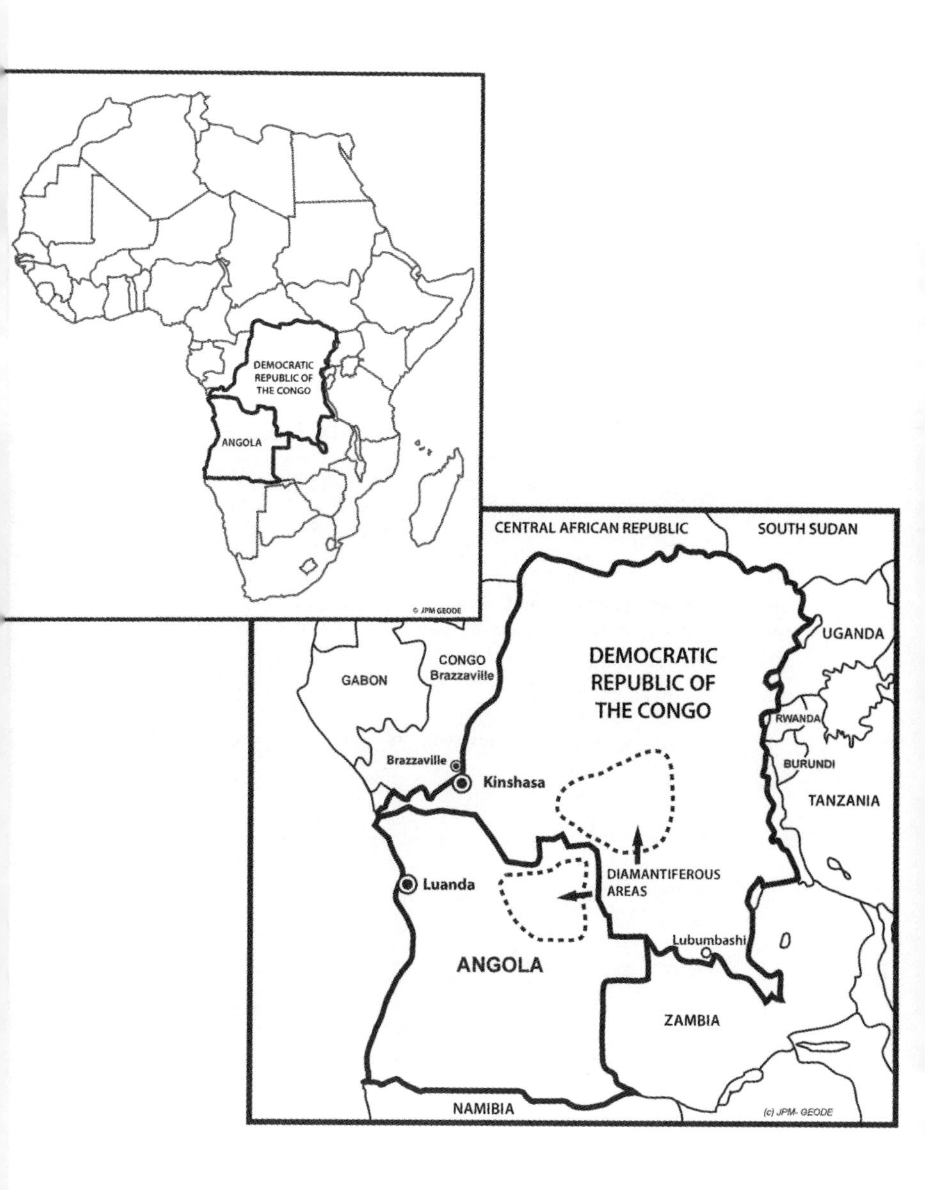
DEMOCRATIC
REPUBLIC OF
THE CONGO
ANGOLA
© JPM GEODE
CENTRAL AFRICAN REPUBLIC
SOUTH SUDAN
UGANDA
CONGO
Brazzaville
GABON
DEMOCRATIC
REPUBLIC OF
THE CONGO
RWANDA
BURUNDI
Brazzaville
Kinshasa
TANZANIA
DIAMANTIFEROUS
AREAS
Luanda
Lubumbashi
ANGOLA
ZAMBIA
NAMIBIA
(c) JPM- GEODE

1. The incendiary and outlandish life of Tshiamuena, nicknamed (posthumously and entirely appropriately) Madonna of the Cafunfo Mines—notwithstanding the jealously of certain diamond panners short on ambition, enthusiasm, and charisma.

The Madonna was not some little madam under the influence of alcohol and other beverages bereft of dosage instructions. She was no prophetess of misfortune and tall tales derived from some unknown gutter. Not even a vendor of dreams, questionable expectations, chimeras . . . well, you're quite cognizant of where such trinkets lead as they stream into your ears without cease. We were only too familiar with the petulant refrains of those curmudgeons who quibbled over such details. They rehashed the same remarks all day long as if there were fuck all else to do on this earth but poke fun at the Madonna—"Tshiamuena this, Tshiamuena that. Tshiamuena's got wings, big wings, and as soon as night falls, this witch takes off and flits about for miles and miles without a drop of kerosene, jinxing us from above and sabotaging any chance of finding diamonds in the otherworld." We'd heard it all! Pointless babbling, rumor-mongering, pure humbuggery; for when it came to Tshiamuena, all ears were pricked; everyone became a scientist, a university professor, a sociologist, a linguist, an ethnologist; each proffered their own two-bit philosophy to dissect her every word and deed. Even the most crestfallen rediscovered a taste for life, the necessary inspiration, the appropriate panache, the smooth words of a politician on the stump. Go hard on the drink if you will, but concocting poppycock just to sink a person (and an authority like the Madonna no less)—that beggars belief. How can people equipped with a cock, a belly, arms, legs, and a brain spend eight hours a day trying to hamstring someone? All the blame for the woes of tropical Africa they laid at her door: miscarriages, failed coups, wars, Emperor Bokassa's delusions of grandeur . . . They speculated without a break, concocted conspiracy theories, strived to detect relationships of cause and effect between the Madonna (blessed be her memory) and any reversal of fortune that befell the Zairian diaspora. And always (and ever still) those rumors of cannibalism. What a topsy-turvy world! The Madonna, a habitual witch with a fancy for flesh and fresh blood? Even if you detest an individual (for plausible reason) it is still insane to make them carry the can for each cave-in, bout of diarrhea, or act of mischief. They'd not even slept off their beer, polished their teeth, and zipped up their pants than they were opening their gobs to erratically gun down a living legend.

They made you want to puke, the whole greasy lot of them. Weirdest of all was that the scandalmongers proliferated in direct proportion to the quantity of energy and cash Tshiamuena expended in assisting the masses. Without going back as far as the Flood, you could spread gossip and tittle-tattle and tell tall tales, yet the truth would not budge by one iota: Tshiamuena was a grande dame, an exceptional being, a mother to many of us, a queen, a powerful woman. She lacked an opera singer's figure, a beauty queen's splendor, or a duchess' imperial bearing, but she captivated and hypnotized as soon as you met her gaze. Look her straight in the eye and you'd be seized with epilepsy on the spot. We Zairians (mostly born after 1960) would burst into tears as soon as we started to chew the fat with her. When Tshiamuena talked of smuggling in the 1970s, just after Angola's independence, not one man dared lift his little finger to challenge the veracity of her words. She rattled off entire family trees of the diggers, be they patrocinadors, dona moteurs, lavadors, plongeurs, or karimbeurs. She was not the memory of Angola, she *was* Angola, the other Angola, the Angola of mines, money, diamonds, cave-ins, the diamantiferous River Kwango; the Angola that any man dreams of at least once in his life (be he a lover of money or not). Tshiamuena was informed of all the rackets going on between Zaire and Angola; she had a detailed knowledge of the Zairians' comings and goings; she knew when such and such had entered Angola for the first time, which back road they had taken, and what capital they carried in their haversack. In her rare moments of madness (for Tshiamuena did lose her marbles, going by her long tirades and her agitated brow) she enumerated the deceased: long lists of kids, all Zairian, felled in their frantic quest for hasty enrichment by way of someone else's diamonds—that is to say Angolan stones. Not a hiccough, credulous utterance, or laugh interrupted her narrative flow, even though it was normal in the Cafunfo Mines to come across young Zairians laughing, mouths agape, for no apparent reason. Her beaming features gave everyone the chance to admire her dimples.

Tshiamuena was born to reign. What a woman! Arms raised, as if a rifle were pointed at her, she pontificated in pizzicato, and we, in our tattered rags, as still as salt statues, indifferent to heat or cold, to famine, fatigue, or fear of the next cave-in, we swallowed her reminiscences like bread rolls spread with soya paste. Tshiamuena was raving, but with such nonchalance. Her fantasies, we lapped them up. Toxic and excessive masculinities were crushed in the bud. Her words touched you, plunged down your esophagus, smashed your cerebral system, and you emerged exhausted, truly breathless, as if you'd escaped a nasty pogrom or done a thousand years' forced labor. Her uncontrolled exhaustions, her nervous breakdowns, her secretions of drool, her vomitings, her momentary losses of speech, of hearing, and of smell too, her tremoring feet and head, and her inopportune drowsiness added grist to the mill of those who accused her of belonging to a sect and sabotaging people's fortunes, not to mention preventing them from hitting pay dirt without sacrificing a member of their family. Her incantations concluded with sumptuous moments of silence that even the foot soldiers of the UNITA rebellion didn't dare transgress. This natural silence fell heavier than starved bodies gorged on digging or the despair of returning to Kinshasa empty-handed. The silence, along with her grating voice and the rare assurance with which she recounted her inanities, was the daily fare of those protracted nights deprived of light bulbs, oil lamps, or even the Good Lord himself.

"In the 1970s," she declared, with a dry throat and an empty gaze like that of the dying or of someone who has lost both parents that very day, "Angola was heaven for audacious and opportunistic Zairians besotted by easy money. Any Zairian from Kinshasa and Kasai old enough to be wed and eat their fill swore only by Angola. The Portuguese colonists had packed up and cleared out in a hurry. Dr Jonas Savimbi's UNITA and José Eduardo Dos Santos's MPLA, which had actually fought alongside each other in the war of independence, were embroiled in a rearguard battle for the monopoly of power. At this juncture," whispered Tshiamuena, with a defeated air and on the verge of tears, "Angola was becoming a colander. Porous borders. A stampede in both directions. Zairians of your age breezed in by the dozens, the hundreds, carrying all sorts of goods. Angola was cut off from the world. And staples such as wax fabrics, cigarettes, beer, transistor radios, tinned foods, rubber boots, sugar, salt, soap, and second hand clothes were snapped up like you haven't the slightest idea. We bartered gems for these products thousands of times."

Tshiamuena was an unparalleled raconteur. She would recap the same tale fifty times. And with each telling, the story took on a different flavor. A living, ancient eyewitness to this golden age (war being the most generous period for doing business: it's double or nothing, you fill your boots or you lose your money and your skin too), she lamented the fact that some Zairians shamefully stuffed their pockets at Angola's expense, yet she herself had no shortage of stones about her person. She said that the Angolans were in a far from celebratory mood and consequently did not keep their eyes on the diamonds. They were at each other's throats while the stones lay idle. Ah, the Madonna! A remarkable woman, Tshiamuena! Any Zairian who had cut their teeth in Angola would have testified for her, even with a gun to their head. The Madonna of the Cafunfo Mines was certainly not of the same flesh as we who strayed for centuries in Angola's alluvial mines. She was a wonderful person. An oasis in the Kalahari Desert. Drinking water. Mother Earth. Temple Guardian. Railway through the scrubland of our dog-eared dreams. Goddess of Grub. Zaire River in miniature. Architect of our opulent desires. Eldest Daughter of money and abundance. Patron Saint of the Zairian diamond panners of Lunda Norte. Ah, the Madonna! Miles of love in the service of the Zairian diaspora. Take the diplomatic service of the Republic of Zaire in Angola, which was out of action—closed, padlocked, null and void—for reasons of belligerency: the Madonna embodied the Zairian Embassy all on her own.

In that period, a whole swathe of the Angolan provinces (including Cafunfo) found itself under the control of the rebellion, which held the mining concessions in an iron grip. They regulated who entered or exited the mines to the nth degree and earned a few kopecks for each diamond found. The quarries were only accessible at prescribed hours. The diggers needed a permit both to stay in the camps and to enter the mines; without it, they could be harassed to the point of death.

It was amid these vexing circumstances that the Madonna entered the scene. She delivered the captives from the rebels' clutches; leveraged her contacts, starting with her Angolan husbands in chronological order (Mitterrand, Kiala, Augustino, José), to enable each and every one to come into possession of the proper papers; cared for the sick and those injured in cave-ins; handed out food to the most destitute; and managed to sort out the repatriation of the mortal remains of those whose families couldn't venture into Angola. The list of her good works is as long as the Zambezi River.

The story went around in Luanda and Lunda Norte that when she was just a slip of a girl she managed to save her parents from an arson attack. Here's how it goes: the fire blazes through the kitchen and spreads toward her parents' bedroom. From her crib, the child realizes the danger. She shrieks and somersaults, but her mother and father are in a deep sleep. With superhuman effort, she climbs out of her cot. Here there are two conflicting versions. Either she crawls to her parents' bedside and, alerted by her screams, they wake. Or—even more fantastical—she remains in her cradle and starts to cry—first teardrops, then tears as vast as the (Zaire) River until they extinguish the flames.

All those who returned from Angola, their pockets empty or brimming with stones, spoke in purring tones when mentioning the Madonna, perhaps to guard against probable sobbing. They were unanimous that the Republic of Zaire should pay Tshiamuena back in her own coin. Render unto Caesar the things which belong to Caesar. Render unto the Madonna of the Cafunfo Mines the things which belong to the Madonna of the Cafunfo Mines. Emotion getting the better of them, they went all in, insisting that Cabu Bridge bear her initials henceforth, that Avenue Saio be rechristened after her, and that on Place Victoire a monument seven meters tall be erected portraying her holding a diamond aloft in her left hand.

## 2. A family distraught, where we learn the damage caused by Molakisi's departure.

Molakisi had split without leaving an address, dispatching a postcard, or even making a phone call—"Dear parents, I've put a stop to my smooth chat, facile insults, and habitual thieving." His precipitous and poorly arranged abscondment exacerbated conflicts among his kin and sowed disorder in their minds. His father stopped getting smashed and clamoring for the carving up of the province (Tata Mobokoli was known for his excesses) and expressed his despondency with much salience:

"There's more to life than the Secession," he lamented. "Sure, my kid's steeped in petty criminality, a lusterless little lout you'll say, but he's my son after all. You'll not make me gloat when I don't even know where he crashes, if he eats his fill, or how he's managing to cope. It's a farce been going on since Babel: the little brats are as headstrong as the river. The river has no nationality. Consequentially, it holds neither vaccination card nor passport. The river crosses whatever country it pleases without due notice. What nationality is the Zambezi or the Danube, which crosses nine countries? The river has that primal insolence, it mills around and wanders according to its fancy. You find children who behave in this manner. They pick their own path: the wise way or, in extreme cases, the smuggler's. You can pull out absolutely all the stops, provide them with opportunity and give them your blessing, pay scrupulous attention to their upbringing, love them to bits; ultimately it's the little brats and them alone who choose which future to embrace. What would you have me do? Am I the guilty one? I'm not holding out for happier days but it seems insensitive all the same to be constantly condemning me behind my back on the pretext that I'm a deficient father."

Tata Mobokoli almost always concluded his jeremiads in the same way:

"All the children marauding the streets of Lubumbashi and Kinshasa constitute a race, the race of the outcast and the destitute; so what's my progeny doing among them? Well, show me a parent without at least one little brat who's flown the coop."

Molakisi's sisters went nearly crazy. One couldn't say for sure that their dissolution wasn't also connected to a poorly assimilated pubescence. They verbally assaulted law enforcement officers, hit on passersby, and pissed in the open air, laughing like mad. Not to be outdone, Mama Mobokoli skipped her Pentecostal Church and boycotted the Good Lord, along with the fasting and praying that characterized her housewife's day-to-day. Many saw in her attitude, as well as in her husband's distress, a grain of cynicism. They were dejected, tearful, physically wrecked, and yet, barely a few weeks earlier, they'd been berating their progeny, calling him butane bottle, amoeba, catfish-faced coward, and other profanities of the same sluice, to the extent that it became awkward to be in their company given that one or the other or both (in seasoned unison) disparaged the kid without pause. The most dreadful aspect of this uproar, however, was that Molakisi couldn't care less. Damien and Ézéchiel, the second-youngest and the baby of the family, were perhaps the only ones who didn't give a shit about the fugitive. Following the departure of their fuckwit brother, they pranced around in his shoes, chests thrust out, faces beaming.

One man's tribulation is another's delight. As Sanza—a pal of Molakisi's who'd been living with the family for a while—was preparing to roll out his mattress, the two clowns turned on him.

"Clear the floor and never set foot in our crib again."

"Piss off and don't bother us no more!"

Despite their seven-year age difference, Damien and his bro hatched all their little plots together, going so far as to parrot each other in any squabble. This earned them the nickname "Clone Brothers."

"Recess is over, it's bye-bye to the comprador-bourgeoisie," declared Damien, while his brother, armed with a chair, stood watch. Sanza turned his gaze on the pair. His left hand quivered. He had an insane desire to let rip. But realizing that sticking up for himself would serve little purpose, he picked up his odds and ends—an empty schoolbag, two pairs of pants, a cardigan—and stepped out the door, shooting them a deathly glare.

## 3. Sanza by a night without fuel oil.

The city of Lubumbashi hadn't aged a bit. Just as back in the day those living in La Cité on the outskirts would pile Downtown as soon as the Angelus struck to their jobs as manservants, child-minders, cooks, houseboys, gardeners, mechanics, builders, and errand boys for the Belgians, the French, or the Americans and had to leave by nightfall on pain of prison or a thrashing, the inhabitants of Kamalondo stepped over the rails separating La Cité (or what was left of it) and Downtown each God-given morning, and rushed to regain their hearths as soon as night fell—in the absence of a cogent car, a bus ticket, or out of fear of fainting amid the monstrous traffic jams. Everything was concentrated in the old town. Taxi drivers, office workers, traders, school kids, bankers, the jobless, robbers (there wasn't much to pinch in La Cité, and also it didn't look good to be caught red-handed by your neighbors) returned from work in a celebratory mood. Automobile headlights clashed like fireworks in a sky deprived of electricity. Hens, pigs, and goats also dashed to doze (some inhabitants owned livestock—nostalgia for the village? mercantile minds? both perhaps). So the animals hurried too. Worn down by the sun, the fatigue, the mud, or the dust, they were basking already in incipient torpor, slumber, mandatory easement, for they spent all day outdoors, snouts to the wind, amusing themselves, bickering, boning, lazing around, nibbling at random detritus and—in the case of the dogs and other canines—barking for trifles. The dust—or the river or the sludge (when it rained gallons)—merged with the black night. Car horns in the African night. Car horns. More car horns, which were met with laughter, sarcasm, or scowls.

"Day go well?"

"Err, Zaire kinda pace."

"And the little one, she's good? Eating fufu yet?"

"How handsome you've become!"

"A lovely romance, you know."

"That's Zairians for you!"

People hailed each other, took the temperature of the country, or waved hello from afar.

Lost in his thoughts, the young man made his way over the railroad tracks—as a vast crowd crossed it in the opposite direction dumbfounded by the sight of this kid doing the reverse at such a late hour of the day—dove down Chaussée des Usines, passed Jason Sendwe Hospital on his left, then the Central Market, and turned onto Avenue du Maréchal Mobutu.

*Might as well sleep in front of the Post Office, when all's said and done!* mused the lad.

Night had already grasped the whole province to its bosom. Downtown was completely dead, its occupants double-padlocked in their hovels as in the ancient days of the Colony.

All the kids who flew the family nest naturally emigrated Downtown until they found a profession (shoeshine boy; pickpocket; dishwasher in a cheap restaurant; detective at the service of cuckholded husbands and ladies in distress; docker at the Central Station; hawker of secondhand plastic carrier bags, sandals, and West African boubous; taxi tout; diamba smoker;

mechanic's assistant; street sleeper), or else climbed aboard the first train for Mbuji Mayi or washed up in a mine as a sifter or a kasabuleur (a diver equipped with an air-supplied helmet).

Not knowing what route to take, Sanza tramped the backstreets blindly. At one point he even contemplated returning to the family home, then recanted. Thinking about his parents who, because of his many months away, would send him packing, dole him out a good hiding, or scold him like never before, he decided to stay out in the wild—*what the fuck would I do back there*? he tried to convince himself, *I'm not giving up my rights and my freedom!*

## 4. Back when the Madonna was living in Angola, it warmed your heart to be Zairian.

The Madonna was engaged in a long rant ("the Lunda Norte of this afternoon, this morning, or even this evening is not the marvelous province we Zairians once knew when we arrived in Angola just after Independence. It is buried forever in the muck of history and will not show its face for anything in the world. There is no lifeline. We're set for centuries of poverty, my brothers; shortages, rotten luck . . . ") when we heard a creak. A filthy young man, whose ugliness was perceptible a mile off, stood in the doorway. The clothes he wore were so dirty that making out their original color was hit or miss. In his left hand he held a suitcase that didn't close, into which was stuffed some underwear, two pairs of pants, socks, and a pair of scissors. The teen blinked as if he were seeing for the first time in his life. As exhausted as he was by the Corta Marta, the route through the back country taken by the diggers and merchants on their way to or from Zaire, he seemed astonished by the spectacle that confronted him. In the course of his incredible journeyings on freight trains, his jaunts around the tortuous streets of Kinshasa's shadiest neighborhoods, and his disreputable frequentations in the Kasai province, the guy had come to hear of this enigmatic woman, but, like any good skeptic, he had underestimated her feats.

Tshiamuena, who, caught in the torrent of her words hadn't noticed the weird arrival, continued in her mourner's voice—deep and languid and peppered with cries—to talk of the land of plenty:

"The Angola of old, the Angola of inexhaustible diamonds, the Angola of fortune, of the days when the stones abounded and were even gleaned from garbage cans; when the few intrepid Zairians who poked their noses into the hive departed blessed, yea, until the fourth generation. It was right at the start of the war, and the Angolans, who were fighting among themselves, did not have sufficient time at their disposal to deal with the stones. *We*, however, were pioneers in the hunt for Angolan diamonds. The Angola that we barely brushed with our fingers after the Portuguese took flight will never return. Today—and you are all better informed than any seer—the earth boycotts us with its diamonds. Worse still, the number of wealth-seekers is increasing so hugely that one wonders who will remain in Zaire if all its youth descends upon Lunda Norte. Ah! Angola, when you hold us in your grip!"

The young man made his move.

"I'm looking," he mumbled, without even stepping forward, "for Tshiamuena . . . "

No one in the august assembly paid him any heed. The Madonna's inanities had the effect of a fine wine. As you absorbed them, you became merry, and then you lost the plot. Tshiamuena preached her head off, and the Zairians (along with a few cherry-picked Angolan subjects) lashed themselves to her incantations, totally drunk on them.

The kid collapsed. The diggers were so beguiled that none of them noticed a thing, or got aggravated, or cried in astonishment, or ran to help. Seconds, minutes, hours passed until

Tshiamuena, in the middle of an anecdote, raised her head and caught sight of the limp body. She screamed then:

"So this is the Angola of today: someone's dying and you sit on your hands!"

Anger, sadness, stupefaction. The vociferations of the First Lady were followed by a general commotion. Everyone rushed toward and pounced upon the recumbent stranger. This one wanted to give first aid, that one second aid, another begged the Good Lord out loud or else set to expelling the demons of disease, accident, and death—"spirits of darkness, leave this body; I order you in the name of Jesus Christ to piss off!"—so that the young guy would breathe again. An opportune moment for each to prove to Tshiamuena that they, too, had a big heart. The masquerade around the youngster made her all the more incensed. She felt offended, humiliated, sickened, and emptied of her humanity.

"Eles são todos mentirosos . . . " she whispered. She only ever expressed herself in Portuguese in cases of emergency. Without going back as far as the Flood, we had heard her make use of this language on just two occasions. The last time was when Zeze, a young Angolan kasabuleur, failed to resurface. His demise caused quite a stir within the Zairian diaspora of Lunda Norte. Every avenue was pursued: suicide, contract killing, human error, equipment failure related to the outdated nature of the watercraft, accusations of witchery, white magic. To put an end to the most persistent, far-fetched, stupid, and inappropriate rumors, the Madonna summoned all the Zairian garimpeiros old enough to make an attempt on another's life or to do something foolish—including those from Kasai, her home province—and furnished us with her four truths. I had never seen that expression on her face before. She grouched in faultless Portuguese about the Angola of the mines and its (intimate!) secrets. Where had she learned to speak Angolan with such finesse?

Two colossal fellows moved the body to the very back of the room, where they took turns administering cardiopulmonary resuscitation without any convincing result. Tshiamuena began to weep, her past as a professional mourner getting the better of her. Fat teardrops streamed down her cheeks. Suddenly, one guy had a brilliant idea.

"A wet flannel!"

The Madonna slipped out, reappearing a second later with a cloth that she herself applied to the kid's forehead, and he soon stirred, to the compulsive applause of the assembled company.

The Madonna was a woman of great moral probity, and extremely maternal. We would all have liked her as our wife, mother, grandmother, sister-in-law, forebear, ancestor, clan founder, matriarch, and so on and so forth. I know guys who'd have auctioned off everything—down to the last diamond carat—to have her just as a distant cousin despite her chidings that were borderline ridiculous: "Franz, you've not had a shower for months and your breath is distracting when you talk to people!"

With Tshiamuena, her emotions were so mixed up it was hard to figure out her misgivings. Even when she was happy, she griped, pouted at greetings, and harangued the Zairians (of both the male and female sexes) and the Angolans left, right, and center.

•

Whereas we stupidly believed that she had left to go and relax, she eventually showed up with a cooking pot full to the brim with spicy beans and sweet potato, an enameled steel cup, a container of juice, a spoon, and even a napkin!

A woman of her caliber never rests, for how can you nap with such a weight on your shoulders? There were the mortal remains of Zairian diggers to be repatriated to Kinshasa and to the Kasai; the dozens of mouths to feed; the rescuing of people pressed into service by the Angolan government forces or the UNITA rebels; the wounds and aching carcasses of casualties (of cave-ins) to be dressed; the brawls and other generational conflicts to be arbitrated; the psychological support for the most vulnerable; the Portuguese and Tshiluba language classes provided for all; the weddings to be overseen; the succor to be given to those struck down by smallpox and typhoid; and so on.

We let her lurch these trinkets over all on her own. Out of jealousy. Why should a boy from some scrubby patch in the sticks enjoy these almost princely honors? The young man licked his chops as soon as he viewed the beans. He sat with his legs akimbo and masticated without taking his eyes off the pot, as if the grub were going to evaporate. Swallowing the last mouthful, he dusted off his mush and, without displaying any sign of gratitude at all, stood up to leave for goodness knows where. The furor cooled his zeal.

Every evening, conclaves were held in her living room. Zairian and Angolan diggers, young and not so young, standing or straddling the benches, smoked, played cards, parleyed and palavered, and recruited potential work colleagues. Back then, the Cafunfo Mines in the Angolan province of Lunda Norte were the most bountiful in central Africa. Zairians who went there got rich in record time. Then they returned to Kinshasa, or left to go live in Libreville in Gabon, or in Europe, and came back only when they'd blown all the cash. The Cafunfo Mines were also known to be a deathtrap which ran at a rhythm of three cave-ins a day. Either way, the operation required a plentiful workforce as pliable as could be. When someone died in a cave-in, they were buried as quickly as possible and new diggers were hired immediately. Digging candidates who'd arrived that day took part in this ritual without which it was hard to get access to the stone. They identified themselves, then answered in turn the sometimes-humiliating questions of the mistress of the house, and those of the diggers who'd come to witness the recruitment test en masse. The diamond panners worked in cooperatives called écuries, or teams, and each of these had its specialty. When a candidate's profile enraptured a gang of diggers, they incorporated him in their écurie. Since mining requires some of the greatest teamwork on planet Earth, each écurie comprised young and not-so-young guys: ace free divers; frogmen; kasabuleurs (for hunting the stone in the River Kwango); dona moteurs who supplied the boat and the diving equipment; karimbeurs, or diggers, who could withstand the fatigue as their excavations progressed ever deeper; muscular mwétistes to haul the gravel out of the river when the kasabuleur had finished filling the buckets to the very top; a highly mobile team not unlike infantry to escort the merchandise to the riverbank where it was sorted and weighed by the lavadors, then transported by the same lavadors or by other mwétistes to makeshift repositories; a good sponsor or patrocinador if the dona moteur wasn't rich enough to supply the work tools, buy food, beer, and cigarettes, and settle the bill for exploitation rights with the soldiers of the UNITA (Jonas Savimbi's rebels who controlled the Cafunfo region), in return for which the patrocinador received a percentage on each stone. The chain of collaborations of diggers and the like stretched as far as Antwerp via Kinshasa and the Bandundu province through multiple dealers and middlemen. A diamond, or indeed any stone in the Angolan province of Lunda Norte or the Kasai, had no value until it reached the international marketplace.

The Madonna suggested—the term is inappropriate, she insisted upon the way of action, whether you liked it or not, whether it fueled rumor or provoked slander—to skip the session devoted to miscellaneous news and start straight into the job interviews. She decided to let the newcomer go first. Aided by the oil lamp, those of us with ringside seats had the remarkable opportunity to admire the boy up close. You had to be there to see the face he made. Incapable of looking up. Shifting about like a rheumatic. Teeth unpolished for eons. Crumpled shirt. Faded, threadbare pants. Ditto the undershirt. Warped sandals. And, as if that wasn't enough, a boxer's nose. We used to say in the mines that money diminishes ugliness, and if you're broke and gruesome to behold, and don't sufficiently stuff your face, the unsightliness increases, deteriorates, and multiplies. Tshiamuena held this view also, though she didn't much go into detail about it. Naturally ill-formed, the young man had kind of broken his own record. Tshiamuena—and this only happened once a year—defenestrated into raucous laughter for no apparent reason. Not wanting to seem dumb, he imitated the grande dame. The perfunctory, poorly spelled laugh lent his face the features of a carnival mask. Tshiamuena had grown into her role—and the extravagant sobriquet of Madonna of the Cafunfo Mines—by force of mixing with this rough company. She suddenly ceased her guffawing and fired off the first question:

"You got a name I can call you?"

"Yes."

"What is it?"

"Molakisi."

"Where you from?"

"Zaire."

"That we know."

"Lubumbashi. I also lived in the Kasai and Kinshasa."

"That's some roll of honor!" came a shout from the room.

The comment provoked unexpected hilarity.

"You looking for work?"

"Yes. They told me I could make a diamond haul too."

Laughter among the congregation. Gibes. A spiteful remark about his nose and his outdated suitcase.

"Your age? Your natural age, from your birth, not your official age."

The Madonna clung fast to age and all that went with it. It was one of her many themes of predilection—"you really can't live without knowing your age or at least making use of some far-fetched dating," she would say by way of excusing her voracity on the subject.

"Sixteen next November."

Tshiamuena stiffened.

"And you want to be rich at sixteen? At sixteen! Sixteen and bourgeois too, isn't that a bit much?"

Molakisi chafed at this.

"Do you take me for your little doggy?"

He had compromised himself by playing the nice boy—which he really wasn't. Back when he lived in Lubumbashi and Kinshasa, and even in the Kasai, he was known as a scrapper who'd pile on you for the merest slight. The Madonna was sort of dazed. She hadn't seen it coming.

"You'll be asking me to show my parental permission next. You don't even know me, yet you're picking my life apart."

Boos. A soldier drew his piece. Wound up, the diggers hammered at the benches: What gives you the right to talk to Tshiamuena like that? Have you ever once looked at yourself in the mirror? Youngsters today! We're in Angola, a little respect for Tshiamuena! Take those words back, Australopithecus! You're not even in the same league as her. You're just a virgin, you've never even had sex in your life, and you think you can look down on your elders? Go fornicate first and then we'll talk on equal terms. These twentieth century Zairians!

Molakisi had confused the mine with the street. He who swore only by brawling, blackmail, threats, and dirty tricks, had happened upon folk who adored those same activities. He apologized:

"I didn't mean to offend you."

The Madonna accelerated the series of questions. The quips enjoining him to return to Zaire intensified. As one might have expected, it was again Tshiamuena who came to the young man's rescue:

"He's only a child."

"A child must learn when to shut it!"

"We've had it with money-grubbers who disrespect you, and you know it."

"It's his face I don't like!"

"That boxer's nose."

Molakisi abandoned his restraint:

"You don't intimidate me. It'll take more than this carrying-on."

Zeze's nephew, Pedritto—who was biting his nails and sucking his thumb with the full weight of his forty years—threw himself at Molakisi, who barely dodged the punch. With a gymnast's leap, the Madonna got between the belligerents. Visibly affected by the assault to which the young Molakisi had just fallen victim, she uttered two or three words in Portuguese before urging Pedritto to vacate the premises. He tried to redeem himself—"I don't know what came over me, it's not in my nature . . . "—but Tshiamuena refused his mea culpa, to the great displeasure of all the Zairian garimpeiros.

You turn up like a hair in the soup at a mine where you don't know anyone, without a penny to your name, unwholesome among the unwholesome—to quote Pedritto's insult—scabby, starving, and scrawny to boot, and Tshiamuena gives you a chance; she gathers you up, keeps a close eye on your health as if it were porcelain; provides you with a bed, a pillow and sheets, sustenance, and clean clothes. All these good deeds, expecting nothing in return. Then you start bringing money in, not even thinking to pay her a tithe, and in the end you chuck her away like a Barbie doll.

## 5. Sanza, the night, and its splendors on the verge of quicksand.

Downtown looked like a wrung-out fruit. Workers were rushing back to La Cité as Sanza made his way up Avenue des Usines. Three boys of about his age strode onto Central Square. The stockiest had a collection of kitchen utensils slung across him. His acolytes on either side each carried a raffia bag full of rations. He walked with confidence. One step after another, arms dangling, neck elevated slightly, jaw clenched like that of a dignitary reviewing troops. His pals talked without pause. They were buttering him up the ass. Clearly they were seeking to extract a smile or perhaps his approval. They clamored away, gushing about the day's proceedings, roaring with laughter, ranting in jubilation. Ensconced in his role as kingpin, the toughie of the three did not appear at all enthusiastic. As soon as he saw them, Sanza remembered one of Molakisi's many warnings—a normal man doesn't laugh every thirty seconds, it kills masculinity dead. The stocky one injected a phrase here, a word there as the conversation progressed, and when his companions made too bold in their mirth, he peered down his nose at them, like they were insects. They processed across Avenue Mobutu, stopped in front of the Post Office, and unloaded their burdens with the same swagger. A stone's throw from Sanza. He tried to establish a connection.

"Hi guys!"

They made him understand they had other priorities:

"Don't get fresh with us!"

"I don't like his face!"

"Lubumbashi's not what it was. Peasants are swarming us from all over!"

"Look at his ugly mug."

They looked in his direction, sniggered, spat on the ground, jeered. Now and then, the stocky one pointed at him, which revived the zeal of the two errand boys. Since Sanza didn't reply, they lit a large fire, cooked rice and vegetables with salted fish on the side, and forgot about the interloper as soon as they set to smoking glue. Stretched out on a makeshift pallet of cardboard boxes, he fell asleep—less from the exhaustion than the thousand and one thoughts that irked him. For over a year, he had made his home with Molakisi's family, categorically rejecting all of his parents' attempts to take him back. Now, in the space of a day, he had ended up on the street, without Molakisi, his protector. He wasn't afraid to find himself on the street for a bit—Molakisi's mentoring had turned him into a daring young man—but what bothered him was the void in which he now floated. Deep in the middle of the night, he felt a kind of presence. Popping wide his eyes, he thought he saw figures flitting about and heard laughter (of the crazy kind) mixed with jibes. He quickly rubbed his face and made out two young men with rippling muscles. They ordered him to stand up.

"Don't even think about trying it on or we'll show you! We're not your cousins, or your grandparents. We're not kidding around. We . . . "

"Hang on, slow down a bit."

At first glance, Sanza thought they had confused him with a third party or needed a little help and that they were doing their utmost to play the alpha males just to wind him up. He flicked his eyes to the right. His three housemates, who were on the point of fleeing, quaked. The stocky one had lost his haughty air. He sobbed with his head in his hands. The two men:

"We're finance inspectors."

"I don't understand."

"We're not going through that nonsense again and again."

"What are you driving at?"

"This city you see here: at night it belongs to us! You a newbie or what?"

"Give us your money, now! Your undies, your pants, your shirt, your clogs. Any objections and we'll do you over once and for all."

Sleep evaporated at these words. Their voices and faces, prematurely tarnished by the glue, made him fear the worst. The youngest had at least twenty-five years on the clock. From their appearance and their disdain, Sanza guessed they'd quit the family home many years before.

"I've got nothing on me."

Everything happened very fast. One of the pair pulled out a pocketknife and stepped closer. Sanza made as if to leg it, and the man with the knife lowered his guard to run after him. Fatal error. Sanza spun around and punched him smack in the face. The guy cowered, his nose broken. His associate jumped on Sanza and they rolled on the ground, but Sanza managed to immobilize him somehow. He sat astride his belly and slugged him with all his might. The guy broke free and tried to take off.

Sanza tripped him up. The attacker stumbled for a few feet, recovered his balance, and sprinted down Avenue Mobutu. His fellow plunderer knelt, sniveling, his face bloody. The three boys approached and ogled Sanza with admiration. They'd treated him as small fry, yet he'd rid himself of two ruffians considerably older than him.

"What planet are you from?"

"It's my first street fight!" the young warrior rejoiced, not comprehending how he'd managed to overcome his assailants.

Sanza would have given wads of dough, all the gold in the world, for Molakisi to have witnessed the clash. It was thanks to him that he was quite capable of putting up a certain resistance in the event of an assault. Molakisi was a genius brawler. God knows where he got his strength. Even when facing off against six bruisers, he sowed disarray in their camp. He used his build and his thick, fleshy arms to fend off fists and even sticks. He could take blows seemingly without pain.

"Why did they attack me?"

The stocky one had regained his imperial sluggishness, but he didn't let slip a single syllable. He inspected Sanza. From toe to top, from top to toe, his mouth a rounded "O" like someone forcing themselves not to puke. His disciples, engaged in puerile competition, talked over each other. They noisily addressed Sanza, all the while dashing desperately after the assent of their leader, who appeared not the least interested in the subject :

"They're street children."

"Not really . . . "

"'Cos they've not been children for a long time now."

"They ran the show until they tired of it and then . . . "

"Now they take advantage of their maturity to patrol the whole of Downtown each night."

"And extort the weakest, the newcomers."

"Like you."

Sanza couldn't believe his ears.

"Are you a little peckish, by any chance?" enquired the stocky one solemnly.

Sanza nodded and joined their little squad. The others examined him with a mixture of fear and fascination. Suddenly, ostentatiously, frowning like you'd stare down an insect, the stocky one asked him:

"Will you be in our gang?"

Seeing the guy's gesticulations, Sanza remembered Molakisi, who was constantly seeking masculine dominance and who reproached him for possessing not an ounce of masculinity: he enjoined Sanza to work on it, on the basis that powerful men (dominant males, to use his jargon) talk softly, stare at others (disdainfully), and never display any joy.

"Will you be in our gang?" the boy repeated.

"I need to think about it first."

"That a joke?"

"I think that's a lack of respect," stated one of his acolytes. "Anarchist they call me, 'cos I know how to mess stuff up. You'll regret it if you . . . "

"They call me Whitey," the other declared hastily. "I got a white man's face."

"Him," they announced together like actors who've rehearsed the same sketch a thousand times, "that's Ngungi. You never heard of him? Pity."

"I'm Sanza."

And the two bambinos:

"He's a living library."

"He knows who's who and what's what in Lubumbashi."

"And he's one of the richest men in Zaire!"

"His wealth is estimated at . . . "

"He's an old friend of President Mobutu."

"Stop your nonsense. Big cheese, sure, but he eats dirt!"

This sparked a breathtaking contest, under their leader's amused gaze:

"He owns carriages!"

"Airliners!"

"Helicopters! Villages! Castles!"

"They say he's the biggest . . . "

"He hobnobs with Mireille Mathieu, Belmondo, Alain Delon, Michel Sardou, Romy Schneider!"

"He's an oilman!"

Sanza turned to Ngungi:

"Is it true what Whitey and Anarchist say about you?"

"Yeah, I've got assets," he went laconically. Then, as if to signify that there was no reason for the debate to continue and that Sanza was already part of his clan, he diametrically changed subject: "We form gangs, the street kids. Our sector is the whole of the Post Office forecourt and Central Square. In fact, you need permission to move in with us. Fortunately for you, we're not uneducated."

"Elsewhere, they'd have defenestrated you."

"Beaten you up."

Ngungi, ever the charismatic and enlightened leader:

"Each clan has its specialty and occupies an area of Downtown—sometimes bought with blood. It's me who gives the orders here. For a long time we lived off stealing. Now we're in international development. Kind of like the Peace Corps. Other groups manage to make a living off begging, or odd jobs as hawker shoe-shiners, matchbox peddlers, porters . . . "

"Thieves . . . "

"Car washers. But watch out," Ngungi continued, "the finance inspectors haven't had their last word yet. You'll run into them, sooner or later. You've caused a hurricane. I'd have handed over my underwear, my shirt, if I'd been you."

"I'll tear them apart."

Ngungi burst into peals of laughter.

## 6. Sanza had had enough of being his parents' puppy dog forever.

Life indoors exasperated me in the end. It was indecently monotonous. After the first few nights in front of the Post Office, I had the feeling that despite the cold, the glue, and the animosity of the soldiers and finance inspectors, my place was not in the warmth of a big house but here in the open air. That's what I endeavored desperately to drill into my mother's cabeza without really succeeding. A few months after I ran off, she managed to track me down, having been notified by Molakisi's family. She was treated to just a few sparse minutes of conversation.

"I can't imagine living anywhere else. You're killing yourself for nothing," I replied to her pleas.

She went on harassing me, deploying imbecilic reasons for a return to the fold. She invoked (with considerable subtlety) the continuing of my studies, breakfast, the morning and evening meals, the family bookshelf, clean clothes, a soft downy bed, a trip to Kinshasa, pocket money, television, healthcare, and so on. I began laughing uproariously when she reeled off this guff. You can't put a price on freedom—neither grub, nor pocket money, nor television. Outdoors, I was my own father, my own mother, my own god, my own ancestor, my own president of Zaire. It was a big world, vaster and juicier than a sad life spent climbing into bed at eight PM, weeding the garden, and grinding myself down on school assignments. And what's more, guys like Whitey and Ngungi: to count them in your inner circle you had to be one of the outdoors crowd. My mother maintained that I was a child.

"You can't even iron a shirt!"

I disliked the word and I made the observation that she was tapped in the head. I was a pup no longer. Bambino was a real hard job. The difference between children and us was one of experience. We had the experience of the street—glue, rivalries with opposing gangs, rain, tangles with soldiers—yet people always insisted on saddling us with the pompous, dreary label of child. Outdoors was always lively, be it run-ins with the finance inspectors, madness, the Villain's Dance, or, of course, the splendor that was the Mambo de la Fête. In the Republic of Zaire, apart from watchmen (sort of) and soldiers, no geezers had experience of life outdoors.

Before I slunk off, she passed me a hundred-zaire note. I headed away up Boulevard Lumumba without returning her goodbye. She stood there stunned. The following day, Louis, my father, turned up. He was so irate he screamed his head off.

"You bring shame on me! You bring shame on your mother! Shame on the Union Minière! On my late parents! On the whole family tree!"

What family tree was he on about? Witnessing this affront, the kids reacted:

"Fuck the Union Minière," shouted Ngungi.

"The Union Minière's a fat bitch!" added Whitey.

At the time, in the face of what I might have considered a joke in bad taste, I made no reply, I didn't even snigger. Molakisi would spout the whole day long that a normal man, a true dominant male, never jokes and doesn't react to even the most slanderous insinuations. My father stared me out. I held his gaze. He wanted to grab me by the collar, I dodged the maneuver. So he tried to hit me. Ngungi, Whitey, and even kids from other gangs came to my defense.

"You dare touch a hair on his head, I'll unleash the pack! Villain, villain!" yelled Ngungi. He always walked around shirtless, which showed off the scar scored across his belly. Louis beat a hasty retreat. We were left snorting with laughter. But I tried not to exaggerate my joy nor extrapolate my laughter for fear of placing my masculinity in jeopardy.

## 7. Ngungi's defenestration or how the wretched Sanza discovers that airplanes take off from the Post Office.

"You really go flying at night?" I asked Ngungi as he sketched out his whole life story.

Back when he still lived with his family, Ngungi was under embargo. As an infant—from birth in fact—his parents had predestined him for a brilliant career in academia. They advised their offspring against bumming around (you must succeed where your mother and I failed!), conspiring with scallywags, and touching that which didn't belong to him. The child didn't eat at the cafeteria—for fear of being poisoned or even catching typhoid—and refused to make friends with the other high school kids.

Next to him in class sat Remy—a boy as thin as the eye of a needle—who spied on him at recess and after class. One day, he decided to tackle Ngungi head on. He offered him a piece of bread.

"I'm not hungry."

"It's not to feed you."

"Leave me be!"

"Taste my bread, it's not bad."

"I can't and you know it."

Remy suddenly began laughing and stared at his fellow student as if the latter had just peed himself.

"It's lamentable, me old coot; still clinging to your mother's skirts at your age. The rest of us have left that tiresome time behind."

"You're wrong," Ngungi snapped back.

Remy upped the ante:

"You lack vision. What proof is there that you're not at your parents' mercy if you can't do anything without their permission? Look how sad you are. You've got no pals, you don't chase the ball down, you don't even know how to talk to girls."

Ngungi eventually gave in. A quite comical phenomenon occurred. In his mouth, the lump of bread transformed by turn into a piece of banana, mango, grape, goat meat (he who never ate that), and salt fish. He was straightaway gripped by such constipation that he couldn't eat anything more for the rest of the day.

"You don't look good," his mother fretted.

"You're worrying for nothing."

"Ngungi, you're hiding things from me."

"A migraine, mama, nothing serious."

Ngungi slunk off to his room, where he fell asleep without even telling his parents. In the middle of the night, he heard a shrill voice calling his surname. He buried his head beneath the sheets. Which only exacerbated the situation. A real racket splattered his eardrums. Eventually Remy appeared dressed in yellow and blue overalls, a helmet sitting snugly on his head.

"You packed your bag yet?"

"What do you want with me?"

"Don't play this game! I'm in no mood for joking around today. You munched my bread, now you come with me."

A long argument commenced between the two kids.

"If you don't come with me, it's your mother who'll snuff it first thing in the morning," threatened his classmate. "Would you like to see her stretched out in a coffin? Have you ever seen the body of a dead person?"

They set off walking, down winding paths half-asphalted and badly lit, before emerging at a large airport. The formalities took just a few seconds. They boarded a contraption shaped like a flying saucer which took off without further ado. Ngungi had lost his bearings.

Remy took pains to reassure him of the benefits of such a voyage.

"You're going to like it."

An hour and a half's flight later, they saw phosphorescent lights in the distance. Dwellings became visible as the plane approached the earth. The landing went without a bump. As soon as they stepped onto the ground, they were off again, pressed for time. At the entrance to the city, a guard of honor awaited them, superbly executed by soldiers, along with a brass band of a hundred men playing the national anthem of an Asian country. The conurbation that extended before them looked neither like Lubumbashi, nor even Kinshasa, and was crisscrossed by clean, spacious thoroughfares. Gigantic bill-boards stood everywhere, all featuring children with smiling faces. Ngungi and Remy were the only ones on foot. Ngungi cast his gaze in every direction, bewildered and disorientated. His travel companion, haughtily:

"If you're adept, your wealth will outstrip my own. We'll stop at my place, then we'll meet up with my colleagues."

"Colleagues?"

"They've been steadfastly waiting. They're very happy to finally meet you, and to count you as one of us."

"They know me?"

"You've been in my sights for a long time. I've been talking about you since last year."

They stopped in front of a villa. Remy banged his fist on the gate twice. A sentry popped out and presented his compliments. Ngungi still couldn't get over it. How come Remy, who lacked even shoes, could enjoy, in this other world, a financial situation bordering on the insolent?

"This house belong to you?"

"Why couldn't it belong to me? It's a pity," he continued, seemingly put out, "that my partner and my children are already in bed."

Ngungi's blood began to boil. He raised his voice:

"No! You, a father already? A child with children?"

"Why not? Is it forbidden to procreate now? Have you looked at me even once?"

Remy pronounced these last words in the manner of someone emerging from a deep coma. As they entered the living room, Ngungi slowed his pace to observe Remy. He realized that, despite his juvenile face and body, the boy moved like a centenarian.

"We are ageless. I am a father. Soon to be a grandfather. Is it a crime to be the head of a large family? You Zairians surprise me!" (As if he wasn't Zairian himself.) "You're Zairian, right? So why are you so spooked?"

"I want to go back to my parents'!"

"I don't like repeating myself. One step outside, and it's your mother who croaks."

Remy flung on some clothes while Ngungi admired the grandeur of the living room: ebony-paneled walls, Louis XIV style furniture, paintings (originals, all!) by Rembrandt, Klimt, Schiele, Monet . . .

They drove to the meeting in a convertible. Again they were welcomed by a guard of honor and shouts of joy. A man in his sixties—who considered himself to be the first Earthling to have walked on the Moon, and in 1958 no less—gave a brief address:

"There is always a real satisfaction when our club gains a new member. On behalf of the whole community, I wish you welcome and remain at your disposal for any questions that you may have."

One after another, the men present at the ceremony—along with a few women, a dozen in all—identified themselves, elaborated upon their wealth estimated in tens of billions of U.S. dollars (castles, wildlife parks, apartments across East Africa and Eastern Europe), and by way of conclusion reeled off the names of the family members they'd sacrificed to enhance their prestige. Lists as long as your arm. The meeting ended with a sumptuous banquet. A horde of majordomos, housekeepers, waiters, and cooks tacked feverishly back and forth. They shifted huge cooking pots packed with meat, set out chairs, laid tables, and came and went with cutlery, wielding bottles of champagne.

Ngungi unraveled himself from sleep, his body bruised—the landing on the Post Office forecourt at his return having been poorly handled, owing to the rotten weather as well as the pitiful quality of the blood which, according to Remy, served as their fuel in the netherworld. Remy also told him that the Post Office functioned as one of the largest nocturnal airports in Zaire. Sorcerers, aides, and apprentices from all over—even neighboring Zambia, Zimbabwe, and Angola (when their airports were overcrowded and there was a shortage of direct flights)—took off from the forecourt. Brothels, markets, bars, hospitals, the Central Station, and many other venues swarming with the common masses acted as full-blown airport sites in their otherworld. I dismissed his mumbo jumbo with a sweep of my hand. He nearly choked himself laughing.

Remy cut classes the next day, but he showed up again come evening. For Ngungi, there was no avoiding the sorcerers' general assembly. The chair addressed the boy solemnly:

"You are now a member of our community. Since you must prove your loyalty to our association, your first test will be to bring about your father's laying off."

Ngungi was taken aback. He prevaricated:

"How will we manage to make ends meet if Papa stops working?"

"Such questions are not for us to answer!"

"You're asking a miracle of me. Without that job . . . "

"Well you shouldn't have grabbed that scrap of bread then."

"I wouldn't be able to . . . "

"Could you bear the full responsibility if your mother succumbed?"

"Give me two days, the time to think about it."

"We have other fish to fry."

One month after this incident, Ngungi's father was summoned by his manager, who offered him early retirement in return for a small nest egg.

"The company needs fresh blood; you're not twenty anymore; you could live it easy."

Which Ngungi's father accepted without thinking twice. He could not do otherwise. Better to take advantage of this final payoff—even if it meant pursuing any old racket—than rely inexorably on the steelworks and that paltry wage. Generally—and this is an open secret—when confronted with money, our ideas and ambitions always exceed the value of the cash itself. Ngungi's father had never touched so much dough in his life. He chose to seal up the money in an iron trunk in the bedroom, and in his spare time would strive to count the bills until sleep overtook him. The more he handled them, the more he lost control. He dreamed up mammoth projects. Initially, he envisaged building an aerospace center—this was several years after President Mobutu's attempts to launch the first Zairian space rocket. His wife opposed this with every fiber of her being. He employed one subterfuge after another to convince her to begin construction work on a luxury hotel, but Ngungi's mother nipped this umpteenth fancy in the bud. Recycling a youthful megalomania, he worked his way around every bar of the province buying beers for guys he'd only just met and who were quite surprised at this fellow's largesse. At the Mambo, the flatterers pushed their imaginations to the limit. As soon as they glimpsed his noggin, they dropped whatever the hell they were doing, likewise whatever amusement they were indulging—smokes, beer, the Villain's Dance, the jukebox, the pool table—called out to each other, whizzed toward his car (like flies), removed their hats from their heads, took a knee by way of greeting, recounted in a clear and audible tone exploits they attributed to him, praised his potbelly and his bulging eyes, extolled his legendary generosity, pointed out fanciful resemblances to James Brown, compared him to the giants of this world, declared that he was one of God's anointed, not to mention chosen among the thousands of Zairians of his generation, proffered—each in turn (and in quavering voices)—a service,

"Might you desire to sit on this chair?"

"Would Sir care to dance the Villain's Dance?"

"If Sir is interested, the latrines have been cleaned today, especially for him."

"Would Sir like to drink something? A Simba? A Tembo? Cognac?"

"Are you going to France for Christmas?"

"Sir must surely have a fondness for music. L'Orchestre Vévé? OK Jazz? L'Afrisa de Tabu Ley?"

"Ah! Sir looks as if he came straight from Lisbon!"

stared hungrily at him, confessed their weakness for his deep dark skin or his turkey gait, smacked each other about or laughed energetically to attract his attention, waited for him to take the floor first at each Villain's Dance before they moved and grooved, sought at any price to pour him his drink—he tipped around fifty zaires when he'd woken up on the right side of bed, thirty zaires when his rheumatism bothered him—and our man, evidently moved to the depths of his soul, ratcheted up his acts of kindness. At the Mambo de la Fête, there were patrons—of the male sex—who sipped the same drink for five hours straight. These fine folk, burdened by debts from head to toe, never let the chance of a piss-up slip from under their noses. Like a diamond panner who, after having tracked and captured the stone, gets sloshed down to the dregs, hands out cash—without counting—and nips upstairs with the staff (of both the male and female sexes) so that the earth spirits will spare him a future cave-in, as well as increasing the chance of grabbing even more diamond carats or extracting cobalt concentrate, Ngungi's father lived the life of a prince. He was running after lost time. Amid his jubilatory extravagances, he realized that while he and his pals had been slaving away in the mines, foundries, and metalworks, other individuals had been enjoying their youth—sometimes thanks to the very stones and workers from these same mines and factories. This was one of the reasons Ngungi's father also swore only by the Secession: all mining production fell into the pockets of the bigwigs of the regime superbly sprawled in their swanky sitting rooms in the capital. Dark thoughts incited in him a great rage. He became aware, to his cost, that the Union Minière, the mastodon, the vile beast, the monster—the one for which folk from all over had forsaken whatever dump they came from to climb aboard any old train to go shift the unctuous earth and melt copper—had sucked his blood down to the last drop and that if he didn't stir himself sharpish, he would end his old days without ever having swayed his body to the frenzied guitars of L'Orchestre Vévé. And so he defenestrated from his bed in the depths of the night, threw everything on—necktie, shoes, housecoat—whatever he could grab, dove into one of his cars, and drove at breakneck speed through the deserted streets of Downtown to the Mambo de la Fête where youngsters, oldsters, the ageless (or those looking more than their age), musicians rendered deaf-mute by the glue, dancers, acrobats, waiters and busboys, the crazy with the green wig, and the barman and all his lineage sang and yelled to his glory until the small hours. All these fauna knelt before him, lauding the youth and beauty that his wallet procured him.

In those days—at the Mambo obviously since it was a world apart—beauty and youth weren't much use if you were broke. The patrons (of both the male and female sexes) were ten thousand times more interested in falling in love, having the hots, becoming infatuated, getting laid, or going out with someone ugly yet rich (their own words), than piddling around with Miss World or the handsomest man on the planet. At the Mambo de la Fête, when the musicians—narcotically perked up—electrified the place, and the dance floor was packed tight, the folk would shout themselves hoarse:

no such thing as beauty
the only beauty's money
no such thing as youth
the only youth is money
nasty boy, quit your hassle!
nasty girl, quit your hassle!

losers, no!
fat cats, yeah!
money better still
money, money, money
nasty boy, quit muddling me!
nasty girl, quit muddling me!

Amid the raging Hawaiian guitars, congas, cymbals, vibraphone, sax, and bass clarinet, the fauna writhed to the rhythm of the Villain's Dance. It was the climax of the Mambo's bacchanalian nights. You couldn't execute the Villain's Dance precisely on an empty stomach. It was even suicidal to try, requiring as many calories as weightlifting. Its tilted postures—excessive, as guys like Monsieur Guillaume or Franz would say—marshaled as many muscles as any combat sport. You stood, slightly bent, arms curved out in front like a pugilist ready to parry their opponent's punches. Then you stepped forward with one foot—preferably the left—and stepped it back again. Then you performed the same with the other foot. Next you jumped with both feet thrust forward, then with both feet thrust back. Lifting your head, you began twisting your hips—gently at first, then energetically—while using the elasticity of your legs to descend and rise again, descend and rise again, hands whirling as if distributing money, a devilish grin on your face.

The cash flowed out, never in, and the iron trunk emptied. The gods and other spirits of the mine refused to replace what Ngungi's father subtracted in order to satisfy (at any price) the voracious appetite of the Mambo's patrons—both male and female. He sold off his luxury cars and, straight after, opened a supermarket. His neighbors and the regulars of the Mambo de la Fête, emboldened by his good faith, now took staple products and other items on credit. When he urged them to settle up, they got cross, inventing and spreading tittle-tattle by way of reprisals. After many months of such disputes, no one stuck their nose in his store anymore. At the Mambo, he experienced an incremental demotion. Undertaking some incredible gymnastics to preserve the slightest rank of his benefactor status, he aroused neither love nor enthusiasm. His stock had plummeted and the patrons had their sights set elsewhere. When Ngungi's father entered the bar, nobody took pains to prostrate themselves as they once did. The waitresses snorted as he passed by. The barmen and their brood chuckled. The musicians and dancers—including Fredo, Mustapha and Kasongo—looked away, or else spat on the floor. The crazy with the green wig didn't run after him either. The busboys and busgirls made it quite clear to him that the Mambo de la Fête was an entertainment venue for youngsters and that if he wanted to take a breather, he should go to Vieux Léopard where musicians from another century performed 1950s rumba—"this place isn't for you, you know, and what's more . . . " The street kids got hysterical when he jostled them on the dancefloor—"I suggested you adopt me, now this is what we've come to!" The disc jockey, who had remained loyal, moped to see him there. That's how it worked at the Mambo de la Fête: you got cash, you got pampered. But once broke, you were odious, a pervert, insulted down to the sixth generation; often they glorified the latest big spender right under your nose.

On the advice of a friend, he turned to a prophet on the outskirts of Lubumbashi who specialized in the lifting of spells. He couldn't understand how, having previously been so organized and incredibly meticulous, he was now no longer capable of keeping his finances in order.

The prophet Singa Boumbou didn't allow his client the chance to unload. Having received Ngungi's father in a narrow, half-lit room, after instructing him to remove his shoes, his bracelet, and his glasses, he took a mirror from a case and recounted his whole life back to him, including his time with the Union Minière and his weird and wonderful outings to the Mambo, with the aim of reassuring his client that he was in good hands:

"You're a former employee of the Union Minière. You have two children. You frequent the Mambo, where the waiters and the owner's children have recently taunted you, and the musicians disown you."

Ngungi's father sobbed:

"What's happening? I bought alcohol for these clowns, can you imagine? And now no one, and I mean no one, shows me the slightest interest anymore! I've become toothless."

The prophet Singa Boumbou in a nasal voice:

"What I see is not going to cheer you up. I must speak with your kids."

"What have they got to do with all this?"

"The eldest," he said evasively, "is not growing up normally."

He stared even harder at the mirror, as if he were deciphering a coded message.

"You know, I receive people from all over the province. And I am always pleased when the solution is close at hand. But in your case, everything conspires to keep certainty at bay. You've got oomph, you're a man of character; but that said, and in light of the current situation, I don't know what I would do if I were in your shoes. We all have children and nothing is less sure than how they will turn out."

He allowed himself long pauses, broke off in mid-phrase, hesitated, and straight-out repeated particular words to raise the adrenaline. Ngungi's father, sitting on a raffia bag, swallowed—without regard—the words exhaled by the charismatic prophet Singa Boumbou.

"I won't beat about the bush. Your boy, the eldest, I see him in the middle of cutting your hair with a pair of clippers."

"Do you have proof?"

"Of course!"

"I want to take a look."

Ngungi's father was already craning his neck in the hope of glimpsing what was going on in the mirror. The prophet pushed his hands away.

"You're not permitted to touch that. The child I see and who is now removing your entire beard has a scar on his left leg."

Ngungi's father grimaced and violently shook his head. The prophet Singa Boumbou placed the mirror back in its case.

"I wish you considerable fortitude."

"Hang on, don't leave me high and dry!"

"You came for a routine consultation. If you want to restore the situation, or at least salvage things, I am at your disposition."

"Absolutely!"

"It's five hundred zaires for the trip and the palliative care, not forgetting that you owe me a new mirror. Your son has ruined mine. It has become almost unreadable."

The old father returned home with the prophet Singa Boumbou, who wasted no time. He pointed at Ngungi:

"Foul fiend!"

Ngungi denied everything completely.

"Then I shall bid you goodbye . . . "

"Aren't you going to take any action?"

"You can see what a dark horse he is!"

"Do something."

From his bag, the charismatic prophet Singa Boumbou withdrew a jar filled with a yellowish clay. In the face of parental pressure, Ngungi ingested the product. Nausea gripped him immediately. He felt as if he was going to vomit up his entire intestines.

"He must continue to take this potion until he admits his wickedness. Only then can we rid him of these malevolent spirits."

Every morning, the prophet came and Ngungi took his dose. Exasperated by the ordeal, he eventually came clean. He recounted his nocturnal travels in minute detail: the banquets, the family he had recently started in the otherworld, his houses, and so on and so forth. The healing process involved the ingestion of a similar beverage three times a day with the immediate effect of vomiting and headaches. One September afternoon, Ngungi left the family home.

"If you doubt my sincerity, you only have to follow me around tonight."

## 8. The apprentice writer and the Madonna.

As soon as she heard that I was a writer and that, as luck would have it, I was in Lunda Norte frantically trying to track down members of the Katangese Gendarmerie, the Madonna sent for me. The grande dame was in no doubt that my presence in Angola was a godsend. She insinuated that everything I had done in my life before meeting her counted for nothing. She had specially prepared a huge pot of very spicy cow foot stew, cooked Cameroon style, with plantains on the side. As soon as I sat down, she opened bottles of beer, without my say-so. This was insane generosity when you know how much a bottle of beer cost in Angola.

"They told me you were a writer."

"Yes . . ."

"I have lived a lot, Franz. Oh, the things I have known, seen, touched, and experienced from my tenderest youth until today. If I pass away, it's not just my own history that would go up in smoke, but complete Zairian family trees."

Intelligence is one thing; intelligence of experience is quite another. The former is acquired naturally or at school. The latter through the vagaries of existence. Tshiamuena was not learned, and her intelligence quotient was less than high. But she had that second intelligence. In the course of her life, she had known so many wayward winters, so many squalls, after-shocks, and botched summers, that she was beyond cacking her pants at any old occurrence. Moreover, when a vital decision had to be taken, such as switching mines in the event of a dearth of diamonds, it was always her who gave the word. Tshiamuena was all-knowing, without ever having attended an American or a Russian university. Was she really a witch? Well, that's another question altogether.

"I see what you mean."

"Wouldn't you like to write my memoirs, boy? Money? I'm bulging with dollars. How much?"

The stew was very good but extremely spicy. I wept as I ate. But I didn't know if my tears were caused by the hot pepper or simply from looking at the Madonna. I hadn't yet finished jacking the first beer, that she uncapped another. Without my approval.

"It's a job that could keep you busy for a quarter of a century. I've always felt I've had several lives. Sometimes in parallel. These past months, Franz, I've felt like I've been living in Angola and Japan at the same time. I even have a Japanese name there—Fumie Ogawa—but I am two hundred years younger. In Japan, I don't live in Tokyo or Nagasaki. Big cities stifle me, they spoil my appetite. Living in Kinshasa, that was already a personal exploit."

There was a knock at the door. Without leaving her stool, she yelled:

"Come in, Molakisi! Why are you so sad, my boy?"

The young man stepped over the threshold, and indeed he looked desperate. It was something of a shock. How could she know that the boy wasn't happy in himself? Molakisi hadn't opened his mouth, yet she was already suggesting he grin and bear it.

"I know what happened. Don't waste your breath telling me what I already know and can see without leaving this stool. Are you hungry, my child? Drat, what's got into me, asking you whether you're a little peckish? I know you are."

Molakisi cleared his plate in one go.

"Come with me."

She walked in front, Molakisi just behind. I brought up the rear. We were off to talk to the diggers.

Nobody wanted to hire young Molakisi. The diamond panners found his immoderate language hard to swallow. As far as they were concerned, there was no question of Molakisi joining one of their many écuries.

"Tshiamuena is a princess, a queen, a mother. If you disrespect her," they'd scolded, "you'll exceed the limits of the plausible, one day or another. You've no sooner zipped your pants up than you're crowing like you've confused the mine with the schoolyard."

"Pedritto, why won't you work with him?"

"It's not that at all, we thought he didn't want to pick up a shovel. Come, Molakisi . . . "

The guys from Pedritto's écurie apologized profusely. He was hired on the spot as a sifter.

There are folk who are born lucky. Pedritto and his crew had been seeking the stone for five years. Ten days after hiring Molakisi—and it was Molakisi who made the find—they unearthed a diamond fragment. The stone has no value in

Africa. It has to land in Antwerp or elsewhere to redeem its true worth. Without even alerting the Madonna, who had contacts among the bigwigs and dealers in Angola and Kinshasa and would have helped them find a serious taker, Molakisi, Pedritto, and their crew cashed in the product for a piffling price. Low would be an overstatement: the dealer acquired the stone for one tenth of its real value. In those distant days, most diggers had a certain innocence. They were unable to distinguish between the different types of diamonds. For Molakisi and his crew, this was the beginning of a new life. They partied from dawn till dusk. Tshiamuena had a fit of hysterics. She spoke with them all together and then individually. The Madonna advised them to return swiftly to Zaire and, thanks to her connections, invest in hotels. She supplied tips and recommendations, provided leads, and raised her voice, but the youngsters couldn't give two hoots about her diatribes.

"You're fussing about nothing, Tshiamuena, we're not in Zaire, quite the opposite: Angola, and bang in the middle of a civil war, so keep these warnings to yourself."

They were not the first or the last to play loose with money from the stone. They were part of a long tradition. Money from the stone is made for being splurged in order to cajole the earth spirits. In such moments of exorbitant and uncontrollable euphoria, the sustained, scabrous image of the Madonna as bringer of bad luck was ripped from collective memory by the effects of beer and cigarettes. But as soon as life resumed its humdrum course, crises struck: a cave-in on Sunday, another the day after; some lavadors sifting gravel, swept away by the swell of the Kwango River; a few ace free divers (who filled buckets on the riverbed with sand potentially brimming with diamonds), suddenly seized by suffocation or hit with heart attacks; a bunch of kondombeurs or mwétistes (who kept the boats steady with long sticks while the helmeted kasabuleurs strained and strove underwater), victims of a mystery malaise; several dona moteurs or suppliers of watercraft and all the digging gear, dead in their sleep; a number of pincheurs (who smuggled people from Angola to Zaire—and vice-versa), declared missing or killed by antipersonnel mines. Wide-eyed, they turned as one toward the Madonna. They presented her with anything that lay to hand—chickens, wigs, high heeled shoes, Dutch wax fabrics, transistor radios Made in China—to ward off the hex. But as soon as the run of adversity eased, the dolce vita resumed and people recommenced their nights of boozing, profanation, rumba, and kizomba.

## 9. What Molakisi and other diamond panners chattered about Tshiamuena.

It saddened Tshiamuena how we were living our lives. As demonstrably indulgent and commiserative as she was, following our interminable nights of boozing, systemic brawling after one glass too many, and dirty tricks engineered by one écurie against another, she would rapidly blow her top as soon as she realized we'd gone too far in our chicanery.

"You jack too much beer," she cautioned softly, wearing the expression of someone who has just missed a step. "You embody a youth crippled by the lure of profit (not forgetting jerking off) whereas you'd succeed if you stopped thinking about rumba and drink for just one moment."

She accused us of idleness (and with what bravura!) and invoked her ancestors for witnesses as if to ward off the jinx from those who snickered at her coercions. She was tilting at windmills. Her advice went in the left ear and out the right (just as hurriedly). Angola and our dreams of speedily unearthing diamonds entranced us to such an extent that her grievances and other rantings sounded like provocations. Everyone was after their own bonanza, far from native Zaire; yet birthright (and its related privileges) becomes null and void once in exile, abroad. Country, family, religious affiliation, and clannish mentoring are ineffective. Junk. And in Angola it was action stations all round, an existential every-man-for-himself, all the more so given that each garimpeiro had entered Angola at his own risk and peril, on his own two feet, by his own means, for reasons of prosperity best known to himself, with his own desires for success or easy enrichment. It would have been ludicrous and senseless to expect good manners. With the exception of various tribal and familial impediments, each was midwife to their own birthing, and for good reason no doubt. We arrive in this world alone and we croak alone in bed or in a banal traffic accident. The Angola of the mines was a different sameness; everyone was their own father, their own mother.

Exile definitively frees and relieves you of the weightiness of traditions and the tight corset of relations and acquaintances. It allows the individual to assay the very porosity of their existence, giving them, for just once in their life, the possibility of being responsible for their actions. Angola has proven this countless times. For it is in your name (and not your uncle's) that you descend ten meters underground; it is in your name that you contravene laws and internal regulations set by the mining police and their digger associates; it is in your own name (and not your family tree's) that you chance your arm at making it back to Zaire, your belly full of stones; it is you yourself who pays the price for a cave-in, a roundup, a systematic snatching of diamonds discovered by the sweat of your brow, or just a run of bad luck. Waiting religiously at mealtimes for the elders to get the ball rolling before munching your first morsel, playing the errand boy all day long, receiving a dressing-down without getting a word in edgeways: these kinds of things didn't take in Lunda Norte.

•

When she phoned her cousins Jean-Pierre and Jean-Jacques, both of whom lived in the Paris suburbs, she declared with the utmost seriousness that they were stagnating in the sticks. And as much as the pair—Jean-Jacques in particular—retorted that they lived in the French capital, with concrete all around, that they took the Métro to work, and hung out at the foot of the Eiffel Tower every Sunday, Tshiamuena didn't relent. She maintained the opposite and continued to brand them "my little dears" even though she, the bicentenarian, the world's oldest woman, can't have been unaware that age counts for naught abroad, and that we are all equal before taxes, the law, and the Kalashnikov.

Her cousins were grown men, over fifty, one of whom was blessed with an offspring of seventeen or eighteen young'uns, the other with an incalculable progeny, but she—with all respect due to her—carried on like a lunatic, reminding them of the imminence and urgency of a return to their native land. Many of us would only learn this much later, but the village was considered to be the center of the world in her ethnic group, and everything outside of it the sticks. In times immemorial, people forsook their dwellings in search of fruits and vegetables, to hunt game, to harvest, and to fish, not forgetting sundry activities such as initiation ceremonies. Those who left always returned one day or another. But Tshiamuena forgot that we were well entrenched in the twentieth century and that nobody, her aside—the self-proclaimed and supposed bicentenarian—took their village to be the center of the world. But let us pause for just a moment. If, in response to her urgings, her two cousins had decided to rapidly return to Zaire (wives and children in tow), how would they have managed to house themselves initially? What would they have lived off while waiting to find a decent job? Who would have met them at the airport, given that she herself was in Angola? And incidentally, if we really want to think it through, Zaire and its many (and unruly) intelligence services wouldn't have issued them a single solitary visa. The agents of the state would have suspected some funny business.

10. The Madonna's gallantry is disconcerting, if it's not already putting you in a position of inferiority. Not only does it befuddle your emotions and shake up your traditions, but it lifts your head unwillingly above the water, no offense to the jealous, possessive, and antagonistic diggers, be they karimbeurs, dona moteurs, or kasabuleurs.

She had put on her loveliest scarlet dress to visit me. It was during the wet season. Rain had been falling all day. The diggers going about their business looked like astronauts in space. We were ankle deep in muddy laterite.

"Greetings, my boy."

"Madam."

"Franz, isn't it?"

"Yes."

"Have you inquired about my age yet?"

"Excuse me?"

Her eyes bored into mine. I straightaway guessed that she was referring to herself. Instead of beating about the bush, I bluntly replied:

"I've been told about a lady who's a little too full of herself."

"They resent me, the Zairians. No one trusts me. They all wait for a cave-in to fling themselves at my feet. Surely they must have told you that I cheat the life holding me fast by the jaws? That I serve as décor to my trash-bag fate? I'm going to tell you the truth. Are you ready to ponder it? Are you truly open to receive it?"

She had climbed up onto a stool in order to look me right in the eyes, so close that I could hear her heartbeat and inhale her kerosene breath, while the incense she exuded made my nostrils and eyes tingle—she had over-perfumed.

"I realize that my frankness makes your head spin, for you men are used to blowing your top and denying everything in bulk as soon as the truth unsettles you. I can see from your gaze that you're bird-brained despite your hooked nose. All that said, let's get down to the nitty-gritty." She began fondling the nape of my neck and my hair, not in a romantic way but with the tact of a mother attentive to her infant when it's naptime and the little one is boycotting sleep. "My boy. Not in all the world, from France to Zimbabwe, by way of Cambodia and Bolivia, will you come across another living being who exceeds me in age. I'm as old as the Zambezi River. I'm as old as New Guinea. I'm as old as the Flood. I'm as old as the sun."

I didn't laugh. My attitude touched her. Her piercing eyes widened suddenly. She seemed to originate from a distant world, known only to her. I couldn't say how long we remained in this posture: me stood, arms hanging; her perched on the stool, dress streaked red with laterite. I kept thinking she was going to kiss me, so close were her chops to my own.

"Do people really go on about Whites loving their fresh meat?"

I no longer recall how I came to ask that out loud.

"All these stories of carnivores enthralled me as much as they gave me the willies," she replied.

Her husky voice had lost its impetuosity. It was exactly as if there were a third party speaking through her. Worn out by her soliloquies, she couldn't even manage to get down off her stool. I carried her all the way home.

A wiser person can always be found. When Tshiamuena had fallen for these flights of fancy worthy of a burned-out pimp, could she have imagined being accused of cannibalism herself forty or fifty years later? And by her own compatriots no less? The very ones she welcomed with open arms, expecting nothing in return, whom she fed their fill, whom she gave clean laundry to—and, this being an open secret, even underwear—provided a mattress to sleep on, catered drinks (red wine, bissap juice, and even the brother beers, Primus and Skol), and cared for when they were sick. She showed a disconcerting beatitude!

"These young Zairians don't know what they're scheming. Youthful indiscretions. Sooner or later they'll bring me flowers and celebrate me with due pomp. As long as Angola's swamped with the stones, I'll not lose hope. Today they upbraid me, tomorrow they'll flock in their thousands."

The reality didn't match her worldview. In the mining concessions, everyone played from their own score, even when guys shoveled as a team. Underhand tricks were ten a penny. The Madonna could in no way escape personal attacks. "Matron or witch, same difference!" they said. Her lion-like charisma among the numerous males and her immeasurable largesse grated on those who weren't part of the happy few and who therefore couldn't benefit from her big heart. Her detractors fueled tons of clichés and nearly always succeeded in establishing a causal relationship between her benevolence and the repeated cave-ins.

"She gives with her right hand and takes back with her left. She helps herself to your luck full time!"

With each cave-in, she earned stripes in the shadow realm.

## 11. The clumsy caprices of a young woman with delusions of grandeur.

"She wants to have her fufu and eat it too."

"She's really pushing it, the old crow!"

"Puberty's gone to her head."

"She's an exceptional woman, you jealous bunch!"

"She's got character coming out of her ears."

"Her poorly contained supremacy makes me sick."

"She's on the same footing as Mother Teresa, Bessie Smith, Billie Holiday . . ."

"C'mon now, she can't sing, she croaks."

"If it wasn't for the Madonna, we'd all be living like in the Paleolithic Era."

"Witch or matron, it's a different sameness!"

"Let her go back to Zaire! Between you and me, Angola's no psych ward."

"She was born in the fifteenth century."

"A grande dame, a queen, a natural-born princess!"

"She was born in 1921 and the argument's settled as far as I'm concerned."

"She's a girl from a good family, you know, which most of us are not!"

Squabbles of this sort occurred often among the diamond panners. Widespread scuffles even broke out when some protagonist failed to put sufficient water in his palm wine. Sure,

Tshiamuena wasn't born yesterday. Her stiffened hands, her baldness, and her attire were proof of that. But this same longevity provoked senseless debates that she herself appeared to sustain. According to her official husband, Mr. Tshilenge, she was born in 1921 or 1923. But the concerned party batted aside such allegations:

"Why are you all going berserk? I've not been a young girl for a century now!"

The Madonna claimed that she felt more antiquated than she looked. She drew on her eloquence and her charisma to convince the doubting Thomases. It was only later at night when you were lying alone on your pallet that her tomfoolery became blindingly obvious.

The Belgians, as Tshiamuena told it, had showed up in her neck of the woods to inoculate against smallpox. Four or five trainee doctors to treat a hundred kids. She bumped into one of them as she wandered around her village. "How old are you?" Not knowing how to respond, she'd given a grudging smile and, shaking with fear, forced herself to hold the man's gaze. It was the very first time she'd come across a White since she was born. Same for her parents, uncles, aunts, nieces, and cousins. And most people in her village.

"As far back in my childhood as I can go," confided the Madonna to anyone inclined to listen, "pale skinned persons were thin on the ground in my region. We were therefore not fortunate enough to view them engaging in any sort of activity. Only a very few elders, traders, porters, and adventurers back from long voyages knew anything. They had a head start on us. We used a particular expression to denote these intrepid individuals: those who've seen the marine animal. They had a singular aura about them and capitalized on it whenever an opportunity arose. Some even made it their stock in trade." The Madonna piled it on, her voice raspy from adulterated alcohol: "Their faces transformed as soon as they opened their traps. Recounting the same anecdote day in, day out, they were gripped by the same malaise each time: eyes gradually widening, mouth agape, hair on end. One fellow would get excessively hung up on the white man's undulating locks; another mimicked his vocal range; another wondered if the white man chewed, smoked, and boozed in the same way we did; another parodied his gait; another confessed how hard it was to figure out their sex; another expressed his pity that the White he'd glimpsed found himself far from home; another still couldn't understand what would possess a person to leave behind father, mother, brothers, and nieces to venture thousands of kilometers at the risk of contracting malaria; another professed that his daftest dream was to see a White on the verge of tears, since the Belgians, by whom he was employed as porter, never showed their feelings in public. Those spinning these tales spiced them up to their taste. They reeled off each little story with bombast and had no qualms about hesitating, right in the middle of the telling, to act out their own role and that of the White in succession. As soon as the speaker took the floor, we clustered round," explained the Madonna. "Women, men, children, no one wanted to miss a single word. People went into raptures, burst out laughing, hopped up and down, stammered, sighed with relief, ground their teeth, listened religiously, shook their heads by way of stupefaction, grouched, covered their mouths with their hands, cleared their throats, became indescribably angry, scoffed for the sixth time, disparaged, scrutinized this or that idiosyncrasy of the white man, cheered the speaker or foisted fresh questions upon him, adopting his phraseology. We larked about," continued the Madonna, "proud to have lived in that distant time, and we mocked their habits unsparingly. Their hair. Their faces. The sweat that coursed down their bodies when the temperature soared. Their shoes. Their garb. When a trader, back from his peregrinations, confirmed, not without sadness, that the Whites used pieces of metal to eat with, this was met with unprecedented hilarity. For more than a year, whenever the fellow revisited this anecdote, we rolled about laughing. 'Come on,' we cried, 'how can any self-respecting individual use prongs to poke at the provender they had cooked themselves? What would it cost them to eat with their bare hands!' The jokes flew thick and fast. But beyond these more or less tangible tales, rattled out after the evening meal, the beliefs, legends, and superstitions regarding the white man erupted and lingered in the collective memory for a long while. The white man having arrived by sea, the river, or the ocean, rumors circulated that they were a marine animal who, after years of solitude and bodily putrefaction, had decided to leave the water in search of a better life on land. The white man was likened to a revenant or even an ancestor—deceased by drowning or by natural causes—whose skin had lost its color in the course of an extended aquatic sojourn and who had returned to the living through loneliness, sadness, and untimely and continual immersion. Even more persistent beliefs about the white man—verging on cannibalism—haunted people's minds. Because the slaves led away onto ships were never seen again, those attempting to explain the phenomenon speculated that the white man chopped them into pieces, grilling chunks which he ate with gusto. He used the leftover meat to confect cheeses, and—never inclined to do things by halves—filled tanks with human blood, from which he produced wine of the same color. He hired thousands of black corallers who, in this bloody commerce, found pleasure in frequenting the white man and above all doing business with him. In their leisure hours, they would take part in gargantuan orgies convened by their masters, which always proceeded in the same manner: the dismembering of the corpses, the filling of the tanks, and finally a fabulous barbecue in the ship's hold that was wont to stretch over several seasons."

Tshiamuena hadn't looked away. The doctor, she recalled after the event, appeared tall to her; he was blond, with a bit of a limp in his left leg. The slightly sticking out ears, small greenish eyes, and huge beard made him seem even more mysterious.

"How old are you?" the man persevered.

The Madonna was on the verge of absconding. She took her courage in both hands, and mumbled:

"I don't know."

"I don't believe you."

He took a step forward.

The child recoiled.

"I would just like to know how old you are."

"Why?"

"For the vaccines."

"The vaccines?"

"Open your mouth."

She did so. The young doctor examined her teeth. The Madonna kept her eye on the fellow, ready to defend herself at the slightest false move.

"Lift up your arms."

She complied.

"You are twenty-five years old, if I am not mistaken. Although, hang on," said the man hastily, realizing that there was not a single hair growing beneath her armpits yet. "You are too young to make it twenty-five . . . No, you are twelve."

This episode stuck in her craw. For Tshiamuena, her body in no way matched the age determined in the course of a conversation. She immediately set to kicking the doctor's reckonings into touch. At school, Tshiamuena soon became the laughingstock of her classmates by claiming to carry half a century on her scrawny shoulders. Her parents tried in vain to reason with her, the girl wouldn't let the thing go. She grabbed hold of anyone who cast doubt upon her claptrap, biting their leg or their arm. At night, she didn't sleep a wink, crying until she could cry no more. She found the world and the Zairians (in particular) unjust for continuing to take her for a big baby when in her little head she was nearly sixty. People in her neighborhood agreed that the girl had a screw loose:

"She's not only stubborn, skeptical, unruly, and impudent, she's downright driven by bad faith. Why does she consider herself her mother's elder? If she keeps on like this, then tomorrow or the day after she'll tell us that all Zairians are her actual children! We saw her come into the world, we saw her crawl on all fours, we saw her boobs form. This is what happens when children miss the boat of a quality education. Those of you who still hang out with that smartass, tell her to quit playing the drama queen!"

They advised her parents to consult a pediatrician, a psychotherapist, or go as far as engaging the services of a soothsayer. In the 1960s, she launched a colossal legal battle against the Zairian State on the grounds that her multiple attempts to change the date (of her birth) on all official documents got nowhere. Her pugnacity produced the opposite effect. She passed for a maniac. After hauling her ass all over the Republic of Zaire, she established herself in Angola. With the same braggadocio. Fearless of ridicule, she continued to swear—on the life of her mother, her grandmother, and her great-grandmother—that she was born in 1885, 1882, 1876, and even—when she'd got out of bed on the wrong side—1492. She did go a bit too far sometimes, particularly when she wasn't succeeding in attracting attention:

"I am the doyenne of humanity!" she screamed beneath the tropical sun of the quarry mines.

## 12. Sanza discovers the pups' gala and their sacred callings of predilection.

The street was ours. It was in our pocket. Our private property, our thing, our merchandise. We filled it with our dreams: gutted dreams, dreams from those nights without fuel oil, dreams lacking heads or backbones. At night, alcohol and glue gave us wings, carried us over rivers and seas, and we landed in uncharted megacities (Cairo, Kinshasa, New York . . . ) seemingly by chance, in the company of our wives and husbands, arm in arm, done up in our fur coats, leather blouson jackets, and cashmere sweaters, pouring one bottle of champagne after another; in tenth heaven. While we're on the subject, I'll say this: we made no illegal seizures of other people's trinkets; we helped ourselves at the source like good colonialists. Misappropriation? Definitely not! How could we have laid hunger to rest if we didn't help ourselves at the source? Indeed, the same people who complained of our plundering lamented not an hour later, weeping crocodile tears and shaking their heads, when they came across the body of a young'un on the asphalt streets of Downtown. Thinking about it, we were no longer Katangese, nor were we affected (directly or indirectly) by the Union Minière and its imbecilic structural adjustments. We were one-night princes, kings, marquises honed by the glue; the glue that gave us ideas, the glue that furnished inspiration, the glue that quickened dreams, and always the glue that allowed us to hold our own in those nights infested with finance inspectors, solipsistic soldiers, vendors of genital parts, and assorted seekers of blood for sacrificial ends.

News of my exploit had spread like wildfire. No numbskull had ever dared stand up to the tax inspectors before. What I didn't know when I had my altercation with them was that they were feared, that they reigned supreme and kept close relations with the police. Should they find themselves slammed in jail, they'd be freed the next minute. They supplied them with information, and even hallucinogens. You follow? My fame grew overnight. As I ambled along the main thoroughfares of Downtown, kids hailed me deferentially, pledging allegiance. Ngungi began to think well of me, vowing an almost brotherly affection. The guy understood me better than anyone, for we had traveled similar paths. Ngungi could read and write without tearing his hair out and had a clear interest in designer clothes. He owned none, and neither did I, but we arranged our tattered garments on our bodies with elegance. Didn't Papa Wemba once state that style is a matter of look and that you can wear any old rags well as long as you know how to put an outfit together? Whitey and Anarchist yearned for the closeness I had with their leader. They had a real go at me as soon as Ngungi slipped away, making it plain that I wasn't welcome in the gang. Several times in his absence, they promised to burn me alive if their leader ever decided to return to his family. Me and Ngungi, we were birds of a feather—save for his jabbering, which he unfailingly failed to keep a lid on in spite of himself. I spent most of my time with him. But whenever he received visits from men of a certain age, he requested that I take a walk while he dealt with various matters—"Come back in an hour; this tittle-tattle's no business of yours. Take ten zaires and live it large." The strangest thing is that he always relied upon Whitey and Anarchist to handle his dodgy dealings, yet I was supposed to be his closest collaborator. I sometimes felt like I was no more than a puppet.

It was a golden time with Ngungi, I have to admit. When we had a little cash, we patronized the movie theater Les Montagnards. This was a whole new world for me, and it took a while to get used to. You could watch a film on credit or settle up in kind. A bottle of beer or four cans of food we'd managed to filch more than did the trick. Les Montagnards operated from ten AM to midnight. Ten AM was American wrestling, free for all the rabble. Around noon, Congolese rumba, or disco, according to public mood, again free of charge. One PM, cartoons. Two PM, first action film. Four PM, second action film. Six PM, third action film. Eight PM, fourth action film. Ten PM, a couple of films for adults only.

I was hooked on French cinema from the start. Mireille Darc, Jean Gabin, Simone Signoret, Bourvil, Bernard Blier, Alain Delon, Romy Schneider: all actors who made a strong impression, expressing themselves in advanced French. Belmondo fascinated me. When he died at the end of his films, as he often did, I cried for real. How unfair, I thought, that Belmondo kicked the bucket each time. At the end of *Breathless*, I was inconsolable. I also appreciated the République de France theater for its romantic feel. When a woman and a man, both dazzlingly beautiful, appeared in the first quarter of a film, you could be sure they'd kiss sooner or later. The pièce de résistance was Jean-Paul Belmondo and Claudia Cardinale snuggled up in bed chatting; Belmondo goes to pour himself a glass of cognac, gets back into bed, looks at her with loving eyes and utters something like "what time is later?" before a tender, a very tender, and saccharine embrace.

Ngungi took much mirth in mocking me. He found it boring if a film didn't contain a single punch-up. He loathed the African cinema of the time.

"It's like theater," he cried. "Even kissing they won't do; it's slow as shit; the backdrops are all forest and plain, whereas we're in twentieth century Katanga. There's goats and wild animals and people drinking from gourds, even though we've been through the Secession here in Katanga and two wars. African cinema is a con. We want reality, the mines, the glue, the Villain's Dance!"

There had to be havoc: an exploding car; a collision between a train and an old jalopy; high-speed pursuits. The lead actor getting revenge for his girlfriend's death or freeing hostages in a doomsday scenario, that went down a treat. The whole theater were beside themselves. People whistled and stamped their feet, demanding the same sequence again and again! When the film ended, everyone hung around in the street discussing the action scenes, trying out holds, and strutting about like the actors.

Money we knew how to ferret out. Ngungi gave me some tips. If I spied a pregnant woman lugging a heavy bag, I would rush to greet her—politely—and offer my assistance. If she hesitated, I would insist. My level of French and how I was clothed proved my good faith. I would accompany her to the bus stop, sometimes even all the way home. "You're an angel. Stay just like you are," she might congratulate me, then give me some loose change without solicitation, perhaps offer me water as well as grub (waffles, fruit, bread). I would then feign refusal so as to complete the seduction. She would dig in her heels in turn and urge me to drop by in case of necessity. I would pocket the coins with a flustered air, but deep down it was quite another story. People of a certain age were my preferred target. I approached them whether they had a burden to carry or not and went away with my pockets full. I only had to ask them a few questions. "Why so curious?" they'd wonder. "It's for a piece of homework," I'd reply. And they would unload, with rare eloquence, on such meticulous and controversial subjects as white mercenaries, the Katangese Secession, and the Union Minière. Weary from having to stand so long, they'd invite me to sit down at a café terrace where they'd spill their guts, and I would listen to the Gospel without butting in—just a word here or there to relaunch the verbal deluge. Many of them were former employees of the Union Minière who had abandoned Kasai province to toil for years and years in the mines and steelworks of Katanga. After sharing their personal stories with me, their own take on the Katangese Secession, they always shelled out. And they paid well! The takings of ten senior citizens and ten expectant mothers allowed us to live beyond our meager means. And that's not counting the business that Ngungi hid under a bushel and which raked in greenbacks.

## 13. A villain always has a plan B, even if it discredits him.

Ngungi caught malaria and hurried home to his family. He'd been crashing part-time at his grandparents' ever since the slanders regarding his supposed witchcraft, heading back to the street when the drudge of family life began to gnaw at him. Overnight, Whitey and Anarchist became quite affable with me. I had never been the object of so many marks of goodwill. Indeed it wasn't so much goodwill as idolatry. They treated me like a responsible adult, revered me, addressed me as "elder," "big brother," "old father," "Uncle Sanza," and more besides! I was delighted by such excessive recognition on their part. Especially after enduring months of bother. They invited me to eat with them, offered me fruits and vegetables, ran to fetch me water at the slightest coughing fit, openly denigrated their leader, Ngungi, calling him satrap, moron, drone bee, bad lay, despot, ass-licker, cannibal, Neanderthal, mirage merchant, impostor, sellout, narcissist, daddy's boy, pervert, megalomaniac, peasant, clown, jealous freak, pithecanthropus, snitch, pimp in the making, highwayman, braggart who pees his pants, marabout, natural disaster, nutcase, turnip head, nasty little squirt, male chauvinist, scrounger. They quacked away about all the dreams, projects, and other life plans they fawned over—Whitey confirmed his imminent move to the United States, while his colleague swore he'd end up chief executive of the Union Minière—and regurgitated babblings that were light years from the truth.

All of us who vegetated in the street possessed innumerable versions of the same past that we sugarcoated extensively to attract the attention of passers-by. Muddling up events as well as personal details made certain life stories ring hollow, not to mention false. We snatched tales from east and west, combining them into one, our own, which we propagated all day long in the manner of the radio until we truly started to believe them. When Ngungi left, Whitey and Anarchist claimed descendance from a royal line—a version which they abandoned after a week. They then asserted that they came from a suburb of Kinshasa; next, that it was not Kinshasa, but Mbuji-Mayi, before rectifying, with some enthusiasm, that it was from Mbandaka that they'd set off for Shaba province. Some nights—when they were hitting the glue hard—they stated that both parents had passed on a long time ago, before they could even walk; other nights, without a shred of shame, they attested to the death of a single parent—in tragic, yet opaque circumstances. The same biographies could be heard in the street, at the Post Office, at the Law Courts, on Boulevard Lumumba, and Boulevard Mobutu: my parents passed away too soon, a distant aunt took us in, but I flew the coop; my father was let go by the Union Minière, we couldn't feed ourselves properly so I decided to go look elsewhere. On two or three occasions, Whitey pretty much recounted Ngungi's life to me. I pointed out that this was not his past and that he'd poached the whole thing. He was mortally offended, but life soon returned to normal after.

I didn't even get the chance to handle the cookware: Whitey and Anarchist suckled me; simmering up sumptuous dishes. The day after Christmas, the two chumps invited me to try glue.

"Try it, big brother, make you wise."

"It won't burn, big fella, it'll give you ideas."

"Just one hit, daddy-o."

"It's not my thing, really."

Together they shouted:

"One hit, one hit, one hit!"

The invitation seemed imbued with good intentions, and I didn't want to reject it for fear of spoiling the sunny mood of my two subjects. Suddenly I felt wings sprout from my back. Everything my gaze touched on was multiplied: trees, buildings, cars, people . . . I began to feel amazing. Next I was filled with a sweet fatigue. I bathed in a quiescence so infinite I could no longer sense my body. Minutes passed, hours, centuries perhaps. Then, a kind of touching on my hands and my belly, which intensified. I stretched my eyelids wide. What I saw did not surprise me in the least. A monstrous hairiness crawled across my body at vertiginous speed. In no time at all I was covered with a generous coat. My face lengthened into a pointed muzzle. My legs and hands diminished to half their size. A sinister bellowing escaped from my mouth. Footsteps. A man and a woman. They trotted quietly along. The man lugging a wheel rim. When they saw me, they slowed. I scuttled off. The woman moaned. The man ran after me, grabbed me. The woman caught us up. We climbed straight into a taxi. I was in the middle, between the man with the rim and the woman. They cuddled me. Just then, I felt a series of irregular and unusually violent blows all over my body, accompanied by gleeful hurrahs. The blows flew thicker and faster. I opened my eyes. For real. Floating shadows. Suddenly, among the horde of kids bashing me with sticks, iron bars, and a motorcycle helmet, I made out the two finance inspectors, plus Whitey and Anarchist. I attempted to fend off the lynching as best I could, but to no avail. I was so enfeebled by the glue that I struggled to give the slightest shout. They were out of control. Hitting and haranguing me. Whitey observed a respite. He paced up and down, as if not understanding what was afoot before his very eyes. After a while, he seemed struck with sudden, daring inspiration:

"Crucify him!"

His pals applauded. Carrying me to a tree, they tied me up with straps and immediately continued the thrashing. Amid the euphoria, Whitey pulled out a lighter and set fire to a plastic bag which he stuck on the end of a stick and hung over my head. A scream. Nothing more.

When I came to, a blazing sun was falling from a sky of azure blue. Whitey, Anarchist, the finance inspectors, and their accomplices, having purloined my things, had taken pains to leave me in my birthday suit. People passed without so much as a glance. I went back to sleep, exhausted both by the glue and the beating up. Later, when it was dark, I crawled as far as the Post Office forecourt, where I dozed some more. Whitey and Anarchist never returned.

"Here!"

A girl of at least seventeen who lodged with her sisterhood out front of the Law Courts (the girls had their own residential area) woke me up in the depths of the night. She handed me a dress and a crust of bread, slipping off before I had time to thank her.

## 14. When Sanza meets the Samaritan, his life takes a dramatic turn.

Outdoors, days and years flitted by without you really noticing. We were, in our way, Sumerians, Babylonians, Gauls, Mandinka, Greeks, and Romans. We didn't have a watch, a clock, or an hourglass. Truth be told, we referred to the ancient calendar, that of our great-grandmothers. Our fucking existence was cadenced by the sun, the moon, the dry season, street fights, glue, police roundups, and raids by finance inspectors. We possessed our own dating system. We enrolled the sun in our lunacies. Sometimes we stayed up all night long and crashed all day. In fact, every major decision in this country is made and executed at night: the collapsing of governments, attempted coups d'état, the suspension or appointment of ministers, the unleashing of rebellions, the takeoff of cargo planes from the Post Office forecourt at nine PM sharp. Daytime was ideal for recharging your batteries. No sleep was smoother, more appetizing and tranquillizing than that which you took in broad daylight—under the influence of glue of course. The thrum of cars only embellished this sublime exercise. I therefore couldn't say how long I remained alone and unhappy until the Lord sent a Samaritan.

I was stretched out on the ground one early afternoon. A big gray car passed once, twice, and yet again before switching off its engine. A man got out and walked toward me. For a moment I thought he was going to tell me to fuck off out of here or give me a kick. The guy was really spindly. Long legs. Tiny head. A stomach quite protrusive for his size. In principle, thin men do not and cannot have a paunch unless alcohol has been a factor, and even then . . . At the time, I'd never have guessed he didn't touch a drop.

"So what's your game, laddie?"

"Nothing."

"Why are you on the street?"

"No reason."

Instead of giving him my own biography, which I considered long, boring, and unimpressive, I undertook to spin him Ngungi's. He was so pained, he shed a tear.

"If all parents did the same, we'd end up with hundreds of children out in the wild. Grab your bits 'n' pieces."

"Sorry?"

"Follow me."

The man walked ahead with a confident gait. Looked back as if to gauge what I was capable of. We emerged onto Avenue des Usines. He stopped in front of a hotel with brightly colored walls. Seeing my hesitancy to enter the establishment, he ushered me inside.

"Monsieur Guillaume. You again! I can't believe my eyes."

A swooning receptionist welcomed us. From the way she lifted her arms and averted her gaze, you could tell she was exaggerating her emotion.

"What else should I do? This is a botched world we swim in."

"But you can't save every child on Planet Earth!"

"If I don't lift a finger, who will?" said the man, his mind seemingly elsewhere.

"The usual?"

"Yes."

"Room 145 is free."

Monsieur Guillaume accompanied me as far as the door. I couldn't quite believe what was happening. Fortune's what you call it. Real good fortune. You're down on your luck and some random guy you've never met shows up and coddles you like his own son. That's when you tell yourself that all is not lost. The world can burn, there'll always be fearless folk to pull the furniture from the flames. People like Monsieur Guillaume. I'm convinced, in my heart of hearts, that if Earth had just a dozen fine fellows like him, things would change of their own accord.

"Papa Guillaume."

"My kids are all grown up, so 'Monsieur Guillaume' will do, if you don't mind. I see no harm in you addressing me in that manner."

"Thank you."

He lived a respectable family life, as he led me to understand. He and his wife had been together for thirty years already. His two children lived in Belgium where they were high-flying medical students at the Université Libre de Bruxelles. His wife worked for an NGO. His own job was sufficient to meet his every need. Monsieur and Madame Guillaume owned at least seven motorcars, resided in a villa a little way out of town, and played golf and tennis in their leisure time. Reading held a prominent place in his daily life.

"I'll leave instructions downstairs. They'll bring you up something to eat and drink. I hope you're not into alcohol yet.

Meanwhile, take a nice hot bath. It'll do you good, body and soul. I'll be back at the end of the day. Don't leave your room."

Around five or six PM, there was a knock on my door: Monsieur Guillaume with a backpack. He handed me it without a word. Seeing that I didn't understand, he stirred from what seemed like a long meditation.

"Get dressed and meet me at reception. Don't forget to bring all your things."

That evening we ate at an upscale restaurant: Italian Gianni's.

"I can't breathe without poetry," he sighed as we entered.

I was over the moon. I think it was the first time in my life I'd been called Sir. Just one look from him and the waiters and busboys came running. Monsieur Guillaume dropped me off in front of the Post Office after.

"I can't have you staying at my place. My wife would take a dim view of that. We've helped kids before who've stabbed us in the back."

"No problem, Monsieur Guillaume."

"But I will look out for your wellbeing personally. I'll come by as often as possible, got it?"

He had already left but he retraced his steps.

"Here!"

It was a fifty-zaire note.

## 15. A quite Japanese solitude.

The way the Madonna told it, in Japan she was born much later—the 1930s—in the small town of Yui in Shizuoka Prefecture, under the name of Fumie Ogawa. Her voice tinged with regret, Tshiamuena would remind anyone who came along that this modest town possessed a tiny little fishing port and that her father was a good, honest fisherman, notwithstanding his immoderate penchant for rice wine. She had grown up eating seafood—miso soup with seaweed, cured mackerel, and many kinds of sashimi. Her favorite was sakura shrimp, a seasonal dish. In her Japanese life, the Madonna maintained a boundless and passionate devotion to Hibari Misora, the country's star songstress. When she wasn't on duty, she listened to her crooning on the radio all day long. She dreamed of having a similar career. But alas, to reach the rank of diva at that time, you had to have charisma, sing very well—no tra-la-la—and migrate to a massive urban area such as Tokyo or Osaka. Young Fumie didn't wish to divest herself of her little town for anything in the world. She said that big cities made her feel like her identity was flaking away; she felt naked wandering the streets of Tokyo (she'd only ever been there twice, as it happened!), it gave her the impression of being a circus animal, trained to play roles. She declared that she felt spied upon as soon as she traveled to a larger town. Aged twenty-seven or twenty-eight, she had started working at the bar of a small motel against the wishes of her parents, who wanted her to get married without delay and become somebody's dutiful wife. She was having none of it. A country girl she may have been, but marriage was like a noose around the neck as far as she was concerned, a prison just like the big city. The men she met at the motel bar fell literally under the spell of her face and her voice which resembled that of her idol—Hibari Misora—to a tee. All of them asked for her hand that very minute:

"You make my head spin, you do. I am ready to sacrifice a part of myself and love you, enjoy a life with you, move to France, to Vienna or Zaire with you . . ."

A man in love can be a pain, a drag, a real nuisance, like a trash can you've not emptied for a month. Some of these gents threatened to kill themselves or cause a scandal if she showed no affection in return, but Fumie Ogawa sent them packing one by one, deriding their exaggerated, clumsy kindnesses—they gave her flowers, orchids to be precise, but also and above all portolan sea charts and geography textbooks in the hope of stimulating a taste for travel and escape. Some nights, it disturbed her, these hangers-about in front of her place of work and all these poorly mounted advances; for she didn't know if these men pursued her for her beauty, her charisma, her big heart, or her face, which, from when she was twenty, invariably reminded them of Misora.

Every weekend, she performed before a throng of motel guests. She covered (a cappella or with a blind pianist) her idol's enka and ballad hits, such as "Ringo Oiwake" ("Apple Tree Crossroads") and "Kanashii Sake," ending with "Mambo de la Fête" for its fast-polka levity that relaxed the atmosphere and the tense, sweaty faces of these lovesick suitors. They, like any captivated audience, sobbed, jacked more beers than usual, and forgot the time and which century and world they inhabited. Man remains a quite extraordinary specimen, feeding off sadness the way you'd binge on bread.

## 16. A call for help.

"Sorry?"

"If you could help me sort out a situation that's been dragging on."

"Are you joking? Me, lend you a hand?"

"I wouldn't have come if I reckoned you weren't up to it."

I was, quite honestly, flabbergasted by Monsieur Guillaume's unexpected visit. He'd promised to swing by, but not before several days' time, owing to his considerable responsibilities, and now he'd popped back just a few hours later. Sweat streamed off him. He must have pulled his office door shut, scrambled down the stairs, dived into his vehicle and driven nonstop all the way to the Post Office. The car door was already open before Monsieur Guillaume had even parked his ride. I realized something was amiss as soon as his mandibles parted. Later, I would discover that Monsieur Guillaume was a very meticulous fellow. He would ponder everything that he did. Simply greeting you required much cogitation.

Monsieur Guillaume took off his sunglasses—which he never removed, even at nighttime—and the next second put them back on, after brushing the sweat from the corners of his eyes. His left eye was faulty.

"I'm just a kid."

"So what?"

"Monsieur Guillaume . . . You've got it wrong. Surely you know more experienced people than my humble self."

"Listen."

He drew a few centimeters nearer, laid his hand softly on my shoulder.

"You're the only kid I can rely on these days. We all have troubles."

"Well, if you say so."

"Thank you, my boy, I knew from the off that you wouldn't let me down. I've been chasing after a guy for ten weeks now. I'd like you to collect a few pieces of information about him. You follow?"

I wanted to press him for further details, but he continued:

"Do whatever it takes to get me his address (it's quite possible he changes lodgings every week), the license number of his car, his contacts. Who he chews the fat with. Tarts? Thugs? Beggars?"

"Don't you have his phone number?"

"What beverage does he guzzle? Does he chat to the barman, and how? Do they know each other well? Is the barman jolly when he talks to him? I'd be grateful if you gathered this data firsthand. From the source. Maybe make his acquaintance? You see what I mean? But obviously don't tell him you know me."

Monsieur Guillaume was sad. Sullen face. A vacant air. I sensed the pain of a father, a man laid low. I pitied him. Here he is, I said to myself, all the money in the world, yet he's unhappy. He adjusted his shirt collar as he continued his grievances:

"I'll be blunt, he likes the ladies. A guy like him doesn't

shoot it on the ground. His wife will be told just as soon as you bring me proof of his philandering. I've been faithful ever since I met my own, you should know. Anyway, my sources tell me the fellow's been frequenting the Mambo de la Fête of late."

With two fingers, he extracted four photos from the inside pocket of his jacket. He leaned toward me. The first depicted a man of a certain age. I'd have pegged him at fifty-five. Sixty tops. He had on a dark gray suit. The photo was taken in the lobby of a motel. Beefy and prominently balding, the man had every appearance of a Minister for Agriculture, Fishery, and Farming. In the second snap, the same fellow, on a bed in the same motel (?) in his birthday suit. With an ecstatic face. The photo itself obviously suggested several avenues: who had taken it? His mistress? His wife? Himself? In the motel? Were they celebrating a birthday? A remarriage? I looked away. Seeing my unease, Monsieur Guillaume sneezed, grumbled, then sighed to loosen the atmosphere, before uttering a laconic:

"You'll get used to it. We've all of us been there."

The man and a woman (his wife?) in front of a swimming pool. An intriguing photograph. They weren't in swimwear. The couple were decked out like they were heading to a religious ceremony. The pool made for a fine caesura with the festive—let's say high-society—look of the man and woman. You could appraise the state of it without much musing. A dilapidated pool. It hadn't been used for years. Wild grass galloped across its belly. The man and his wife (?) had their backs to it. The alignment of the bodies clearly highlighted the desire to depict the swimming pool's fate. The last snap was scratched almost bare. You could see the man in profile. Monsieur Guillaume casually put his photos away.

"This guy's a lowlife. He calls himself Alain Delon."

Such indelicacy surprised me. Monsieur Guillaume was not the type to bandy insults about. He gave me a friendly pat on the back. Rummaged through his pockets without finding anything. Then asked me to take him back to his car. Gestured to me to get in. On the back seat, a pile of books, newspapers, documents, a bottle of water, and a pair of spectacles.

"You won't understand anything. It's poetry. Kosovel. Do you know him? Yes? No? At your age, he'd already created a whole world."

He found his wallet, handed me a ten-zaire note.

## 17. A border marriage lasts only as long as the words "I do."

The Madonna's life could have been brought to the screen or adapted for radio: widowed twice by the age of twenty-five; divorced five times in Angola; twenty-two years spent as a math teacher in a Kinshasa school, then defenestrated like filth; went mad for a while; arrived in Lunda Norte province aged fifty-five with the hope of gathering diamonds herself. Two days later, she had joined a crew of diggers as dona moteur, a position almost exclusively reserved for men. Soon after, her écurie snagged two diamond carats. That same year, she met her second husband, or rather her first Angolan one. Instead of making merry, she threw together this restaurant of sorts that was a restaurant in name only.

The Madonna was doggedly determined that all should vaunt her praises. Franz should have told her: "Tshiamuena, you're a powerful woman, an extraordinary being, a rare character, an endangered species even; without you there'd be carnage, scarcity, and dysentery, for you provide us not only with food and booze but also joy and the hope of tomorrow stuffing our pockets, of becoming responsible fathers, the most faithful husbands, and zealous patriots. But with all due respect, I couldn't give a shit about your phantasmagoric tales."

Instead, when the Madonna asked him to write her memoirs, a tearful Franz furiously scratched his head. He behaved like that when gripped by emotion. The young man looked hard at the Madonna and, his voice husky, almost stammering:

"Ever since our paths crossed, I can't stop thinking about a character from a novel, the female protagonist of *The Wall* by Marlen Haushofer, a writer from my country. Cut off from civilization in the wake of a disaster, she imposes her own liturgy on the world, or what is left of it. Making do with what she has to hand, she arranges things as best she can to withstand oblivion."

That same month, the Zairian diggers were surprised to see the Madonna and the Austrian keeping company. She dictated whole swathes of her eventful life to him, starting with her birth in Japan during World War Two up until her entry and triumphal establishment in Angolan territory. Nothing predestined her for such adventures. Tshiamuena had got herself summarily expelled from the high school she taught at for claiming to be the biological mother of Napoleon III. She tried to keep her household going by conventional means, but couldn't quite manage to. "We'll die of hunger at this rate," she declared to her husband. "I'm going to go to Lunda Norte at the end of the month." He had tried to discourage her ("What're you going to concoct over there?! Angola's in the middle of a war, and anyway, there's no guarantee you'll return with any dough!"). He knew in his heart of hearts that she'd not retreat an inch. Her charisma was innate. Once she'd made a decision, she didn't chicken out. She auctioned off the household furniture, along with her shoes and her wedding dress, and bolted aboard the first bus for Tembo on the Angolan border, where she bought merchandise: condoms, bottles of beer, cigarettes, salt, sugar, palm oil, matches, and soap. She struck up friendships with other Zairians who swore only by Angolan diamonds and—like her—awaited the smugglers' instructions to cross the demarcation line. "Back then," she eagerly recounted with haughtiness and sometimes a false melancholy akin to that of a faded soccer luminary whose memory has remained sharp, "we entered Angola like you'd go to the bathroom. You didn't have to wave your passport or any document at all. The Portuguese colonists had only just skedaddled, and the Angolans were shooting at each other." After a few lonely days in the company of the smugglers and a host of porters loaded with merchandise, she reached the first Angolan villages. They traveled only at night. The smugglers went off to negotiate with the villagers who had the diamonds while the others remained hiding in the bush. As soon as the deal was done, they went and exchanged condoms, beers, children's toys, and second-foot shoes for diamonds. In wartime, people drink far too much, smoke double the weed or cigarettes, and thoughtlessly barter anything that allows them to escape or latch onto an illusory slice of civilization. But this magnificent, epic, prosperous period very soon crumbled. The Angolans were waking from a long sleep. They established the laissez-passer system, erected barriers, and took a dim view of a single woman venturing into a conflict zone. It was compulsory to be accompanied by your husband.

"We had several strings to our bows. In Tembo, Kikwit, and many other little towns, as well as in the Angolan villages, marriages of convenience were made, marriages that disintegrated of their own accord as soon as the lovebirds set foot back in Zaire, with or without diamonds in their pack. In wartime, sexual urges are intense. People seek distraction—even the soldiers. Drinking Primus beer or wearing new or second-foot shoes no longer suffices to soothe the soul. When you start putting sugar in your tea and salt in your pot after many months of privation, you aim high. Soldiers looked at us with puppy-dog eyes even when we stated ten thousand times that we were married and that ours was the most rock solid, blissful, faithful union on the planet. As we brandished our marriage and remarriage certificates, they looked away, spat on the ground, and exhorted us to divorce in exchange for diamonds. That's how I met my second Angola husband: one Mitterrand. He proposed at the Zairian border. I could see no objection. My first husband, a UNITA soldier, was given a posting and I refrained from following him, despite his many suggestions that I do so. Mitterrand was of that breed whom nature and society decline to favor and who forge themselves through pain, courage, and perseverance. He carried no academic baggage of any consequence, but was possessed of such strength of character that all his initiatives succeeded.

Anyone who spouts off about diamonds without having touched one is a hopeless liar talking crap. If you lack grit, then when you see and touch a diamond for the first time, freshly plucked from the hole, you may well puke, piss yourself, or laugh insanely at the idea that such an altogether insignificant stone is worth stacks of cash. A diamond will make you lose your mind. It creates disturbance and contradictory feelings in the brains of those who (irrespective of age, profession, and degree of charisma) fondle it. I've seen folk stutter then faint in contemplation of the stone's radiance. Ah, Angola . . . "

Franz was so obsessed by the Madonna's life that he no longer showed his face. He would pass without greeting you. Glimpse him pulling his suitcase through the red sand of the mine and you'd guess (without being a savant or the school principal's oldest son) that he was either off to see the Madonna or else returning from her. Once, when he was taking notes, the Madonna kept jumping from pillar to post and, as if these ramblings didn't suffice, began talking in Japanese, Tshiluba, and Portuguese, screeching and weeping as she went, before returning to Japanese again. Franz experienced the scene as a miracle.

The next day, the Madonna found the words to apologize—an unprecedented occurrence. ("It's not easy for me to talk about all of my lives, dear Franz. They are full to the brim just like the Zaire River. They have dark sides, but sometimes they gleam as bright as an alluvial diamond.") With the weight of her many centuries, the Madonna favored long dresses, and gold chain bracelets on her ankles. She removed one and held it out to Franz, who declined. She insisted.

"Take this, you'll need it before the year is out."

## 18. The beer jackers reveled into the small hours.

Me and my pal Ngungi showered only during the rainy season. In the dry season, scrubbing and sprucing up were of no interest to us. The public standpipes were out of commission anyway. And we couldn't see the point in showering, since we almost always ended up getting dirty one way or another: dust, sweat, a random brawl . . . We used deodorant to suppress body odors. Our skin grew calloused from lack of proper care. Long fissures we referred to as "the geography" spread across our stomachs, hands, legs, and even the soles of our feet. The first rain of the year caused us as much anxiety as it did impatience. When it fell, we ran about, stripped to the waist. Our skin cracked upon contact with the water. It streamed down our bodies before penetrating us to the bone. That particular afternoon, I unwillingly took a cold shower. I was drifting around the vicinity of the Salesian College when a torrential rain—the first of the season—came pelting down. The time it took to make it back to the Post Office or find some sort of shelter, I was soaked like a sponge. I shivered with cold. Quickly I pulled on a pair of dark blue velvet pants and a white shirt—gifts from Monsieur Guillaume—while waiting for the deluge to end so I could head to the Mambo de la Fête. For him, I was prepared to sell my soul to the devil.

On Rue du Marché, I was splashed by a speeding car. The road hog reversed. I was expecting some apology, even a little loose change in compensation. He wound the window down and stuck his head out:

"Another microbe!"

He pulled away in a sheet of spray, nothing but contempt in his gaze. It was clear to me, without a shadow of a doubt, that the guy was a bigwig of the regime. If he'd run me over, he wouldn't even have stopped.

The Mambo de la Fête was totally crammed, as per usual. Gathered outside was an enthralling array of car washers, beggars, plain clothes policemen, street thieves, a half-naked nut, itinerant peanut sellers, and patrons waiting for a work colleague or friend (male or female) clutching bottles of beer and pulling on cigarettes. Whitey, Anarchist, and their pals battled at checkers right at the bar's main entrance. They flipped me the finger by way of greeting and yelled war cries, pillorying me down to the fourth generation. They were spoiling for a fight. You could see in their faces that they hadn't scrapped for a good week and that a maddening desire to see fresh blood was gnawing at them.

The Mambo remained standing despite its fifty years on the clock. You could easily feel the presence of those who had long frequented the club—the raucous laughter, the sashays, the perspiration—and who in the meantime had become senior state officials or found themselves locked up in Kasapa Prison (you can live ten lives in one in Zaire, things change at vertiginous velocity and sometimes in radical fashion). The former—when they had a few hours to kill and the urge to wet their whistle or dance the Villain's Dance—flocked to this establishment wherein they'd nurtured hope and other dreams of grandeur; the latter—as soon as they regained their freedom—came here to celebrate their release and kickstart new rackets. Huge mirrors hung from the walls and ceilings. You felt like you were in a glass cage. On one side were the usual tables and chairs—decrepit, made of ebony, some bearing the names of patrons who'd reserved them for life—and on the other, the heaving dancefloor. The patrons—of both the male and female sexes—swayed, strutted, sweated (like pigs), crowed in jubilation, and shouted without divesting themselves of their attire. They danced, reeled, and ogled themselves in the mirrors, admiring their hairstyles, their jewelry, their outfits, even their supposed beauty. Not one of these men and women, all dressed to the nines, slipped out of their threads despite the tropical heat, the wreaths of cigarette smoke, the breath from fetid mouths, the body odors, the assorted whiffs, the soot, the hiccups, the vomit, the piss, the sweat, the snot, the hacking coughs, and the loudspeakers spewing the same rumba they had for years. The latest find at the Mambo de la Fête was the most-beautiful-wedding-dress competition (held every Saturday), where the lucky woman received a car as well as five hundred zaires, not forgetting the many consequential opportunities that might lead to remarriage, cooptation to the highest spheres of power, and trips to Algeria and South Africa.

## 19. The Madonna knew about Franz's life from A to Z.

Tshiamuena reasoned by reductio ad absurdum and this was the first thorn in Franz's sleeve which impeded his writing about her. She would say one thing then recant it, contradicting herself as her tale progressed, mixing up her other life in Japan with her time in Zaire and her day-to-day in the mines of Lunda Norte. Sometimes she would actually go into a trance in the course of the telling and begin to read Franz's life in a skuzzy, unintelligible voice.

"Franz, you were born in Sankt Pölten, a few stone throws from Vienna. As a little boy, you already liked to travel. You dreamed of becoming an explorer or a carpet dealer in order to roam the world. A classic dream. Since your feeble resources didn't permit such a privilege, you enrolled at the University of Graz, in the geography department. Two years later, you packed it all in. Did odd jobs left and right, yet still didn't manage to satisfy your ego. You are an eternal malcontent. Each time you start something, you tire of it fast. You turn your back on love and break off friendships overnight. On a trip to Vienna, you met a young woman and moved in with her the following week. Two months later, you put the relationship on pause and immediately enrolled in the anthropology department of the University of Vienna. It was there that you met your Zairian friend, René. Miraculously, you completed your studies. But the demons of indecision regained the upper hand.

You knocked about Austria from one end to the other before returning to your hometown. At an African party, you fell for Mujinga, the daughter of a Katangese gendarme. That's when your idea for a novel took root."

Franz was caught in his own trap. He wanted to kiss his past goodbye, but Tshiamuena endlessly reminded him of it, which compromised the writing process ("My little man, you know that it was a shock to your parents when you hastily left Sankt Pölten with 447 shillings!" "Darling, when you don't want to continue a relationship with a girl, you tell her, you don't sneak away like you were coming back from the john! Valentina Schneider's crying because of you!" "My little Franz, you broke Lotte's heart." "My little Franz, what was the point when you were living in Graz of going to drink coffee with Verena at the Grand Café Kaiserfeld or listening to good jazz at Stockwerk and breaking off the relationship from one day to the next?" "My sweet Franz, the heartbreaker.").

## 20. Between rumba and rumba, Sanza chooses rumba.

Suddenly a man dressed as a chick—or a woman clothed as a little lad, whatever—screamed with all their might:

"The Villain's Dance!"

The poor DJ would have preferred not to yield to the childishness of these fauna in heat, but they bellowed and insulted his lineage down to the fifth generation. At the very first chords of the Villain's Dance, the people lolling around outside the building—beggars, mangy rogues, amateur thieves, fallen pimps, faded Zairian soccer luminaries, penniless alcoholics, potential spies, small-time crooks, rich kids, engineers, and schoolteachers, in suits or wedding dresses—poured into the Mambo. You'd have thought they were being shot at, or that some maniac had hurled a gas canister, so unreal was the haste. The scene unfolded as if all these fine people had never heard a note of music in their lives. A rapture verging on madness. Like it was the last rumba of their existence. One voice stood out amid the pandemonium. A bare-chested guy with a wig on his head wailed:

"The lagoon is a phony river! The lagoon, the lagoon, our lagoon!"

There were two versions of the Villain's Dance. The longer one lasted an hour and thirty-seven or thirty-nine minutes; the shorter one, eighteen minutes—sometimes ten when the DJ was blasted on glue.

No (intelligible) words, just cymbals, a baritone saxophone (dominant, excelling in the solos, with each solo ending jaggedly like an old crate entering the station), the psychedelic riffs of Hawaiian guitars, a majestic accordion rescuing a below average trumpet, three cajóns (splendidly handled by a Peruvian trio: Sandro, Raquel, and Selestino, imperial in unison, separately, or solo), a bass clarinet, two double basses (which alternated with each other), a conga, a triangle, a grand piano, castanets, banjos, trombones (four in number), two alto saxophones, two tenor saxophones, cornets, a kora (played to perfection by a Senegalese citizen, Soriba Kouyaté), percussion (crazy licks and blasphemous breaks in the manner of Günther Baby Sommer), and a tuba; this whole hullabaloo mixed with the shrieks and howls of zebras, antelopes, crocodiles, and polar bears—the seething crowd echoing the shrieks in parody. A cerebral earthquake. I couldn't restrain myself. The track was quite simply irresistible. Feverishly I drummed my fingers on the table I was leaning against. Like waves breaking on a beach, the population of the Mambo advanced two steps, then back four.

Thrilled, I couldn't stop myself shimmying. Somebody jostled me. I turned and was transfixed by the landscape of knocked-over chairs and tables. In a corner: the guy who'd yelled at me after showering me with muck with his car, in deep discussion with a lady. He spoke with arms raised, all hopped up. The woman tried to reassure him, but the guy, clearly not believing a single word, spasmed and stuttered.

"We're walking on eggshells . . . Can't you see we're going too far?"

Suddenly, I had the impression I'd met him before, perhaps

in a past life. *The photos!* I exclaimed. It was the fella in Monsieur Guillaume's pictures. Right after the Villain's Dance, I moved closer to the couple, as the waitresses and busgirls wrung out the dancefloor to receive the most-dazzling-dress parade. I sat down and faced the man. He was becoming more and more obnoxious, grouching about the waitresses and busgirls, and declaring, with no fear of ridicule, that the Villain's Dance was not a song, but rather a conglomerate of coarseness:

"This ain't no rumba, it makes your head hurt. Rumba is vocals, guitar, conga, and, if you like a little spice, the sax of Manu Dibango or the accordion of Camille Feruzi. What a waste! You can't understand anything, and the maracas—one of the clearest of instruments—are almost incomprehensible!"

He was selling the illusion of a better world without rumba, that opium of the people. His arrogance disturbed me. In this country, you dance to celebrate life, to clear despondency, and to scoff at malaria and typhoid; and this guy here wanted to lecture us with his third-rate philosophy. I was on the brink of getting up and asking him to shut it. I have never understood these people who go clubbing, but don't jive, who sit squished in their chairs jacking beer, watching (with disapproval) the others as they dance, and, like this guy, wrecking the rumba. I remembered what Monsieur Guillaume told me, that this guy will pay, that he thinks he's fooling everyone, but that his wife will come to know all about it. I decided to accomplish my mission in the most beautiful manner. I opened my ears wide and recorded the entirety of the conversation.

•

They took their leave of the establishment after roughly an hour. Their freshly vacated chairs were claimed by two middle-aged men. One of them sported a blue jacket. His companion a three-piece suit.

BLUE JACKET: "You're trying awfully hard there . . .

THREE-PIECE SUIT *(gruffly)*: Admit at least that without colonization we would still be living in the bush. It brought us roads, hospitals, railways . . . "

BLUE JACKET *(smugly)*: "Africa has known large empires and immeasurable kingdoms: Dogon, Bambara, Ségou . . . "

THREE-PIECE SUIT: "That old tune! Empires without cars, without portable stoves . . . "

The man with the blue jacket drained his glass and whistled to a waiter. Who came running with a bottle. He surely knew the two fellas, was well aware that the pair of them had been clashing over the same themes for years, and wanted to take advantage of the opportunity to expand his knowledge.

"I've gotta retake my exams in a week, it's my third try. Who was the most sadistic, Leandro? Léopold II or Hitler? It seems there's still a monument to the king in the center of Brussels."

You never entirely forget someone who nurtured you as a child. Even twenty years later. You sense a presence as soon as they roam the vicinity. When your eyes meet or you hear their voice, a whole chunk of the past shoots to the surface. I recognized the guy with the blue jacket as my former schoolmaster, an enthusiast of political history on whom we'd slapped the nickname of "Magellan"—at school we would take an encyclopedia and attempt to find resemblances between historical figures and our teachers. Magellan and his pal had barely sat down before reengaging their debate.

LEANDRO: "It's thanks to him you can glory in this vast, magnificent country."

MAGELLAN: "Thanks to a bloodthirsty monster, you mean."

LEANDRO: "Without Léopold II, Katanga would be a Rhodesian province perhaps, or a Zambian territory. Zaire in its current borders wouldn't exist. Instead of moping, be brave enough to . . . "

MAGELLAN: "Look at Congo-Brazzaville, that's a paltry country. Or Gabon, a tiny country too. *(He pondered, busted by the drink.)* Who else? Oh! Zambia, but you don't see them all rushing to top themselves in the ocean, do you? And have you ever met a sad Ivorian?"

LEANDRO: "Stop these racist comparisons!"

The crazy with the wig entered the Mambo de la Fête and made straight for the dance floor as the brides paraded—their reflections diffracted in phosphorescent splendor by the mirrors—yelling:

"The lagoon, the lagoon, the lagoon is red!"

The patrons—of the male sex—disdained him down to the fourth generation.

LEANDRO *(without a care for the bouncers struggling to control the crazy)*: "We're not going to rewrite history. If we sliced off Katanga like you wanted to in your childhood, it would still be a debacle. Just consider the picture. The River Zaire would belong to you no longer. Can you imagine the humiliation? You give birth to a river yet control none of it!"

MAGELLAN: “Katanga is rich, my boy, very rich, with its diamonds.”

Chatou, the doyenne of the busgirls, who had dressed up as a bride, won the competition hands down. An event equal to her reputation. Whistles. Applause. The Villain’s Dance again to end the evening (or to start the day—it depends—being four in the morning already). For the pickpockets who hadn’t worked much, this was a propitious moment to top up their turnover.

21. Tshiamuena knew the destiny of every human being in such a way that for some she could predict marriage, easy money, and recovery from chronic gonorrhea; for others, such as Franz, a cave-in or arbitrary detention.

When he first arrived in Lunda Norte, Franz had taken her side before very quickly becoming disillusioned. The diggers were busy jacking beers—she only took mint tea—when she addressed Franz without paying them any mind: "Franz, my friend, your first contact with Zaire dates back to the 1970s, at the anthropology department of the University of Vienna. One of your departmental colleagues, René Botsilo Bosili, was the son of a Zairian diplomat posted to Vienna. A straight-up guy, by the way, sure of himself, always smartly turned out. You got to chatting one Friday. 'What are you doing tomorrow evening?' asked René. 'Not much, at any rate,' you replied. 'My sister's getting married. It would be really great if you came. I'll sort you out an invitation. Actually, you won't need one.' The civil ceremony was at eleven AM. The party at six PM, not far from the Prater Park. And the entrance of the bride and groom, expected at seven PM. You showed up at six PM, Franziskus, to find nobody there. Which somewhat surprised you. Around six thirty PM, you headed home. You told yourself that the party had been cancelled at the very last minute, or that René Botsilo Bosili had played a trick on you. The following Wednesday, you see him from afar. He avoids you. In class, he gives you the cold shoulder. You manage to corner him anyway. You take tram 43 to Skodagasse. It's packed and René can't escape. He makes the first move: 'I invited you to my sister's wedding and you didn't come, and what's more you're giving me the cold shoulder!'

"In the heat of the moment, Franz, you didn't grasp what he was getting at. 'No, I turned up at six PM as agreed. After a bit, I went home. There was no one there!' René broke into raucous laughter. 'What an idiot! I told you six PM but you could have guessed for yourself that six PM is a bit too early for the guests and even the bride and groom to have time to get themselves dolled up. The party certainly happened.' From that time on, Franz, you did the rounds of wedding parties with René, all scheduled for seven or eight PM where the guests and the happy couple showed up at ten PM or much later even. The same for concerts scheduled for eight PM where the Zairian musicians came on stage three hours late. Those were fine times, weren't they, Franz? When you broke girls' hearts without a care! Fridays, you took the night train for Paris, Geneva, Firenze, and partied with the Zairian community before making it back to Vienna on Sunday night, sometimes Monday morning. There were very few Blacks in Austria back then, African immigration being a recent thing. As a somewhat remote country in the heart of Europe, it doesn't have a colonial history like Belgium. But when there was a Zairian party in Vienna, Graz, Bregenz, or Innsbruck, you always had a ringside seat, my Franz. At an African party in Salzburg, you fell for Sylvie Kalombo, a Zairian whose father was a Katangese gendarme living secretly in Angola. In the wake of Zaire's independence, Katanga had proclaimed secession (at Belgian instigation). An army, the Katangese gendarmerie, was formed to defend the gains of the new state. And Sylvie's father had been among the first of these gendarmes, led by white mercenaries. After many months and a series of battles between the Katangese forces and UN troops, the mercenaries and gendarmes crossed the Angolan border. On two occasions, in 1977 and 1978, under the label of the Congolese National Liberation Front, they invaded Katanga with the support of Cuba and Angola. Zaire, for its part, thwarted them, backed by the United States and France, among others. Ah, that was the golden age of the Cold War, when the diamonds sprouted like mushrooms. And then Franz, my dear little Franz, after René Botsilo Bosili returned to Africa, you came and joined him in Kinshasa. You had that passion tourists have who arrive in a country for the first time and have boned up on it so much, they pay less heed to the advice and suggestions of the natives. René assured you he'd find some people to guide you all the way to Luanda, but you were so impatient, you set off on your own and found yourself here, for you'd confused Luanda with Lunda! Tell me, Franz, with the diggers for witness, tell me if I lie. Ah! Franz. Antonia, little Antonia from Linz, how she swears she'll have your head!"

Franz completely lost himself in his writing. He started evading Tshiamuena. As she entered left, he exited right. A comical situation. One day, she caught him by surprise and pretty much castigated him. ("You're not going to spend your whole life avoiding me! It's no disaster if you can't carry on scribbling . . . ") But that was to misjudge Franz. He defended himself fiercely. ("Madonna, you mean a lot to Zaire, your country of origin, and I will write these memoirs.") That was Franziskus for you. He was incapable of saying "no" and wanted to please at all costs even when it wasn't worth it.

"It's no big deal if you lack inspiration! Prison is the only place in the world you can get your ideas in order. You'll see clearer once you're there."

The phrase rankled with him. For Franz, it was obvious: he had to leave Angola at any cost. He ended up going to see the Madonna of his own volition.

She had cooked for two. Fish braised Cameroon style, with rice and cassava sticks. Red chili pepper.

"Molakisi has been telling me about his hometown, Lubumbashi, these past months, where most of the Katangese gendarmes come from. I'd like to go there, will you let me?" Franz gabbled.

The Madonna's answer was quick in coming:

"Sit down and eat. I knew you'd need money for your trip. Which was why I gave you the bracelet. You'll meet loads of people there: Magellan, Ngungi, Sanza. And you'll have all the time you need to write my memoirs." She abruptly switched subject. "Your parents, Franz . . . "

"My parents?"

"Yes, your parents," continued Tshiamuena solemnly as only she knew how. "They're racked with sorrow. You'll send them a message? Oh, I almost forgot: Angelika Bauer . . . You broke her heart like it was porcelain. You'll send her a few words in mea culpa?"

Franz grouched:

"You're asking too much of me."

The Madonna raised her voice:

"Do it for me, Franz!"

As Franz understood it, Tshiamuena would try anything to prevent him leaving. He had nothing more to say.

An ambiguous phrase left his mouth:

"Are you a Buddhist, Tshiamuena?"

"Why?" replied the Madonna, applying herself to the uncapping of a bottle of Primus without his say-so.

"I was just asking," the young man remarked, "it's something I'm thinking about at the moment."

"Why would I be a Buddhist, my little Franz?"

"Why couldn't you be," Franz persisted, tears in his eyes.

The Madonna, sighing like someone who's answered the same question ten thousand times and can't take it any longer:

"BECAUSE I AM GOD."

## 22. What Tshiamuena was the name of.

The family name—or belly name, to be precise—is a wish, a vibrant desire, an intention. The hope when granting it is that the child will follow the example of who they're named after. Some guys jack beers without counting or go burgle, pre-destined by the name they bear. Tshiamuena was no exception to this state of affairs.

According to the beliefs of her native people, God is nuts about names. He accumulates a multitude of attributes. He bears some names that are his alone. He also bears by derivation the names of elements of nature, of trees, animals, illustrious personages, drums—the list is long—to mark his many qualities. Thus he is also called "Tshiamuena" to refer to his omniscience, and in allusion to a memorable lady.

The way the old-timers told it, Tshiamuena was a powerful and resplendent woman. She had a big heart. Her arms were always open wide. She loved men with a love that was real. Tshiamuena was always ready to lend a hand. But people didn't want to have a damn thing to do with her. As soon as they glimpsed her in the distance, they took another route. They didn't even want to talk to her, still less meet her gaze. When she passed by, they whispered behind her back and eyeballed her until she vanished from their view in order to pursue their chinwag. They'd be jacking beers beneath the palm trees, Tshiamuena would join them, and they'd set to scratching their heads, spluttering incomprehensible phrases, and professing a bellyache, fish to fry, children to put to bed, a neglected saucepan on the hob . . . Tshiamuena was capable of reading, with surprising casualness, the past, present, and future of people with whom she conversed. She was as familiar with their lives as she was the back of her hand. Talking with you, she'd discern your thoughts, plans, dirty tricks, skullduggeries, and below-the-belt secrets. Tshiamuena knew when and with whom you had messed up, and even what naughtiness you were presently concocting. Under these circumstances, people preferred not to have a damn thing to do with her.

## 23. Franz and the art of getting into the Mambo at ungodly hours of the night.

There was a huge crowd in front of the Mambo de la Fête. The crazy with the wig welcomed everyone with sardonic laughter, exaggerated gesture, and his perennial remarks: "the lagoon is an aerial territory. The lagoon is the juxtaposition of our dreams. The lagoon in its corrupted impermeability will save the world despite its simpering. The lagoon is no excrement, it's a world in motion."

They celebrated the independence of South Korea—even though no South Korean had ever set foot here. That was the Mambo de la Fête, the Mambo de l'Amour, the Mambo de la Débauche, the Mambo de l'Insomnie . . . The patrons (of the male sex), the barman, and the waiters seethed with inventiveness. They always found an excuse to party. All these fine folk lived with the illusion of a better world. Asceticism, sexual abstinence, fasting, and prayer, all such baubles were nothing but cock-and-bull tales in their view. The Mambo's patrons (of the male sex mostly) scorned lost souls, beggars, (street) children, the elderly, the sick, train crashes, natural disasters, dogs and other pets; in short, anything that made them face up to their own humanity. They feared dying in their sleep, having a serious accident, or ageing, which meant an inability to dance the Villain's Dance, jack beers, and celebrate the independence of Sudan or Bolivia.

Franz (in his checked pajamas) made his entrance with his suitcase full of papers that he lugged everywhere, even to the latrines and onto the dance floor. According to the Mambo's indiscretions—principally from the people he rubbed shoulders with, including the owner's children—he took it to bed with him. Slugged with sleep, he zigzagged his way across the bar, trailed by the crazy with the wig—"The lagoon is a green heaven! Meaning it irradiates the sun with its siren beauty!" Franz lived a few blocks from the Mambo. He'd had a bad dream such as occurs when you start taking glue—dreams where you're chased by warthogs, crocodiles, tigers, and two-headed gibbons; dreams where the ground gives way beneath your feet and you find yourself falling endlessly into a ravine, dreams where the boat capsizes and you're the only one to be drowned—and had come down to the bar with his (strapless) suitcase in the hope of jacking one or two beers, then leaving—suitcase in tow—still sloshed with sleep. It wasn't the first time he'd showed up at such an hour. A warm welcome awaited him.

"Three beers for Franziskus!"

"You in good shape?"

"A bolero, a rumba, a polka piquée, L'Orchestre Vévé, a gin 'n' tonic, anything to resuscitate our dear Franz."

"Franz! The Zairian lads and ladies admire your courage."

"Franziskus, you haven't seen the Incubator, have you?

Embraces with Magellan and Leandro who managed to sort him out a chair. One of the owner's sons, a law student, offered to prescribe him some medication to lift his languor even a little. That was Zaire for you—a country which was self-educated in times past. All Zairians were self-educated in at least one specific field. People stepped out of their comfort zone to try their hand at a field in which they possessed no skills.

"I did six months at the faculty of medicine and I can recognize the symptoms."

## 24. Franz and the nostalgia of the blank page.

Even after changing the subject of his novel, he still felt like he was getting bogged down. His other problem was that he over-thought things. Insane perfectionism. For him, the sentence was what really counted in a novel. He gauged each one in the manner of an ophthalmologist examining his patients' eyes. Every sentence cost him three hours of concentration. The words in his mouth and beneath his pen weighed tons. It was an almost physical effort to get the writing out. He was used to holding forth about the Madonna, but as soon as he began writing, his hands shook and his head exploded. A ringing in his ears. He wrote, sweating. He would jot down a sentence and immediately cross it through—or simply remove a comma. His big suitcase contained in reality just a hundred or so sentences that had been rewritten, crossed through, ruined, patched up, gutted . . . The same hundred sentences, as mucked up as can be, scrawled in his crib amid the symphonic throes of passion, or at the Mambo with the Villain's Dance in full swing. Even when abandoning his project on the Katangese gendarmes for the one on Tshiamuena, and after that, a text about his beer-jacker friends or the vagrants Whitey and Sanza, he still had the feeling of getting bogged down. Like a cave-in that catches short the diamond panners deep in their hole.

## 25. A nocturnal farandole.

"Were they close?"

"Yes, they were chatting one on one."

"Did they dance?"

"Not that I know."

"Did they neck?"

"I don't think so."

"Does it seem like they're sleeping together?"

"I don't know."

"Pity, no damning proof to break up a marriage," muttered a dejected Monsieur Guillaume, before doubling down: "It would have been a godsend for us to fell him from the inside."

Monsieur Guillaume spoke in a monotonic manner that betrayed the many years spent at the Petit Séminaire de Kabwe in the Kasai region. Blank prosody. A voice devoid of surprise. You'd think he was reciting a breviary. On several occasions, I wondered how his wife, his brats, or indeed the rest of his family managed not to flip their lids at this niggling, annoying voice. When, in a rare moment of complicity, the guy would utter a jibe, there was no fatuity, no fervor, not even a hint of a grimace or a smile. In fact, as far back as my memory will allow, I only ever saw him guffaw on two occasions. One weird morning in December, a large car failed to brake in time and hurtled into a clothing store. Cries of panic and distress as people rushed from all sides to help the injured. Not budging an inch from his vehicle, Monsieur Guillaume broke into hysterical laughter. The second time, we were in his office and the radio was on. He was guzzling his coffee, anxious. A bulletin interrupted the music program announcing that three students had drowned; Monsieur Guillaume exploded with the biggest laugh ever.

"Monsieur Guillaume?"

"Yes, my friend."

"I forgot what I was going to say."

"Ah! The barman: tell me, did he look like someone who'd mislaid his wallet? Who'd won the most-beautiful-dress competition? Who'd demanded L'Orchestre Vévé? And the disc-jockey, what expression was he wearing? Was he chatting away with the musicians (on the sly)? What kind of music were they pounding out? Funk?"

"The Villain's Dance."

"I know that, it's the only tune they play!"

Monsieur Guillaume wanted to know everything about the evening's proceedings. Information, as far as he was concerned, only retained its quality if reproduced from beginning to end. It was all in the detail. "Even a banal fact could solve a riddle several years old," he declared. "You must never leave anything to chance when you want to probe the world in depth." He raked over the same questions, examined each of my answers (under a magnifying glass), dug through my hesitations in the hope of an unshakeable certitude, sighed deeply, and shrugged his shoulders. Having taken his leave, Monsieur Guillaume retraced his steps, very edgy:

"You didn't notice anything unusual?"

"No . . . "

"Think, Sanza! Those things that appear to be the least important are the ones that hide the most treasures. You saw nothing else?"

"After the couple left, two men grabbed their chairs. Later on, a white man joined them."

"A white man?"

In a flash, Monsieur Guillaume's eyes snapped wide. He looked like a fella—a pickpocket, for example—caught in the act.

"A white man? Why didn't you mention it? You should have started with that. A real white man? Or an albino?"

Monsieur Guillaume was almost shouting.

"It was my first ever white man. On TV, sure, a bunch of times, in films. But I can't be sure about it. It was gloomy, the music, the screaming . . . "

"So Lagoon was right!?"

"Lagoon? Who's that?"

"The crazy with the wig. Don't know if you saw him."

"I did. But he's mad, isn't he? Do you believe the things he says?"

"He works for us," he replied (seeing my astonishment) as if it went without saying. "He gave me a report on the matter. I didn't believe him, 'cos he often kids around. I thought he'd had one brandy too many or that he was out to take me for a ride. And what was he doing, your whitey?"

"My whitey?"

"The one you saw!"

"He was scribbling down everything the other two guys were saying. But one of the men was familiar. He used to teach me."

"Try to gather some scraps of info about these three clowns. His Excellency the President of the Republic has announced a tour of the province. If the guy's a journalist and he cranks out a scathing article, we'll be left with nothing but the shirts on our backs."

Two or three days later, Monsieur Guillaume picked me up on Avenue des Usines. (It was on this major thoroughfare that Molakisi had convinced me never to return to my parents'). He was at the wheel of a spanking new BMW. This was the first time I'd seen him smoking. He dragged on his cigarette, quite calm. Behind us sat two tight-lipped giants in tuxedos, sunglasses glued to their heads.

"You know," he said in a confessional tone, "this is the first time in my life I've roped in an individual who's not part of the firm for such a perilous mission. But you deserve this acknowledgement, after all."

"We gonna nab Alain Delon?"

"Him we'll leave to play the hero a while yet."

"Let's just lock him up and move on," I replied, bewildered by his new stance.

Monsieur Guillaume had been swearing to lay his hands on the guy day in, day out. He exhaled a (long) stream of smoke from his nose and responded:

"What's the rush? You've got a lot to learn, kid. Patience is what matters in our line of work. If we bust the joker, his accomplices will continue to operate and could still strike. Plus, in neutralizing the guy, we risk no longer knowing what's afoot. My own method is quite particular. I like to let a situation molder. Leave the mastermind to go about his business, flex his muscles even. Then we start squashing his accomplices. It's the best way to deal with someone who's bothering you. You shake up his collaborators, his children, his wife. And if his head's screwed on, he'll throw in the towel on his malfeasances, and that's the country liberated from his germs."

Suddenly relaxed, Monsieur Guillaume sighed:

"These are things I wouldn't tell my wife. Never in a million years. She works for a so-called NGO in her free time and even campaigns for the advent of democracy, poor thing! Do we really need democracy in Zaire? It's premature. Democracy engenders euphoria and euphoria promotes chaos. Everyone opens their trap and believes they're entitled to attack the institutions of the Republic!"

We drove for another half hour before feigning a mechanical breakdown in front of a house with large windows. Monsieur Guillaume ordered us to hastily disembark and to gesticulate around the open hood. Cars stopped and offered to lend a hand, but Monsieur Guillaume curtly declined these marks of solidarity. All of a sudden, a vehicle braked a short distance behind us, just in time. The driver, a man whose age was impossible to guess, berated us, quite enraged:

"How am I going to get my car in?ow am I going to get my car in?!"

The two toughs discreetly drew their guns, to the great amazement of the guy, who could only stand there, mouth agape. He would have expected anything—a punch, a threat, an insult—but not the barrel of a pistol pointed at his paunch. Monsieur Guillaume addressed the fellow in an almost paternal tone:

"If you don't want to end up at the morgue, hop in, and no messing."

He attempted to flee. The goons, having anticipated this reaction, stopped him in his tracks. Grabbing him by the wrists, they threw him in the back of the car and began roughing him up before Monsieur Guillaume had even turned the key in the ignition. Sobbing in every language, he apologized for his misconduct while playing down his role in the conspiracy.

"I'm just a link in the chain. It's not me who produces the flyers."

"When you tarnish the image of this country's authorities, you must bear all of the consequences."

There was no need to insist: he began to confess, gabbling so fast he cut off his own sentences. Monsieur Guillaume switched on the radio and turned up the volume of the music program, which was playing a number by L'Orchestre OK Jazz. As with any self-respecting Zairian rumba, in which the narrator (man or woman) bemoans a romantic misadventure or some other social rejection—edged out by a rival, turned down flat, spurned on the spot, reviled by the in-laws, or despised by their family for their good fortune, their expertise, or their frenzy for jewelry and designer clothes—in "Salima," a young man expresses his sorrow at having to leave his partner to go on a long journey.

When we reached Lake Kipopo, "Adiós Tete" was on.

Yet another man weeping over the departure of his ladylove. Monsieur Guillaume lowered the volume. His henchmen scrambled over a wall. Three or four gunshots rang out. They came running back weighed down with a sack full of flyers. The car took off at full pelt.

"What a dog's dinner! I warned you before about the improper use of your weapons."

"They insulted the authorities of this country, we couldn't help ourselves."

Monsieur Guillaume overtook a few cars before veering left down Avenue de la Révolution. He turned the knob on the radio. Another rumba track. Majestic guitars filled the vehicle. Monsieur Guillaume dropped me in front of the Post Office and headed in the direction of his office with the flyers, the captive—who'd screamed so much, his voice had become inaudible—and his men.

## 26. In the offices of the DDD.

Outdoors, your belly was a garbage dump. We ate anything we could get our hands on. Sanza threw up most of what he'd gulped down that day: two cups of water, a slice of bread, a scrap of meat, bananas he'd pilfered from the Central Market, peanuts, vegetables, a glass of juice, a rotten mango, salt fish . . . The mewling of the tortured guy in the back of the car had overwhelmed him as soon as he'd set foot on the forecourt. After rearranging the poor sap's face, Monsieur Guillaume's goons had stretched his fingers with pliers. At each yank, the man yowled. The memory of his bulgy, bloodied mug—puffed lips, swollen eyebrows, one ear ripped off—haunted Sanza. The crackling gunfire also echoed in his head. It's not at all nice to hear the sound of gunshots close by and for the first time in your life.

Bereft of news from young Sanza, Monsieur Guillaume took a detour into town. Traces of vomit still streaked the Post Office forecourt. Monsieur Guillaume stepped out, arms dangling, looking happy (already a personal feat), uttering repetitive snatches of Kosovel, as was his wont. He believed in all honesty that Sanza would be grateful he'd brought him into this very particular profession.

"Sanza, are you well, my friend?" he called from a distance.

The latter took him to task, pulling no punches.

"Murderer! Get out of my sight!"

"Listen, Sanza . . . "

"Filthy killer! I want fuck all to do with you."

Monsieur Guillaume sniggered. He wore the smile of someone who'd fallen off his pushbike and got up again. Not a snarky, jaded, or forced smile: when a person tumbles off their bike, they stand up very fast and grin in order to prove (to themself as well any witnesses to their fall) that there's nothing broken and that they have the situation under control. But at the same time, the posture of their upper limbs, their legs, their face is at total odds with their laugh. A laugh that's as congruous as an oil stain on a shirt. A laugh that is out of place. And the very first reflex when you get back to your feet is to vanish into thin air. That's why, despite the testy protestations of the fallen fellow—no, it's not worth calling an ambulance . . . I'm OK . . . I'm alright . . . —next day you learn that the guy broke a leg or is hospitalized. Falling off your bike can be extremely humiliating.

Notwithstanding Monsieur Guillaume's impatience, Sanza didn't put so much as a jot of water in his red wine. On the contrary, he dissed the guy down to the fourth generation. Being torn off a strip by a kid barely out of puberty was a picturesque situation for one of the most feared men in the province. His serenity spoke volumes. Like a father dealing with a son who's messed up but still sticks to his guns, Monsieur Guillaume knew that he'd talk him round one way or another and that Sanza's badgering and prevarication were temporary.

"I understand you, dear friend. I just wanted to . . . you know"—at that instant, Monsieur Guillaume scowled, his voice shook—"I wanted to help you take your destiny in hand. The first time I spotted you, my aim was to make you a leading figure of this country. I realize my error. I picked the wrong person. I thought you were ambitious. My fault. What a waste! You've chosen your path, good luck."

Monsieur Guillaume turned and headed back to his car, a little hunched over. He seemed unhappy. Sanza watched him go before giving in.

"Monsieur Guillaume, wait! Where are you going?"

"To our offices!"

"Can I come with?"

Monsieur Guillaume always drove in fourth gear. As he moved off, he was already in his own world. He didn't say another word to Sanza for the whole trip. He just muttered. Was he praying? Placing his plans in the hands of God? Reciting poetry? Kosovel? Rilke? Mallarmé? Rimbaud? He parked the motor and stepped out with little enthusiasm. Sanza trailed him like a dog who—having long displeased his master and being convinced that the man wants to get rid of him (to his eldest niece perhaps) and sensing the danger—would like to redeem himself.

The DDD had its offices in a disused and unfinished building. Popular gossip had it that the building's erection in 1971 had been initiated by a Japanese subject, Shinji Tanizaki, who had a reputation as a party animal. He bought such prodigious rounds at the Mambo de la Fête that his name remained etched into the collective memory a long while. It was an open secret that the guy had no offspring. To the considerable stupefaction of the populace (of the Mambo), he made a hasty return to the country of his birth, supposedly to attend the wedding of one of his twin sons, Ryota and Kenta. He never set foot in Zaire again. Two or three years later, the new buyer died in a mysterious traffic accident. His vehicle slammed into a tree. Those who discovered the body observed with some dread that he was driving half naked—pants undone, underwear inside out, shirt creased and unbuttoned to the waist. Two main rumors emerged at his funeral. According to the criminal police (who dropped the case) he was already dead before the vehicle struck the tree—a version rejected by the Mambo's drinkers who reckoned the fella had some talismans at home (notably a snake) and had kicked the bucket for non-adherence to their precepts. Pedro Kavungu (alias Pedro de la Rosa), an Angolan who'd resided in Lubumbashi for thirty years, acquired the building straight afterward. Just like Shinji Tanizaki, he made a sudden trip abroad—to Tanzania or Italy—to attend his nephew's university graduation, and took advantage of the occasion to settle in Lisbon until his dying day. The building was then purchased by a prominent storekeeper. The day following the acquisition, Louis Umba jumped into a lake leaving neither a will nor the slightest explanation to his only son, Leandro Umba. The site passed into the hands of a young Belgian-Zairian chap with big dreams. Cyrille (for it was he) planned to construct a three-star hotel and recommenced work on the place with great fanfare. Two teams of laborers relayed each other, the first operating at night, the second working during the day. Cyrille himself slept on-site. One afternoon, he left to withdraw some cash from Shaba Bank. It was the last anyone saw of him.

•

A phone call awaited Monsieur Guillaume. He picked up the receiver in one smooth motion.

"It's about my neighbor."

"I'm listening?"

"I'm suspicious of him."

Monsieur Guillaume flipped through a notebook, pen in hand, ready to take down the details. The call was from a sixty-something. Monsieur Guillaume was able to get an idea of a fellow from their voice and how they pronounced their words. From listening to a person's delivery and a few odd sentences, he could guess their age, their profession, their level of studies, their temperament, and so on. As a technocrat of the intelligence services, Monsieur Guillaume knew how to sort the wheat from the chaff. His office was flooded with false alarms.

"I've got a bad feeling about my neighbor. Every time the Zairian authorities appear on TV, he gets angry and switches it off. Yesterday I heard him say that he was prepared to do anything to bring change to this country."

Monsieur Guillaume recognized the man on the other end. He worked for the DDD part time. Reassured:

"Is he a danger to the safety of people and property?"

"No idea."

"I'll discuss it with my colleague and get back to you."

Monsieur Guillaume to Sanza:

"He's a casual informer. We have outposts in every neighborhood. It seems there's a guy who's always criticizing the Head of State. Shall we act? It's your call."

Nobody had asked his opinion for months and months. Sanza, awed by this sudden trust:

"Like you, I cannot stand badmouthing of the people who actually run this country."

Monsieur Guillaume dialed his informer's number.

"Give me the address and tell me what your guy looks like."

At which, pimply Sanza burst out laughing. Monsieur Guillaume dialed another number:

"Did you cook anything? I'm with someone. Ngungi? No, not him, don't even mention that little shit. He's obedient, this one. Sanza's his name."

Before leaving the place, Monsieur Guillaume gave him a tour of the premises. Spacious offices fitted with huge cupboards crammed full of documents.

MONSIEUR GUILLAUME: "Do you want to see the hotel?"

SANZA: "The hotel?"

MONSIEUR GUILLAUME: "The jail. Our jail. We call it the hotel. The folks we put up here are always in transit. We've got to stick them somewhere, the guys we nab. This stays between you and me, promise?"

Sanza was about to smile. Monsieur Guillaume stopped him dead. Contempt in his eyes, only contempt. That was Monsieur Guillaume. He would offer you candy, tell you saucy tales—which didn't make him laugh—yet the next minute clam up so tight that no one could release him, not even his wife. As they were heading for the jail, he changed his mind and told his errand boy to fuck off:

"I trust no one. Not even my wife."

## 27. Every human has a double.

They say that every human has a double. They might be elderly or of a different sex. Some people have two or three. In general, two people sharing the same features never coexist in the same area—unless they be blessed with biological kinship. It's a law of nature. Sanza was therefore more than surprised to discover the physiognomy of Mère Antonine, Monsieur Guillaume's wife. She and the woman conspiring with Alain Delon at the Mambo were as alike as two peas in a pod. Very large. Fluffy down beneath the chin. Thick head of hair. Stentorian voice, too. The only major difference was that the woman from the Mambo de la Fête was a smooth talker. She'd been the one calling the shots.

Sanza didn't take his eyes off the fine woman all through dinner. He looked like a doggy starved of affection. He ate greedily, talked loudly, and snorted with laughter, despite Monsieur Guillaume having forbidden such behavior. It was in his nature to do what he was advised not to: if you told him not to wake you in the morning, he'd set upon you at daybreak and then apologize. But Mère Antonine assiduously ignored him. Then, while her husband was busy clearing the table, she addressed him:

"How long have you been working together?"

Sanza, who was dozing, jumped:

"You know, Madame, you've got the most respectable

husband in the world. Have you ever gone on one of his missions with him? When he's reading the riot act to some rude boy, he sure don't mess about."

"How old are you?"

"The official age."

"Which is?"

"Which one? Fifteen? Ten? Sixteen?"

Mère Antonine got up.

"Madame, did I say something to offend you?"

She berated her husband:

"Yesterday it was Ngungi, now you bring another one home."

MONSIEUR GUILLAUME: "We have no choice, you know?"

MÈRE ANTONINE: "I won't have you involving kids in your business!"

MONSIEUR GUILLAUME (cold as always): "It's a matter of national security."

Monsieur Guillaume whistled twice. Sanza joined him in the kitchen.

"We've got a long day tomorrow. Take some fruit. I'll drop you off."

28. Scheming like a sorcerer or a cannibal's apprentice, Ngungi throws a fit at the sight of his teammate's spectacular ascent.

He thinks he's reached the Himalayas, that he's the first among us to collaborate with Monsieur Guillaume when we've all of us been there. But actually, if we're really laying it on the line, Monsieur Guillaume was closer to me than to any street urchin. Where was he when Monsieur Guillaume was taking me to swanky restaurants? Monsieur Guillaume gave me pocket money, had me over to his place for dinner, bought me such fine items of clothing. I, Ngungi, was the only one out of all those zealots, be it Whitey, Sanza, or Anarchist, to be held in peerless esteem by him. So when I learned—even if water had flowed under the bridge since then—the drivel he'd spouted regarding me, it made me furious. I was the first street kid out of all of them to meet Monsieur Guillaume's wife. She paid me ten thousand times more attention than she did this dodo. So it's a fiction, a black and white movie to say that I was Monsieur Guillaume's flunky. He respected me. There! Young Pimples can molder in his vagrancy. You can't compare the ocean to some paltry river in the backcountry. The ocean is the ocean. A river is a river.

## 29. The intelligence services dislike one-upmanship and they don't do things by halves.

The Pierrot affair was one of the first missions Sanza was involved in. Over the course of a conversation, Monsieur Guillaume gave him free rein to plan and carry out the operation from A to Z. The hunt began quite by chance though. They were driving fast down the half-empty streets of Downtown, snatches of rumba sputtering from the radio. The musician, in his crooner's voice, sang of his forbidden love for one Marie Louise. He's dying to live with her, but her father is opposed to their union. Heartache is all he has left. Monsieur Guillaume switched stations. The discussion program *The Open Debate* had only just started. One agitated participant was accusing the country's authorities of governing Zaire without rhyme or reason and threatening to join the resistance if the situation persisted. Monsieur Guillaume was shaken. He couldn't stomach people laying into those running state institutions in this manner. Any form of criticism leveled at the Zairian authorities cut him to the quick. He glared at Sanza.

Pierrot worked as head warehouseman in a stationery store. Sanza suggested dismissal. Monsieur Guillaume phoned the storeowner a few hours later:

"Your employee's talking twaddle on all the radio and TV stations."

The man tried to cover for Pierrot:

"What our staff get up to outside of working hours is absolutely no concern of ours."

MONSIEUR GUILLAUME: "I get it. I'm not asking anything extraordinary of you. Just give the bastard the boot and things will very soon go back to normal."

THE STATIONERY STORE OWNER: "I won't lay a finger on my staff just because of you. And I don't give a hoot whether you like it or not."

MONSIEUR GUILLAUME: "Hang on . . . "

THE STATIONERY STORE OWNER: "This is Zaire, you know. You can't go around pestering people all the time!"

MONSIEUR GUILLAUME (measured yet deliberate): "It's a funny thing, but while working on this case, it came to our knowledge that you haven't been paying your taxes promptly. How many months of arrears? Ten . . . wait, let me check. No, fifteen. And without going into details, we're in possession of some information we would like to share with you. We know from trustworthy sources that your wife deals in knockoffs and she's never been hassled for it. Your older brother, the one sentenced to five years in absentia, we know where he's holed up. Your son, it appears that . . . Hello? Hello? Anyone there?"

Utter silence at the other end of the line. The guy was knocked for six, incapable of reply in the face of these multiple revelations. In his idle moments, Monsieur Guillaume asserted that any regular Zairian had skeletons in their closet; that you only had to dig a little; that it was up to the intelligence services to fabricate them, and, if need be, use the skeletons of close friends and family members to exert pressure on the individual. Monsieur Guillaume spoke without betraying the slightest emotion:

"It's up to you to choose between Pierrot and your wife, your brother, your son, and your maternal aunt."

Pierrot was unceremoniously let go that very day. Less than a week later, he landed a hotel job, thanks to his connections. Such obstinacy grated on young Sanza.

"This guy take us for losers or what?"

They contacted the hotel's general manager and applied the same method. Pierrot very swiftly found himself in the doghouse with his brand-new employer. But he was not discouraged. He called upon a garage owner, who straightaway found work for him. Monsieur Guillaume upped the ante. He set Miriam Lenge—nicknamed Mimi the Incubator in the trade—in hot pursuit of him. A smooth, swift operator, the Incubator was famous for her beguiling ways. She had been the DDD's trump card, until her first wrinkles appeared. The rumors about her ran into the hundreds. It was said that she was the one responsible for the downfall of the governor of the Banque Centrale du Shaba. When Monsieur Guillaume got in touch, her approval rating was on the slide. She wasn't expecting any glory from the mission, just a posting to Kinshasa and a fresh start.

The Incubator didn't even have to put all of her expertise into practice. Pierrot succumbed to her charms on the dance floor.

"I know a nice little hotel," he suggested, "the Vaudeville de l'Amour, just five minutes away. We'll not be bothered there."

The Incubator declined his proposition—"I'm not that

kind of girl, you know!"—to ramp up the emotional tension. Pierrot: "I thought we were on the same wavelength . . . " The Incubator: "Look me in the eye, do you think I get off with the first guy who comes along?"

A week later, Pierrot's aunts, uncles, mother-in-law, and wife received the unpleasant surprise of a certified letter enclosing photographs of the adulterous pair. Overnight, Pierrot found himself out on the street. Sanza had a brilliant idea for a death blow that would impress Monsieur Guillaume, who continued to underestimate him. Pierrot had shed a fair bit of weight in the course of his various misadventures, so Sanza and his mentor put the word about that he was afflicted by an incurable disease, in addition to shingles, tuberculosis, and typhoid. At the Mambo, Pierrot found the door barred—a phone call from Sanza himself having deterred the owner.

Pierrot went insane in the end. It happened out front of the Mambo de la Fête. Inside, the dancefloor was packed to the brim with a seething fauna grooving to the psychedelic rhythms of the Villain's Dance. The occasion was the fiftieth birthday of Criticos, a Zairian of Greek origin lionized in the shadier parts of Lubumbashi. He was a guy who went all out. Like most parvenus, he sought to shock at any price and reveled in his reputation as an outrageous figure. Criticos offered to buy six rounds of beer for patrons (of the male sex) aged fifty like him, and ten rounds for female patrons of forty-three, as his wife was. He had caught people off guard with this improvised birthday party. Most of the patrons hadn't brought their identity cards with them, which was one more reason to provoke animosity and ruction—already discernible at the Mambo de la Fête even when there was nothing to celebrate—some lowering their age, others raising it in order to benefit from this binge at all costs. On the dance floor and outside, the waiters attempted to sweet-talk the patrons (of both the female and male sexes)—around thirty in all—who swore they'd make serious trouble if their ages weren't recognized snappish. Leaning back against a car, Pierrot soaked up the mayhem without a word. He was seen wandering away from the vehicle, ridding himself of his clothes one by one, screaming with all his might, and rolling on the ground. For a while, it was thought that drink had got the better of him, before the realization that the guy hadn't imbibed one iota of beer the whole evening.

He was never seen again.

## 30. When you've got rhythm in the blood it's plain to see.

Franz was a hopeless devotee of Zairian rumba. His ears pricked up whenever a refrain reached him (from a bar or a habitation) while out on his strolls. Upon landing in Lubumbashi from Angola, the very first thing he'd asked about was a place of entertainment.

"Where might I go to shake my hips? You've no idea quite how much I miss rumba."

Without even looking him in the eye, Ya Bavon, receptionist and owner of the small hotel—a short-time joint—where Franz had dropped his bags, who was chatting with his fiancée or wife:

"Take the first taxi. They're all party animals, the driver will tell you where to go."

Franziskus hailed a vehicle and jumped in.

*"One love, one love, one love!"*

Djibril must have had a couple of beers under his belt that evening. He was quite perky and wore clothes befitting his age—well tailored, not his usual baggy pants and outsized garish shirts.

*"Where are you going, my brother? Are you Belgian? French?"*

He spoke in a flawless English learned from reggae.

*"I'm from Austria."*

*"Australian?"*

*"Austria!"*

*"I know your country. My uncle was a diplomat in Vienna."*

*"When?"*

*"It's been years."*

*"First time in Zaire?"*

"*My second.* We can speak French if you like."

*"English, if you don't mind. I want practice my English."*

"I want to practice my French too. Where can one go dance rumba?"

Djibril started, like someone who's just missed the last train.

"If you all want to dance rumba, who will dance salsa? *One day I'll going to Jamaica."*

*"Have you ever been there?"*

"I will take you to the Mambo de la Fête."

"I'm beginning to like this town."

The taximan drove at full tilt. He overtook one taxi, then another, before purposefully running a red light. Djibril handled his wheel like a Formula 1 driver, zigzagging about to stop a police car passing him. He giggled wildly, convinced of his superiority, and started honking and shouting "*One love, one love . . .* " Guffawing, he accelerated down empty boulevards, and whistled each time Franziskus mentioned the discreet charm of Katanga. He was very proud of the place. Djibril had carried all kinds of customers that day: depressives, phonies, government functionaries, priests, school students, Union Minière staff, bread sellers . . . Some straight out called him ignoramus, railed at him, shouted into their phones, and evangelized at him; others let him know they'd rather endure a scorching foundry than drive a car around from morning till night; others handed over insufficient cash or got themselves a free ride by claiming to have mislaid their wallet; others said he was a secessionist; and some sympathized with him, even inviting him to the baptism of their first son, an engagement party, an academic grade conferment . . . Franziskus's declarations at the end of a hectic day were the best things a taxi driver could wish for.

He made an improper passing maneuver on Avenue de la Révolution where it crossed Lumumba. A headlamp-less crate bore down on them, honked two or three times, overtook the taxi, and slowed. The driver of the gas guzzler flipped them the finger, stuck his head out, swore. Djibril pleaded sincerely for his province: "We don't all respond the same way in Katanga. You must get used to such hopeless cases." Djibril's cab screeched to a halt in front of the Mambo de la Fête and the crazy in the green wig rushed toward the vehicle: "The lagoon is a multiplicity of dreams. But not all dreams match the multiplicity of the lagoon."

Addressing the Austrian:

"I don't frequent these sorts of places, but I'll buy you the first drink. We're in Zaire, after all, I'll not leave you stranded!"

When Franz Baumgartner entered the establishment for the first time, they were doing the Villain's Dance. The song arrived just when the accordionist, as prodigious as a tropical rainstorm, was covering the trumpetist's hesitations. Franz had the face (ears, eyes, dimples, mouth) of someone who hasn't swallowed a drop of water after three days of drought. He ran onto the dance floor like a bat out of hell. The crazy with the wig—"The lagoon is a blues; the blues of the hounded"—followed him. The Mambo fauna didn't take their eyes off him all night long. They jacked beers and gawked like in a museum. At around three in the morning, the Austrian was seen deep in conversation with Mimi the Incubator. Would they end the night at a hotel? In any event, they never made their relationship official.

But unlike that pimply Sanza, I didn't clutter my brain with who humped who.

## 31. The boy in knee-length shorts and his bourgeois urges.

Sanza and his new poodle, Monster, had been roaming the alleyways of Kamalondo all day long. He had received the animal the previous day as a gift from Monsieur Guillaume.

"What would you like me to do for you?" Monsieur Guillaume had whispered coldly.

"I've always wanted a little dog, ever since I was little."

Monsieur Guillaume hastily left his office. He reappeared barely an hour later with Monster.

It was late at night when Monster and Sanza entered Italian Gianni's. The joint stayed open till two in the morning. They settled down at a six-seater in the center of the restaurant's main room. Sanza sought at all costs to draw attention to himself. He had donned a loose linen shirt, navy blue pants, and double-buckle shoes. He removed his sunglasses so that nothing would escape him. Right in his eyeline, a couple of highbrows gnashed their teeth before bursting out laughing. The young man didn't allow himself to feel intimidated.

"Something wrong with you?"

"Don't use that tone with us!"

"Made a big splash and now he's wimped out."

"You're the same age as my grandkids."

Sanza didn't back off:

"You're the same age as my grandparents! You owe me

respect. You're pathetic, you know. I can see why Zaire's not going anywhere."

They put their heads down, aware that the teenager wouldn't back off, that he was looking to pick a quarrel. Street kids love a confrontation. They'll employ any trick to push you into a corner and force you to open your wallet by way of compensation. Ultimately, the street remains the best remedy against timidness, false modesty, and embarrassment. Who would have wagered just a few months before that Sanza would castigate adults so condescendingly? Who would he be without Molakisi or even Ngungi?

"It's not like we're at a station waiting for a train!"

A pudgy waiter hurried over, a shifty look in his eye:

"Sir, we thought that you . . . "

"What sort of a place is this?!"

" . . . that you were with your parents who were parking the car, and . . . "

Sanza didn't let him explain himself further:

"So you don't believe a teenager can have a nibble of something without his parents around?"

"Sir, you must know that the average age of our clientele is fifty. What's more, it's late, nearly midnight. You should be at home in bed already. Anyway, it occurred to us that you were waiting for people to join you for a family dinner . . . "

"Does it bother you that I'm alone?"

"We most humbly apologize. Do you know what you'd like?"

"You've ruined my appetite. A fruit juice. After that, we'll see."

Sanza stroked the poodle's coat and leered at the patrons (of the male sex). Shattered with fatigue, Monster had nodded off.

Sanza was imperious. He lapped at his glass and hailed the waitstaff (of the male sex) every five minutes with some inanity or other . . .

"What fruit is your juice made from?"

"Have you worked here long?"

"What year was that?"

. . . while stroking his dog. But as the night continued, he glanced furtively at his watch and could no longer hide his edginess. Three men eventually showed up. Sanza adjusted his shirt collar and slugged the rest of his drink. Franz (dragging his suitcase), Leandro, and Magellan sat down a few tables away. Franz took a bunch of papers from his case. Sanza was in such a rush to get stuck in that he joined them immediately. A real beginner's error, as Monsieur Guillaume would tell him later. Convention advised sitting tight for at least a quarter of an hour until the prey became aware of you, got used to your presence in the setting, or caught your eye more than once. Things always had to be done in such a way that the encounter with the quarry was struck with the seal of happenstance.

SANZA *(happily)*: "Don't you recognize me? High school . . . "

MAGELLAN: "I don't teach anymore! *(He made the introductions.)* Sanza, a former pupil . . . Franz, a pal of mine. Leandro Umba, my right-hand man. What on earth are you doing here?"

SANZA: "Nothing special, just drinking my juice. *(To*

*head off any possibly embarrassing questions, he pre-empted.)* This is my dog. Monster's his name. A gift from my father."

MAGELLAN: "Are they well?"

PUDGY WAITER: "Have you decided what you'll have?"

SANZA: "Who?"

LEANDRO: "A gin and tonic."

MAGELLAN: "Your parents!"

FRANZ: "A beer for me!"

MAGELLAN: "Your parents!"

SANZA *(with a sneer and a reproving look)*: "They're hanging on in there, like all Zairians. Dad's lost it since he was let go. Mom runs around like a headless chicken to grub for us. Fucking country!"

FRANZ: "Let's continue; you know that in Kolwezi . . . "

SANZA *(a little discombobulated)*: "What's your pal scribbling?"

MAGELLAN: "Ask him!"

FRANZ *(in broken French)*: "An interview for the purpose of a novel on the Katangese gendarmes."

The discussion went on, but Sanza was elsewhere.

LEANDRO *(addressing the young man)*: "Are you OK?"

SANZA *(sad)*: "I'm thinking about my mother! It's awful what's happening in Lubumbashi. People vanishing with no forwarding address."

LEANDRO: "You shouldn't be so pessimistic."

MAGELLAN *(to Franz)*: "The Shaba War was a thorn in the boot of General Mobutu. He appealed to the Moroccans . . . "

SANZA *(broody)*: "Here am I with three stout fellows waiting for someone else to do something for this country."

MAGELLAN *(surprised by the kid's shrewdness)*: "It's not quite that simple. We're trying to solve the problems as best we can."

SANZA: "And your friend, Franz, can't he help you stage a coup? Surely he knows some mercenaries?"

FRANZ, LEANDRO, MAGELLAN *(as one)*: "A coup?!"

MAGELLAN: "Forget it."

SANZA: "We could try something all the same."

LEANDRO: "I agree with him. We must cut the Gordian knot."

FRANZ: "Happily. But I'm just a simple intellectual."

SANZA: "If we can't stage a coup; I mean, if hefty guys like you are incapable of undertaking such a thing, we're screwed."

MAGELLAN: "Speak for yourself! I was in the war of . . . "

FRANZ: "All the more reason to attempt something."

LEANDRO: "Planning a coup's not like organizing a wedding party."

SANZA *(to Leandro)*: "After everything they made your father go through."

MAGELLAN: "What do you know about it?"

SANZA *(scoffing)*: "Pussies! You're gutless! Lumumba was younger than you and he was already getting things done. Miracles. Even if we can't pull off a coup, we can at least try something else."

FRANZ: "A protest march."

MAGELLAN: "Which will be bloodily quelled."

LEANDRO: "Flyers, like those handed around last year."

SANZA *(reciting from memory Monsieur Guillaume's suggestions)*: "Burn some cars in front of City Hall, go flyering, cut off a bridge, take the governor's children hostage, spill red paint down Avenue Lumumba."

LEANDRO: "A lightning action wouldn't be a bad idea."

MAGELLAN: "I'm . . . "

SANZA: "I'm going to try something, with or without you."

MAGELLAN: "How about jacking a beer at the Mambo?"

LEANDRO: "Cool."

MAGELLAN *(the former Katangese gendarme in him now speaking)*: "I'll plan something so tight, the whole province will hear of it."

## 32. Monsieur Guillaume and his sense of responsibility.

Sanza wasn't surprised to stumble upon the crazy (with the green wig) in the DDD's facilities. The man was dressed to kill, wearing all blue with shiny shoes and sunglasses—a registered trademark of the intelligence services of the time. The crazy rushed at Sanza like when you greet a pal you've not seen for a decade:

"I heard you're doing a real pro job. Hats off! We need eagle-eyed kids like you."

Monsieur Guillaume was on the phone when Sanza walked into his half-empty office. He was the picture of frugality. A table, two chairs, and a large bookcase—KOSOVEL, KLEIST, RIMBAUD DAVID DIOP, KEATS, SAINT-EXUPÉRY, WERNER SCHWAB . . . He didn't conceal his fascination for Kosovel, the Slovenian poet, as well as for writers and poets who died in the flower of their youth. He said—his voice shaking—that in just a few years of existence, they'd furnished enough for a century. With considerable reverence, he signaled to his little puppet to sit down while he continued with his phone call.

"No, what's the urgency? He's my colleague. Yes, our new recruit, the young man I was telling you about."

Sanza felt honored that as powerful and feared a guy as Monsieur Guillaume held him in such esteem.

"I'm telling you, national security is the Gordian knot of any country that stands on its own two feet. National security is its brain, its heart, its backbone, its belly, and its cock. A country's intelligence services are to it what the kidneys are to the body. They're the plumbing of a nation. We expel, sometimes by medieval means, the toxins that pollute the Zairian Republic. But instead of raving about the work achieved, the population baulks at the handful of petty blunders committed by our agents. Sometimes I think I'm dreaming! We have so many irons in so many fires, we barely shut our eyes of a night, and still there are grumblers. Answer me this, and yes, I want an answer straight away: where would Zaire be without its valiant agents? We already know where. No country in the world—and certainly not France, the United States, Bolivia, Colombia, or Sudan—would last a single day without the intelligence services. Zaire would be a sieve without us. Not even a sieve, a river mouth."

Monsieur Guillaume abruptly ceased talking, as if hit by a sudden brainwave. The man at the other end of the line went on berating him, trying to back him up against a wall. Probably unearthing things that Monsieur Guillaume would have preferred were left buried. Large drops of sweat formed on his already tense face. He listened, impassive, then riposted:

"No, you're talking crap there, who do you take me for? Pope John Paul II? I'm telling you, we don't play mommies and daddies! We have the heavy responsibility of ensuring the security of a whole people and we are aware of the role allotted to us. Ah! I knew you were waiting to trip me up. The children? They wander the streets. Was it us who brought them into the world? They're real collaborators. You underestimate them for no reason. They're sponges. They pick up and record everything that goes on in this city. We just keep them busy."

Monsieur Guillaume let the guy get two or three words in before shooting back:

"I'm telling you, every human being is a potential snitch. An informer, in other words. You just have to condition them to spill the beans. Honestly—and this is not unique to Zaire—every man has things to tell, every man knows things about his office colleague, his boss, his sister-in-law. See what I mean? Listen, listen . . . I've got a colleague here, cooling his heels, we'll talk again!"

He hung up.

"You well, my boy?"

"Yes, sir."

"If you ever consider you're in danger at the Mambo, you've got the barman to fall back on. He'll know what measures to take to ensure your safety."

"The barman?"

"Just tell him it's on behalf of Monsieur Guillaume."

"He's working for us too?"

"He doesn't know you. You don't know him."

"He works for the firm?"

"Who won't plug away for us if we want them to?"

Sanza couldn't imagine a gorilla like the barman bending over for anyone. The guy was a real colossus. One meter ninety five and a hundred and twenty kilos. With his clientele, his dough, his contacts.

"You joking?"

"Do I look like I'm joking?"

Monsieur Guillaume and his crew had gone to find the fellow. "You graft for us!" "Leave me the fuck alone!" the beefcake shot back. They turned the pressure up a notch and had the Mambo sealed shut the next day. The barman didn't budge, so they switched into high gear. His second-youngest kid failed to come back from school. They looked for him everywhere. Without success. Even today, no one knows where he is or what happened to him. A month later, his eldest son evaded a kidnapping. In the week following the incident, the barman agreed to cooperate with Monsieur Guillaume. He supplied info on his customers in return for protection. And he was not alone. Beggars, peddlers, street kids, and good-time girls: all these beautiful people worked full or part-time on behalf of the many intelligence services, including Monsieur Guillaume's DDD.

"I've learned that you hang around with a certain Ngungi."

"We're not friends," the young man replied.

Monsieur Guillaume persisted:

"You don't know Ngungi?"

"I lived at the Post Office with him. But we're not fast friends."

"Well, it's reassuring to hear you say that. Try not to let on about what you get up to with me. If he finds out anything, he'll spread it about and it'll be me who pays the highest price. I risk losing my job; my wife risks losing hers. Anyway, back to the topic in hand, you were saying about the European?"

"Franz."

"We must look into that!"

33. Ngungi was so conceited that he cried foul and cursed his lineage whenever his charisma began taking on water.

You can see for yourself where bad faith and ingratitude can lead. When Sanza showed up on the street, it was me, Ngungi, who received him with open arms. It was me again who convinced Whitey and Anarchist to enlist him in the gang. It was me, too, who routed the finance inspectors come nightly to fleece him, even if he's convinced of the contrary. It was yet again me who gave him food and drink. And who taught him the ABC of a life outdoors. Now the miscreant is in Monsieur Guillaume's office ignoring me, disparaging me, ragging me down to the tenth generation. In life, you must keep close watch on the taciturn. Still rivers flow deep. Sanza humiliates me in his pal's office, calls me every wickedness under the sun—"N-gungi this, Ngungi that!" It's pretty sad (and violent) to learn that he calls me "filthy rag," curses my lineage, and considers me vile! This is an error. I see no other word for it. Him, Sanza, handsomer than me? What a con! A pretty boy, him? With that gash across his face? And those abscesses! Can you be pimply and handsome?

## 34. When Whitey talks, everyone pipes down.

"Whitey, bro! Long time, no see!"

You won't believe this. We were there in front of the Mambo jacking beers when Sanza hailed me. I couldn't help laughing. It was a pitiful sight. He'd rolled up the sleeves of his loose linen shirt and swapped his double-buckle shoes for second-foot espadrilles and his navy-blue pants for half-pants—or long shorts, it depends how you look at it (the garment extended well below his knees, but it's a question of individual perspective). That he was now running after me was unthinkable. When you've lived on the streets for years, nobody's going to show up one morning with hopes of colonizing you. Sanza was way off the mark. We'd washed up on the street long before him, hung out at the Mambo and Italian Gianni's long before him, sampled glue long before him, hustled marks long before him, squatted the forecourt long before him. No way in hell could he have the upper hand on us despite the bruising he'd dished out to the finance inspectors. The street has its own ancestors. And they're owed considerable respect. You might be forty years old, but if you end up on the street, then overnight I'm your elder. Sanza thought that since he came from a well-off family—although he was yet to exhibit any proof—he'd make short work of us.

"What do you want with me?"

"I'm just happy to see you again."

"We pass each other every day, and it's now that you notice me?"

"No, Whitey, we haven't seen each other for months."

"Something bothering you? Spit it out, why d'you want to see me?"

"I feel really sorry. I behaved very badly with you last time. When we were with Ngungi and even after he left. There, I ask your forgiveness."

It killed me that he was already conjugating Ngungi in the past tense like you'd talk of a fossil discovered somewhere out in the bush, an ancestor, a parent you'd never known, or even a mislaid sock. It was his wont: as soon as he stopped giving a toss about you, he'd flush you from his mind. When we'd taken him in at the Post Office, he harped on endlessly about Molakisi and his family: "we didn't eat our fill at the Molakisis's; there wasn't enough room to sleep at the Molakisis's; it was infested with field rats at the Molakisis's . . . " He had employed subterfuge to spark discord between ourselves and Ngungi. When the latter had gone, Sanza began deprecating him. And he wouldn't stop once he had the wind in his sails. Now it was my turn to endure his tyranny. He took me at my every word, examining each sentence: "Whitey, why do you recount different things about yourself each time? Yesterday you said that your father lives in Kananga, today in Kinshasa, and last week in Mbandaka!"

Between you and me, by what right did he cast doubt upon my own life? And even if I was lying, who was he to judge me?

"How about I refuse your apology?"

"Why?"

"Because your apology is not sincere."

"Yes, it is."

"No, it's not!"

"It is! It is! You must believe me. I messed up. My apology is sincere."

He looked even more pathetic in his doggedness.

"No, it's not!"

"But it is, Whitey!"

"If you're truly sincere in your apology, then give me your dog."

Sanza turned pale.

"My dog?"

"Yes. What's he called?"

"Monster."

"Is it a boy or a girl?"

"Who?"

"Your dog of course, Sanza, have you turned deaf? Is it a boy?"

"Yes, a male."

"Well, come on then."

"Whitey . . . "

Sanza handed me the lead:

"Take him if it suits you."

Sanza wasn't done surprising me. He dug around in the back pockets of his half-pants and exhumed a crisp ten-zaire note. Straightaway, the crazy with the wig headed our way holding a stick he brandished at the sky, drool all down his thorax, mouth agape: "the lagoon is an ecstasy, the lagoon is a featherless bird, the lagoon is a celestial cavity, the lagoon is vaster than the ocean, it bears in its breast the seeds of expansion . . . "

"Hey Whitey, you know people. I've got some pals need help with something."

"Should have said so sooner, my friend. They pay well?"

The old sedan was speeding so fast, it was almost flying. The radio was dispensing music. A tune unknown to the public at large. In the back of the vehicle: Franz, Leandro, Magellan, Sanza, Anarchist, and Monster sprawled all on top of each other. In the front of the taxi: me and two pals. The driver—past fifty, skinny as a nail, tiny hummingbird eyes, dreadlocks tumbling across his shoulders—was identifiable by his sartorial style. He wore pants exaggeratedly large for his hips, a multicolored shirt, and rubber boots. He was so drunk he could barely see. He drove with his head bent over the steering wheel. Eventually he turned on the windshield wipers. "*One love!*" Djibril cried each time they took a bend badly or narrowly missed a chicken, a sheep, or a passerby.

Downtown hit the hay somewhat early. La Cité and its dependencies—excretions of shanty towns with no precise demarcations, deprived of electricity and drinking water—stayed awake till the small hours. The driver guffawed, accelerating down the empty boulevards, honking for pleasure or to lighten the mood. Not one of the passengers uttered a word. All of a sudden, Magellan, or Sanza—the two rascals shared the vocal register of a diamba toker—broke the silence:

"We're in the country of rumba, that's provocation!"

A cascade of reactions:

"It's very slow, this music."

"Playing reggae when we're in Zaire?!"

"Makes you want to sleep more than dance."

"Want to pee, you mean."

"Rumba is languorous too."

"What's the musician singing?"

"Is that English or Polish?"

"How do you say *one love* in Lingala?"

"Franz, Franziskus, how do you say *one love* in German?"

"The problem with Zairian rumba is that the track lasts fourteen minutes; we've got stuff to be getting on with."

"Zaire would be an empty shell without rumba."

"Bullshit!"

"Franziskus, do they dance rumba in your country too?"

"Leave Franz the fuck alone!"

"Franziskus . . . "

"It's all down to beer. Without beer, rumba would just be sinister funeral music."

"You're generalizing, Leandro!"

"Beer and rumba are twin sisters."

"Beer is her big sister. She existed before rumba."

"You'd do better to keep your mind on reggae."

"We're in Zaire."

"Someone farted!"

"Well, it wasn't me."

"It's a sign of good health. You don't fart when your body's in a bad way."

"All these Zaireries are tiresome. Under other skies, people take everything philosophically. They study rocks, snakes, saliva, even farts."

"Good point, Djibril."

"Now that's what I call a fart!"

"So silky smooth."

Djibril lost control of the wheel—the car was heading into the countryside—before wresting it back, braking, then letting in the clutch. A frightened Monster began barking.

"We're not going to listen to this music for hours, are we?!"

"Franziskus . . . "

"He's pissed on me, Monster's pissed on me."

"Lucky beggar; it's good fortune if a dog urinates on you; don't be shocked if you become a multimillionaire overnight!"

The charismatic prophet Singa Boumbou was waiting for us, barefoot, in front of his concession. He had a three-piece suit on but was wearing it inside out. He apologized briskish:

"My life's been something of an ocean these past few weeks. I had a vision yesterday, in the early afternoon. An angel appeared, around thirty years old, black skinned, and strongly urged me to receive you like this. It's not easy being in constant communication with Heaven, you know. I hope you won't hold it against me."

Singa Boumbou's main residence was every inch the cabinet of curiosities. Hundreds of incongruous objects filled the place, stowed in order of arrival: balloons, ten-foot mirrors (a dozen), doorless wardrobes, toilet bowls, syringes, maps, torches, wheelbarrows, firearms, masks, a car engine, three or four fridges, a stack of flags—those of Colombia, Afghanistan, Germany, and South Korea prominently placed.

"A consultation at this hour? Is it really urgent?"

Magellan got straight to the point:

"We need a miracle. And Whitey has sung your praises. Is there a way of making City Hall vanish? So that people wake up and realize the building has disappeared."

Singa Boumbou seemed distant. He had the habit of saying nothing and looking elsewhere to make himself appear important in his clients' eyes.

"What has City Hall done to you?"

"We want to strike a blow that will grab people's attention for centuries to come, as a reaction to what's happening currently in Zaire."

"But City Hall?"

"We have no issue with City Hall as such. It could be the Post Office or the Law Courts."

"Ah! I understand," sighed the charismatic prophet.

"We want to protest against authoritarianism, but the buildings are guarded and we have no munitions . . . Also, we don't wish any act of vandalism."

Singa Boumbou stared at us, pained at being unable to furnish the appropriate solution to our request:

"Expiration. Does that mean anything to you? The building dates back to colonial times, see? And June 1960 is when my powers start. I cannot act outside of the continent either—for example, when I'm asked to neutralize a crook living in Europe, my power can't cross the ocean. I can give it a go but there's a huge risk."

"You mean . . . "

"Say I make City Hall disappear, maybe I can't return the structure to where it was."

Magellan took a step back:

"What if we stuck to our initial plan? Whitey told us that at least two of your followers are on duty at Police Station No. 2. Since they're on guard and you share the same morals . . . "

"You Zairians complicate things for nothing! A grievance like that can be resolved in a flash. My men respect and obey me."

"We want to try and do something. Maybe paint the building red."

"Do you have any beer money? Let's go talk it over."

## 35. The Mambo de la Fête rumor-mill.

Throughout the City of Lubumbashi, one piece of news was on everyone's lips: the attack on Police Station No. 2. When an info, rumor, or idle report dropped into the Mambo de la Fête, it was somewhat fatter when it left. People recounted the incident as if they were eyewitnesses or even leading protagonists. Franziskus, Magellan, Sanza, Leandro, and myself had trouble believing that we were even involved in the maneuver. The crazy with the wig had his own version of events—"the lagoon, the lagoon, the lagoon, and Police Station No. 2 are red with blood." Mimi the Incubator, lolling triumphantly at the Mambo bar (makeup like a Barbie doll, ever-present blonde weave), took all the credit—"it's old hat that attack, inspired by a film I know well; they've pinched my ideas." The patrons (of both the male and female sexes), the waitstaff, indeed the whole Mambo de la Fête pontificated (with considerable scorn)—and in the first person too—on the subject of the sacking of the police station. According to the Mambo rumor-mill, the assailants embraced the officers on guard duty at Police Station No. 2, then watched a soccer match or a porn film and necked gin and tonic with them before tying them up. In general, when you tell a story with much condescension, it tends to become true.

Here's what really happened. Singa Boumbou conferred with his two policemen after dining together. He explained the situation.

POLICEMEN *(as one)*: "Are you sure about what you're proposing?"

SINGA BOUMBOU: "An angel came to me. He requested that I help these young people. The country's in a bad way."

When we went along to the police station, the two men let us cuff them without proffering the slightest resistance. We painted the place red and daubed a mile-long message on the door:

DEMOCRACY HERE AND NOW.
THE BLOOD OF MARTYRS AND INNOCENTS
CRIES VENGEANCE LATE INTO THE NIGHT.

## 36. The return of the mystery-child and his dumbfuck bro.

When your girlfriend, your sister, your first cousin, or your son-in-law wakes from a long coma, or even—to take a less contentious example—returns from a long stay abroad, your face lights up and you want to leap into their arms and tell them every single thing they missed while they were gone: marriages; divorce ceremonies; baptism or birthday parties; infidelities made public or nipped in the bud; blowing of fuses; the rise in alcoholism in this district or that; the migrations of some to prison, and the return of others upon release; former gigolos become bootleggers or business leaders or turned childish or got religion; ex-prophets now working in the illicit trade of minerals. That's the feeling of happiness which overcame me when, crossing Boulevard Lumumba, I happened to spot Ngungi progressing with a confident step. He was filthier than ever. A kid heading back to the street is usually spick and span—you can smell the clean shirt on him. Ngungi was wearing that fur coat which never left his shoulders, football socks, kicks sized larger than his feet, and two pairs of pants as per usual. The spitting image of Ngungi. He generally wore one pair of pants over another. Even all his clothes sometimes. This gave him the air of an astronaut walking on the moon, despite him making a herculean effort to appear haughty.

With him was his younger brother who, unable to keep up

the pace, bobbed along behind like a car trailer. Ngungi was even sterner than the first time we met. I ran to greet him.

"Ngungi, my man!"—a car nearly took my leg off—"Ngungi, Ngungi!" I shouted at the top of my lungs, but instead of being stirred by the same enthusiasm, the sorcerer, to my great sorrow, began deriding me down to the fourth generation.

"You've gotten paunchy and you think the street's your due; your daddy's gotten crazier than anyone could have imagined; your mother doesn't even know what she wants from life; your next-to-youngest uncle drinks like a fish; your aunts sling rotten food at the Central Market; your ancestors are the worst crooks the nineteenth century knew; your nephew François is a public menace; your offspring will live off begging; if you have boys, they'll end up sifters in a diamond mine; your grandsons, maggots all, will bring shame on Zaire and every Zairian."

Ngungi excoriated even those family members of mine he didn't know (incidentally, apart from my mother, whom he'd only met once, not a single person from my clan had ever made his acquaintance), even the dead and the disappeared. Worse, his weedy bruh repeated each invective to the T, like a newly bought parrot. Without going back all the way to Noah's Ark, there's not a street kid I know so free with insults as this boy. He would lay on a great spread. And he was capable of any quirk, I knew that. It wouldn't have surprised me in the slightest to see him return to the street with his grandparents' television set, with flowers, or a wardrobe, just to show off. In fact, one evening, Ngungi had turned up with his grandfather's cane and two pairs of his shoes which he began wearing on Sundays to play the fancy boy. Still, seeing the kid in this state, railing at me for no reason at all, that really hurt.

Even today, his words echo in my head: "you're not worthy to be a Zairian, Sanza. You make me expend my saliva in vain. Just look at your head; that's not a head, it's a lump of fufu, a real mountain."

There are people who are part of your inner circle. They have your trust. You innocently believe everything's fine and dandy up until the day you realize they've been sliding the rug out from under you for years. Perhaps I'm rambling, but what mechanism could explain Ngungi's rancor?

You never get over a night spent under the stars, particularly after receiving a hazing and trying glue. Those who returned to square one after being persuaded by uncle, mother, parish priest, or father very quickly tired of the monotony of home life. Television set, radio, family meal, table manners, the seven AM wake-up: all became archaic rituals, the habits and customs of a civilization on the way to extinction. The blather and servility at home—birthright on the pretext of this or that—smelled off and wasn't far from pointless brainwashing. Like dressing up the old as new. After months, even years, of abstinence (beer, glue, brawls), every sort of asceticism and natural cowardice, they stormed out again, without the least regret. When they made it back Downtown, it was blindingly obvious from their way of walking—as if they had on new shoes that pinched or even a ball and chain—that they hadn't been in circulation for a while. They talked incessantly, outlining career projects and basking in the sun while inhaling the traffic fumes, arms spread, eyes closed, shirt unbuttoned to the navel. They scampered about every which way like dogs without a master or who had been caged up too long, and strutted, heads held high—and chests thrust out—in front of the Cathedral of Saints Peter and Paul, the Government Building, and City Hall, checking (from afar) if the Law Courts had been repainted in their absence and in which color, dashing to make sure that such or such a bank was still operating, or that Jason Sendwe Hospital was still accepting patients. Everything seemed different to them: schools, people, smells, car horns. If they realized you were a street kid, they'd stop you and, with an accusatory look, call you to account:

"What happened to the blue tanker truck that used to park at Central Square?"

"So they finally did lay a lawn on the City Hall forecourt?!"

"That tops it all, and here's me thinking I'd be grazing on the mangos from that tree!"

"The grass at the Cathedral of Saint Peter's growing well."

"Is Father Ambroise still standing, with his ninety years of age?"

"What's driven the city mayor to complain about Criticos? He's the most legit Greek I've met in all my life! He's officially married to Rama, a Senegalese girl from Touba, raises his offspring well, pays his taxes, runs his store according to the dictates of Zairian law, and parades (like all good workers) in front of the Governor or the President during the Independence commemorations—if the latter makes a trip to Lubumbashi."

"What's got the mayor's goat that he's had Criticos' store placed under seal? Doesn't he have the same right as us to make a living? I'm proper aggrieved, what's the mayor been smoking lately? The Republic of Zaire is a hospitable country. He's got no business, the mayor, dragging us into this song and dance of his. Don't the Pakistanis, the Indians, and the Lebanese have the right to trade on Zairian soil? If this mayor—and I weigh my words—continues with this shameful harassment and pathological concupiscence, I'll give up my Zairian nationality until the next mayor comes along."

"Downtown's aged like an ancestor."

"I'm happy that Thomas's puppy's gone back to his dog dad. Someone just told me that he scampers about on three legs now."

"Is the crazy with the wig still living?"

"You're podgy, the lot of you; what you been stuffing yourselves with, rat poison?"

"That shows how good the living is in Zaire. Everyone's bought themselves Mazdas."

"Really they should prohibit under-sixteens from vagrancy. They piss and crap everywhere. I've only been back four hours and I've seen at least a dozen shits."

They had the visage of guys who've worked every day for two years—Saturdays and Sundays too—and are taking their first ever vacations. The visage of convicts released that very day after years in the clink and who're free to walk in the open air. The look and the gait of Zairians born in winter in Europe visiting their country of origin for the first time as an adult and going door to door to greet their matrilineal grandfather, their mother's distant cousin, their next-to-youngest uncle, or the youngest on their father's side who they know only by a voice and a photo. They had the visage and that bittersweet feeling peculiar to exiles coming back to their country following the fall of a dictatorship or even a civil war. They had the visage of people returning to their little town after heavy shelling only to find a familiar place that is no longer theirs, and who, almost fascinated by the shambles, walk slowly through the midst of the ruins past carts blasted by flames, hunched buildings, streets strewn with all sorts of stuff, their attention caught, amid this marvelous debris, by some often insignificant detail, be it a half-burned banknote, a schoolbag, a woman's high-heeled shoe, the baker's walking stick, a television screen . . .

Ngungi couldn't not return to the street. His eyes had seen that which a child should never see; heard things far outside his world. Ngungi collaborated with the police and the army generals. The son of the Mambo's owner was his right-hand man. He was pally with nearly all the Lebanese in Lubumbashi. Was welcomed at Italian Gianni's and, surprisingly, by Mamou Nationale, whose joint even normal (yet hapless) folk would never stick their nose in. He was received and waited-on like a prince. The principal of the Lycée Les Aiglons, who'd known sixty-five summers, addressed him as Sir and bowed slightly when he held out his hand. Those who did their time in Downtown Lubumbashi during those years were intimately familiar with the following anecdote. A highly capricious music star visiting Lubumbashi demanded Cuban cigars—making a whole song and dance and threatening not to play unless her grievances were met. The concierge of the hotel where she was staying teetered on the edge of dismissal. Having collaborated with Ngungi on other cases, he went to find the boy: "One of our guests would like some Cuban cigars, do you know where we could get some? Lubumbashi's an island, Havana cigars simply can't be found!" Ngungi burst out laughing. Two hours later, he was back with the goods.

Ngungi couldn't not show up. There was too much going on in his head for him to stay at home twiddling his thumbs or playing the obedient child. With his feelers out all across the province, he was in the know of everything that happened Downtown, in the poorer neighborhoods and their excretions, be it serious or shady. Like all street kids, he knew that the staff of the Banque du Zaire took a two-hour break and that at lunchtime, without exception, they poured into Italian Gianni's or Mamou Nationale's to graze Zairian; that those of the Banque du Shaba were paid sparingly and couldn't allow themselves to stick their nose into Italian Gianni's or even Mamou Nationale's and that it would have appeared suspect if they stepped inside even just to pee; that the teachers of the Lycée Imara got their wages the second day of the month; that all the Lebanese opened their stores at ten AM and that they stood by each other to the extent of applying the same prices (to the nearest centime) on the products they sold and that when an employee did a runner, no other Lebanese could hire them; that no freight train left the Central Station after six PM; that all trains arriving in the course of the morning provided a very fine opportunity to make some money (what with the traders requiring bodies to unload the goods, their comings and goings were to the advantage of opportunistic thieves); that this one Post Office employee spent every Thursday night shacked up with a lady on Avenue du Soleil; that Father Jacques of the parish of Sacré-Cœur didn't eat goat meat; that every day, Marie Boulogne, a native Frenchwoman, walked her dog (who went by the incongruous name "Monster"); that one of her children had neighborly relations with a woman who worked as an assistant at City Hall; that Simon the Zambian only opened his store from midday (something to do with his diabetes); that Criticos, who was born in Kasenga, spoke Swahili better than your average Zairian; and that his brother Nikias had gone into the cobalt trade after a long time working in fishery. Indeed Ngungi would compare himself to Nikias when the Greek sped through Downtown in one of his many cars. Frowning, he trumpeted that he and Nikias shared the same taste in girls, sleek wheels, and fur coats.

## 37. The child nostalgic for trains.

Ngungi carted his brother Simba everywhere with him. Since living on the streets, he'd not enjoyed an ounce of freedom. Even when he slunk off to defecate behind the Law Courts, he made sure his brother stayed close by. When you ran into these two, the image that sprang to mind was that of a mother hen with her chicks, for a normal hen attacks anyone who makes a move toward her brood. She flaps her wings and scampers at you like a real flamenco dancer. Ngungi was quite aware that any street kid who encountered junior would subject him to a proper hazing. That he was so intent on protecting Simba was chiefly because he knew in all good conscience that as the brains behind the most sensational band of rookie reprobates, as the orchestrator of manhunts, the snaffler of money and glue, and as debt delinquent supremo, the whole of Downtown dreamed only of exacting payback on his brother. Indeed, no sooner had he and Simba stashed their clutter at the Post Office, than news of his return began to spread like wildfire. Within an hour, every rival group was informed of baby bro's appearance, triggering a (tacit) race to be first to lay hands on the kid. Not to be outdone, the girls who crashed on the Law Courts plaza were also intent on taking the sorcerer's sibling to the cleaners—once, while conversing with Bibi, their den mother, whom they idolized and held in the utmost regard, Ngungi had slapped her.

Simba was happy with these privileges at first. He didn't

work. Working meant pickpocketing, rummaging through garbage cans, telling tall tales to old gents and pregnant ladies in order to pocket the proceeds, washing cars, selling information to women and men who wanted to check their partner's fidelity status, hawking matches and garbage bags, begging, faking blindness to encourage passersby to shell out more, confiscating schoolbags from high-school students and returning them in exchange for cash, flogging glue, toiling as shoeshine boy or docker at the Central Station, and engaging with informers. Later, he began to weary of this third-rate protectionism. When everyone was dancing the Villain's Dance at the Mambo de la Fête, Simba wanted to execute a few steps too, but his brother was having none of it. He feared he would lose him in the crowd and that someone would seize the chance to break his arm.

When Papa Wemba and his band played the Mambo, an immense euphoria preceded the concert. Everyone was talking about the show and the clothes the musicians would wear. All the street kids made the journey for the gig, with the exception of Ngungi and Simba. For weeks, Simba had been consumed by a tremendous sadness because a rumba played in a bar against a landscape of bottles, frenzied patrons (of both the female and male sexes), waiters, busgirls, the barman (generally stout in stature), and coiling cigarette smoke, is a hundred times better than that listened to at home, within your four walls. Rumba is an outdoor music. A music synonymous with joy and euphoria. Zairian rumba was invented to be listened to and danced to with others. Chamber music it is not.

Simba bemoaned the strictures of his existence, akin to that of a premature baby in an incubator. Whenever Ngungi engaged in conversation with his pals, Simba was never able to get involved in the discussion. He had neither the code, nor the gift of the gab, nor the slightest scar, let alone eyes frazzled by glue—another of his brother's prohibitions. Simba felt as if he were in the shoes of someone who couldn't speak a language—Russian, Wolof, Turkish, German, whatever—but must smile or nod his head to show the participants in the discussion that he gets the subtleties of the jokes.

"Let's go see the locomotives, Ngungi!" he exhorted his brother one day, angling for an excursion to the station. He had never boarded a train, had never even seen one—except on television.

"I haven't the time. You demand a lot, you know! That I feed, clothe you, and now act as your tour guide!"

The words stung. And so, as his brother drowsed in the glue's grasp, Simba slipped away. He was damn lucky. From the Post Office to the Central Station, not a single street kid crossed his path. He'd have caught the drubbing of his life otherwise. At the Central Station, Simba was dazed by the triumphal entrance of the shuddering freight trains, most of which dated from the colonial era. There was something animalistic about the noises they made. Lewd railroad men with grease in their hair slipped beneath the machines. The train that came to a halt on track five was so packed that some passengers had climbed onto the roof to escape the crush. Four bambinos around his age alighted. They were not accompanied by their parents, and this was clearly the first time they'd set foot in the province of Katanga. They couldn't get over the fact that Lubumbashi had such a population. They stopped to scan the station, not without disdain, then swaggered and strutted about in the manner of conquistadores and other discoverers of rivers, peoples, mountains, and tributaries. Simba watched, stunned, then followed them. An intense rage gripped him. My bro is a dumbfuck, he brooded. Stuck right on my ass the whole fucking time. Even twins don't do everything together. One farts, the other watches TV or washes their face. Of all the street kids, I'm the only one without a pseudonym. When Ngungi was my age, he was already living it outdoors!

A customs agent took them to task:

"Now look here, you're bringing shame on the Republic of Zaire!"

The boy who appeared to be the chief—every gang has one leader, and only one, who provides the directions, ideas, and craftiness to keep raising the bar, and to whom respect is a given—retorted straight off the bat, as if he'd hoarded the insult in his mouth for years and was waiting only for the opportunity to spit it out:

"Did'ya mutha send ya, ya fat fuck?!"—while the rest of them snickered and ran about in circles giving him the finger. In their tiny minds, they were ancestors. Before winding up in the street, they'd all wanted to age as quickly as possible. Old age: how it fascinated them. It was that inaccessible paradise, the flipside of the childhood that kept them apart from real life. You'll wait eighteen years to jack your first beer; you'll bide yet more time if you're itching to leave your family; eighteen years you'll wait for smokes; and you have to be home by seven PM. Consequently, they wanted to collect some wrinkles as quickly as possible. The slightest bit of facial hair was carefully tended;

sometimes they'd resort to a soap-based product that supposedly hastened its growth. They yearned to become toothless old men at any price, endowed with a salt-and-pepper beard. Add to that an awkward, stiffened gait, and the benefits of the resulting aura were palpable: a nod received at every street corner; at mealtimes, the assembled company wait for old pops to kick things off; a whisper from old pops during a squabble and everyone pipes down. The street was an age accelerant for many.

Simba stepped aboard one of the machines without an ounce of hesitation. The train (registration Z4754) was leaving for Ilebo via Mbuji Mayi—more than one thousand kilometers away or three weeks' voyage in the event of derailment, the engineer's syphilis, or attack by trainjackers.

Ngungi had a heavy head. It weighed a thousand tons. He was dreaming that he was at the Mambo. They were all shaking their stuff to the rhythm of the Villain's Dance. Amid the pandemonium, he saw Sanza deep in dialogue with the crazy with the green wig. Then he distinctly glimpsed Monsieur Guillaume, dressed all in black, holding a flower in his right hand. In a fit of excitation, Monsieur Guillaume elbowed his way toward Simba. He greeted him and made to hand him the flower. In a fraction of a second, the flower became a dagger. The time it took Ngungi to react, run, and throw himself on the assailant, it was too late. Monsieur Guillaume had vanished into the viscid masses, their pores gushing sweat like water from a faucet. Ngungi woke abruptly from his sleep. He raised his neck. No one in sight. His brother: gone. He lost his shit. Set to running about, screaming, in his fur coat.

•

I had been out on assignment with Monsieur Guillaume all day. Usually we operated at night. Monsieur Guillaume would show up whenever and take me with him on his operations. So I spent most of my time in the offices of the DDD. I was sagging with fatigue when he dropped me off in front of the Post Office. Ngungi, who'd been waiting, resolute, approached, then rushed forward as soon as he recognized my profile.

"Where's my brother?"

I hadn't been informed of his bro's disappearance. He and his brother no longer spoke to me, yet it was me he turned to now that Simba had gone missing. He was extremely worked up yet desperate at the same time. He'd scoured every alleyway of La Cité and Downtown, bars and restaurants, without finding the slightest trace of his brother. He fell back on what he knew best: proffering insults.

"You're just a lame foreigner. I've been on the streets for four years. I gave you water and something to munch when you came across me in the street, I gave you a meaning to your life, the opportunity to persevere and succeed, I lavished you with love like a premature babe; and to pay me back, not only do you snatch my place but you even go after my baby bro."

I began to smile. He didn't quiet down.

"Where's Simba? Where's my brother, Sanza?

I realized he wasn't joking. At the same time, his grievances seemed somewhat abstract. Did I give a shit if Simba had taken off? How was it my problem if his brother had gone and winged himself?

"Go fuck yourself, you and your excrement of a Simba!"

Ngungi was not expecting such a reaction on my part. He turned red with rage.

"You wait right there, I'm gonna give you such a walloping!"

He stepped out of his clothes with considerable tact. First, his coat; next, the first pair of pants; then kicks; then second pair of pants; firefighter's helmet; socks. He grabbed me by the neck, we rolled on the ground. People who've never grappled don't know what a fight truly is. In the street, a minute lasts for an eternity. In our case, night had already fallen and there was no one about to pick the winner. Neither of us emerged victorious from the clash.

Ngungi was not a man of subtlety. If he liked you, he'd show his appreciation in the most brazen manner: lending you his fur coat at night from two till six; inviting you to Italian Gianni's and disbursing his entire capital there; introducing you to all his new friends; fawning and flattering to foster the friendship. But if he wished to have no further dealings with you, it was a complete horror show. He'd insult your descendants; taunt you; dish dirt behind your back; machinate all sorts of funny business your way. Since his return, I no longer recognized him. He'd forbidden his asshole brother from speaking to me or diddling around with me. At night I heard them talking me down and laughing fit to burst. He even stopped mentioning his nocturnal rambles, and I missed that deeply. Upon waking, Ngungi would observe the same ritual. He'd babble utterances in an unknown language, then, leaping to his feet, he'd slowly stretch his left leg, then his right, spit two or three times onto the pile of cardboard boxes and garbage bags which served him as a mattress, and slug in one go the residue of whatever liquid lingered in his bottle, be it water or juju juice. It was only at the conclusion of this choreography that Ngungi knew serenity and peace of heart once more. He would then greet the whole gang—starting with me, much to the chagrin of Whitey and Anarchist—employing the grand gestures of a President of the Republic on walkabout, and recounting, quite unsolicited, what had occurred in the night while we snored.

"I slept in the Zaire River yesterday, I was so tired," he sneered in his falsetto voice.

The Zaire River was not only a reservoir of dreams. Suicides and other dissenters of the Republic were chucked in, dead or alive, as confirmed by Mambo rumor. The river, as Ngungi himself described it, was a metropolis. In the belly of the river, there was another world: megalopolises better mapped, erected, and equipped than the Republic of Zaire. Boulevards sunlit by innumerable streetlamps; restaurants; weight rooms; brothels; bakeries; in short, everything that a cosmopolitan city can boast of. And, doubling down: "The river's population is as vast as all of tropical Africa combined."

## 38. Luck is an animal.

Luck is an ugly little animal, stubborn and sly. Once it appears in front of you, don't let it scuttle off. Arm yourself with anything to hand and do whatever it takes to hold onto it. "Any normal man," said Tshiamuena, "has three major strokes of luck in his life. But alas," continued the Madonna, "luck doesn't sound an alarm when it arrives. Some people are so inattentive that they fail to notice when chance smiles on them, or at least they don't know how to profit from it. Years later, they'll find themselves high and dry; spending their days and nights brooding over the number of times they caught some luck and didn't really know how to take advantage of it or were too meek with it. But there can be no pity with luck. You must seize it, berate it, thoroughly drain it of its juices, exploit it in every detail and without the slightest compassion."

Tshiamuena cried when she spoke of luck. She would say that luck is one of those pets that every man should have. "Fate," she went on, after having taken two gulps of a mixture, the recipe of which was known to her alone, "is characterized by several types of luck: the luck of rapid prosperity, the luck of an iron constitution, the luck of meeting an ideal partner. Coupling up with certain people when you have no luck is like felling the tree in which you're lazily sitting. You get wed and straightaway every door closes one by one; money slips through your fingers, sickness catches you on the hop, your plans and dreams go up in smoke, and at fifty-five you look twice as old." The Madonna was adamant about the luck of wealth. You enter a mine one morning, and that evening you unearth a diamond, and not just any diamond, a buffed-up, spotless one. "You did nothing to merit that," declared Tshiamuena, "but money flows at your feet. You open a store or a bakery, customers scramble to get through the door; a newspaper kiosk, the cash pours in."

## 39. The sidereal and mercantile ubiquity of men and things.

The incredible thing about the world is that at the very same hour, minute, second, more than five hundred billion actions occur simultaneously: people get laid; jack beers; switch on the radio; foment coups d'état; read Bofane, Mabanckou, or Musil; watch a movie; smoke their glue; curse each other; dance the polka-mazurka; board trains; drown; pass on; end up in prison. In Africa—particularly in Angola and Zaire—events also took place concurrently.

While Magellan and Co. jacked beers in the Republic, and Sanza snitched, those of us in Angola led a more or less balanced lifestyle too.

Molakisi had run out of luck. After gambling with the money from his first diamond, he had fallen into decrepitude. One day, while they were sieving and shifting gravel on behalf of the UNITA, a soldier shouted at him. He and his fellow diamond panners were in single file carrying tubs of potentially diamond-bearing gravel to the storehouse when this soldier cursed at him—even though they were on familiar terms—and told him to piss off.

"I don't want to see you here no more! Move!"

Molakisi made to put down the tub; the soldier aimed his weapon:

"Pick up your crap and get out of my sight!"

Molakisi didn't realize at first blush what had occurred. He left the mine and went to find Tshiamuena. He was crying. Tshiamuena laughed initially.

"Why did he kick me out?"

"He didn't kick you out! He gave you your chance. Sift through your tub."

Molakisi lifted three handfuls of gravel. A diamond winked at him, clean as a whistle. He placed the diamond in his pocket and, without even thanking the Madonna or saying goodbye, ran off to sell the product. That evening, he went to find a young man who was returning to Lubumbashi via Kinshasa.

"Take this!"—he handed him eight hundred dollars, along with his parents' address—"Tell them I was buried by a cave-in along with five of my workmates. We were busy getting the sand out of the ground, but since we were tired we piled it up right around the hole instead of throwing it a distance away. It had rained the day before and suddenly the hole caved in. My parents will surely mourn me, but tell them I'd become a lowlife, a ruffian, a bandit. They'll feel less sad that way. I'd like them to forget me fast."

## 40. When Whitey reports, everyone pipes down (cont.).

Monsieur Guillaume smoked cigarette after cigarette, entrenched in his habitual silence, save the occasional muttering of a Kosovel line. Sanza was in no mood for joking around either. He amused himself by juggling with the two pens he'd picked up off his mentor's desk.

"You know what, son? It's the first time I've felt so bad in all my career. Thirty years of service, and for the first time ever I feel like I've missed the boat."

"I get your frustration. I'm disappointed too, but we've got the situation under control, no?"

"The intelligence services operate through anticipation. They read the facts, the events, they interpret them and extinguish the flames before the fire even breaks out."

"But we're in control of the situation. We're continuing the operation as planned. I'll make contact with them again to arrange another attack. We'll bring out the big guns this time. Right?"

"We've taken a hit, it must be said."

"No point you moping about for no reason. And you said yourself the intelligence services are defined by the glitches they encounter."

"Sanza, I am tormented by an insane desire to burn the Mambo to the ground."

Imitation was the defining behavior of the inhabitants of the Mambo de la Fête. If a patron (of the male or female sex) was glimpsed sporting a sweeping silk dress, overalls, or super long shorts, the following day would see dozens of people displaying the same get-up. The attack on Police Station No. 2 had created copycats. A dozen police stations were painted red. As if that wasn't enough, people came along to the Mambo dressed all in red. Sanza and Monsieur Guillaume's plan was a classic seduction operation. You want to lay your hands on some very specific people, so you infiltrate them, ferment pernicious ideas—a coup d'état, a sabotage, a hostage-taking—furnish them with the means and the intelligence to realize the plot, even though maybe they weren't even dreaming of undertaking any action, gather the evidence to charge them, then stop the plot and place all these fine folk under arrest. Or else you let the situation deteriorate and, confident and heartened by an initial success, these fellows embark upon a much more extensive operation, with spin-offs—remotely guided by you—and there you dismantle the network by arresting the main players since you have solid proof against them and reasons to pursue the most delightful crackdown.

Sanza arrived around ten PM.

"Have you heard?"

"What?"

"Two more police stations."

"Two more what?"

The Mambo de la Fête was drowned in decibels. You had to use all of your vocal cords to be heard.

"Two more police stations were daubed. The guys were caught in the act, but the deed was mostly done."

We congratulated ourselves and had a good laugh about it.

"Franz, Franz!"

Sanza wanted to tell him something, but the Austrian was in his element.

"Franziskus, come here, my man!"

Sanza took him aside. I wasn't dancing myself, I didn't really like prancing about anymore. Ever since Franziskus first appeared at the Mambo, my popularity had been hanging by a thread. Westerners frequented the Downtown bars, so I was one of the few fair-skinned people at the time to stick their nose into the Mambo. I watched Franz and Sanza from afar and, from the movement of their lips, guessed what they were speaking about. It was one of the things the street taught us: to interpret what people were cogitating in private. When they returned to the dance floor, they suggested striking again—"we must strike again." Since the suggestion emanated from two people, Leandro and Magellan opted for a hit, without much thought. As if to encourage the guys to act expeditiously, Sanza began alluding to the sufferings endured by Leandro's father. I attempted to alert Leandro, Magellan, and even Franz to the danger of such an operation. I was sure that Pimples was playing a dirty trick on us. The techniques he was deploying were known to all the kids who had grafted, directly or indirectly, for Monsieur Guillaume.

## 41. A mission too far or the necessity of finishing with things before they finish you.

The gang planned an attack not far from the Post Office. After jacking some beers, they had Djibril escort them Downtown, where they headed toward City Hall on foot. Having made a reconnaissance mission, Magellan whistled twice. Sanza, Franz Baumgartner, and Leandro fumbled their way forward and began painting the building's columns, fear in their bellies. A dozen minutes passed.

"The lagoon!"

The word slipped out of the Austrian's mouth. They burst out laughing. It eased the tension.

"Hey, Franziskus, you mustn't forget to include this episode in your book!"

"Don't make that Djibril the main character, whatever you do. If you could only cut off that shock of hair of his in your novel, it would be a good start."

"Don't write that Sanza's just wearing super-long shorts. That stays between us Zairians."

"And the crazy, how does he appear in your novel?"

"Who'll play the role of the baddie?"

"And Mimi the Incubator?"

"The day you make up your mind to ask for the Incubator's hand, I'll stop wearing my super-long shorts."

"You need at least some excuse to change . . . "

Again, they burst out laughing.

Suddenly, Magellan stopped his teasing of Franz. Former Katangese gendarme that he was, the guy had sensed an unfamiliar presence in the vicinity. A car was approaching silently from the direction of the Lycée Marie-Josée. Another from the direction of the Post Office.

"Scram!" he went.

It was a proper devil-take-the-hindmost. Despite having a head start on his companions, Leandro tripped and tumbled. He picked himself up, but it was too late to give anyone the slip. He was nabbed unopposed and thrown into the trunk of the vehicle.

"Someone's ratted us out!"

"I can't believe that," Franziskus broke in, his breath short.

"You're awfully quiet, Sanza, say something!"

Magellan let fly with his left leg; Sanza dodged. Franziskus stepped between them. Sanza recalled some advice dispensed by his mentor once when they were shadowing someone. Monsieur Guillaume had slipped him a tip that had stuck somewhere in his skull: confessing can be one of the most credible strategies for denying the facts. So Sanza simply exploded with rage.

"Yes, it's me who sold you out! It's me who put you up to this! Me, that's right. I've always been a snitch. I ratted you out, no regrets."

He was a born actor, this boy. He cried and rolled around in the sand. Franz got jittery. Magellan backtracked:

"I'm sorry, I don't know what came over me."

They walked back to the Mambo de la Fête. Magellan wouldn't let it lie:

"I can't get my head around this screwup! Cars parked at either end of City Hall!"

Sanza, softly:

"What if it were Whitey? He looked happy not to be coming with us."

"I can't conceive of anyone else . . . "

"It did cross my mind for a moment," Franz added.

Monsieur Guillaume wouldn't touch so much as a drop of beer. He energetically warned his protégé against giving himself over to alcohol of any kind. Sanza forestalled as he stepped into his office:

"That was one crazy evening, how scared they were!"

Monsieur Guillaume was sprawled in his office chair, head tilted slightly, feet on the table.

"It pains me to have come so close to the goal."

Sanza minimized this fresh Pyrrhic victory.

"They had a close call there, they'll not try anything else."

Monsieur Guillaume, with the expression of a brat who refuses to go to bed:

"The aim was to collar the lot of them and draw a line under this episode for good. Now I seriously fear they'll counterattack."

Sanza, dreamily:

"Where is he?"

"Who?"

"Leandro?"

"Well we're not putting him up at the Karavia Hotel! We stuck him in the lockbox with six other knuckleheads our department reeled in from their ramble. I've just been looking at the TV. Those buffoons have seized Kisangani. It was the last stronghold."

Monsieur Guillaume popped the cap on another bottle of beer and poured half of it down his throat. He was vexed. Throughout his career, the man had known not a single setback, even when coordinating operations remotely, but he remained constantly dissatisfied with his success. It seemed to him that there was always a missing element preventing the achievement of the perfect job. Fake coups d'état and arrests and abductions that left no trace were among his specialties, but he had to add a hobby—destroying couples. The recent lackluster operations had destabilized Monsieur Guillaume and he experienced each imperfection with the pain of the lovelorn. As if that wasn't enough, the offensive against Zaire initiated by the rebels of the Alliance of Democratic Forces for the Liberation of Congo laid bare the nonchalance of the intelligence services. Since 1996, the soldiers of the ADFLC had been invading the national territory from the east of the country. Each time some forlorn dump of a place fell into their hands, the news was welcomed with jubilation across the Republic. The plebs were sick to the back teeth with "Le Maréchal"—in power since 1965. At the Mambo de la Fête, every patch of earth the rebels conquered was a fine occasion to jack beers.

"I feel like shaking people up some. How about we pay a little courtesy visit to the sisters of the parish of Sainte-Thérèse?"

42. An epidemic of lost cocks.

One Sunday in Downtown Lubumbashi, a man neither young nor old—handsome, svelte, frizzy hair—was strolling leisurely down Avenue Kimbangu on his way to a wedding or a birthday party. Suddenly, he felt something like an electric shock in his pants. Sticking his hand down his britches, he realized, to his disenchantment, that his cock had gone.

"Help! Help! Help me, my cock's been pinched. Help!"

A throng gathered—intellectuals, muggers, students, and policemen among the gawkers. The traffic was blocked. No vehicle could get through, so thick was the mob that flooded the avenue. The policemen took things in hand.

"Take off your pants. We'll check."

The young man protested.

"Liar," screamed the crowd in fury.

He complied.

Total stampede. Even those who hadn't seen anything of the young man's privates scooted. As the day progressed, National Radio reported the same phenomenon in other towns across Zaire. A wave of panic swept the province. There were damaging repercussions at the Mambo de la Fête. Patrons (of the male sex) drank beer, competed at pool, and played drums or sax with their hands down their pants. Similar reactions elsewhere, with additional animosity. People (again of the male sex) walked around with their hands in their pockets to avoid having their yuca detached. The word went that it was done by other men for sacrificial ends. To guard against it, people took public transit with their hands outstretched, ready to protect their property; they boycotted restaurants, eyed up other passers-by of the same sex from afar, and avoided greeting anyone. An international conference—with massive attendance from the French, Belgians, Austrians, Portuguese, Croatians, and Senegalese—was hurriedly convened, bringing together specialists and other éminences grises from fields of research as varied as anthropology, mechanics, ethnology, sociology, botany, and anatomy, under the pithy title LOSS. The proceedings were broadcast live on National Radio and Television. Among the seasoned scientists, the prophet Singa Boumbou—in a sensational demonstration that left a lasting impact—explained with brio the loss of the male member as an ambulatory, magical phenomenon that occurred only in the heads of the people concerned.

## 43. Kicking a dead horse.

Monsieur Guillaume maintained more than one mania besides poetry. Driving at breakneck speed gave him a feeling of invulnerability. The vehicle circled the synagogue four times before entering the tunnel and emerging onto Chaussée de Kasenga. He felt several years younger. All of their activities (shadowing, sabotage, wanton destruction of people's assets, blackmail, kidnapping, raids) had been taken to half-mast for strategic purposes in order to lend wings to potential troublemakers and take them by surprise. Monsieur Guillaume was himself amazed to have lasted a whole month without raking in anything at all.

"Dear friend, what are we going to do about that crank Singa Boumbou?"

Sanza turned down the volume on the radio:

"We'll start by cutting off his beard, his hair, and his nails in front of his followers to humiliate him. Next, once we've put him in the lockbox, we'll make him write out this sentence ten thousand times: "I shall refrain from furnishing assistance to delinquents."

Sanza creased up. He thought his mentor would join him in this fit of hysteria, before realizing that Monsieur Guillaume remained silent.

"The security service is not a seminary, you know. If you still feel compassion for human beings, you should pick another path."

Monsieur Guillaume turned the knob on the radio. The velvet-voiced musician was singing of the bliss of living in the Zairian capital, a city that pulses to the party beat. Monsieur Guillaume breathed deeply. He always indulged in this little exercise when he wanted to say things that were close to his heart:

"You need to get out of your comfort zone, laddie. Travel, for example. Travel enables a man to get the measure of himself and learn something of his fellow humans, their habits and customs, philosophies, cultures, and ways of being: how they live, drink, eat, and get their rocks off. My very first passport was literature. My father was a simple manservant and I'm proud of that. He worked for the Portuguese, the Belgians, and the French his whole life long. Invariably, he would come home bearing books. And me, idiot that I was, I read and I read. I read to defenestrate myself from the penury into which the family was squashed. Each text disclosed itself to me like an invitation to exile, to exoticism, to travel. I dissected an Argentinean writer and found myself in Argentina—no visa required! A Greek writer, I landed in Athens; a Romanian, in Bucharest. As I pursued these acquaintances, there crystallized within me a desire—burning, uncontrollable—for the literatures of Central and Eastern Europe: Rilke, Kafka, Ingeborg Bachmann, Paul Celan, Josip Murn, Canetti, Wolfgang Borchert, Dragotin Kette, Kosovel, ah! Kosovel, Kosovel, the sheer epitome of the sublime. His entire oeuvre is an architecture of regret. Literature, savored almost in spite of myself, was a passport to (sometimes pointless) exiles, clandestine voyages, quaint vagrancies, one-way journeys through unknown lands, ambulatory transhumances. Baccalaureate in hand, I enrolled at the Petit Séminaire de Kabwe, before flying off to Strasbourg thanks to a grant from the Zairian state. I liked Europe—but without spring and summer. I've always been a man of the night for as long as I can remember. Light burns me, makes me anxious, defenestrates me into the scum. A few years later, I came back to serve my country. What matters about the work I put away is not whether it is commendable or execrable, but whether it is accomplished with passion. You're so far off understanding, you might as well have not been born. Read Kosovel, Rilke, Dambudzo, and then we'll talk."

The last sentence he uttered like an affront, with a kind of contempt in his eyes.

He slowed, and parked the motorcar on the verge of a dusty road. Before stepping out, he took care to shove a pistol into the inside pocket of his jacket.

Singa Boumbou and his confederates had taken up residence on a steep mountain. Among the members of his cult there were bankers, former soccer players, musicians, hawkers, policemen, and teachers. Every Thursday in the month, three trucks loaded with grub and non-alcoholic drinks replenished the concession. He forbade his followers from lapping so much as a single drop of beer to prevent them profaning their bodies; from consuming the meat of goat, pig, turkey, beef, or lamb; from smoking, even passively; from watching television whatever the program; from practicing any sport at all; and from talking to or trading with any person considered impure. The charismatic prophet did, however, vigorously recommend that each one wash themselves at least seven times daily, and refrain from copulating on New Year's Day—which he himself had ordained as February 15th, the date of his birth. One of his biggest (medium term) aims was that they cut themselves off from the world. Definitively. They would consume vegetables that they grew themselves; make their own clothes; erect schools and universities for their own children; mint their own money; and speak a language used solely in their world—in other words, concoct a language from scratch. The charismatic prophet warned everyone of the perils of a putrefying body and soul. He had his stock phrases, such as "Nobody chased after a ball in the Garden of Eden." Or indeed: "I am staggered that the Zairians dedicate themselves to rumba—a satanic music, given that none of the instruments used in this musical genre, be it guitar, drum, maracas, or trumpet are mentioned in the Book of Genesis." Or indeed: "Heaven will be denied to those who wear neckties." Or indeed: "The body must remain free from all stain. Working to earn more than one actually needs is a sacrilege."

The main residence in which the charismatic prophet lived for five days a week was located in the center of this fifty-acre conurbation. Sprouting around the main residence were the misshapen little trapezoidal two-to-four-room apartments in which his retinue dwelled.

The resounding silence disorientated Sanza. When he'd gone there with Magellan, Leandro et al, almost at the same time of day, the yard had been all a-jabber, the inhabitants writhing to music played on instruments they'd fashioned themselves; snoozing outside on rocking chairs; or standing around, in pairs or in groups, parleying, cuddling, and joking about.

Monsieur Guillaume and his agent quickened their step toward the main building. Nothing but a deafening silence. Not a mouse. Not a cockroach. Not even a mosquito. This incongruity didn't dissipate a jot, even as they combed the other plots. Silent apartments. It all felt as if the population, warned of an imminent danger—huge hurricane, deadly storm, volcanic eruption, earthquake, or breaking-out of civil war—had skedaddled in haste, not even bothering to close their suitcases or take a single thing with them. Most of the doors were still ajar; large stockpots bubbling away; lightbulbs on; a table laid—plates, wooden spoons, a container full of cassava leaves, two bottles of some homemade beverage.

They exchanged a look but made little comment. In the half-light, the two clowns appeared even more outlandish. It was the physical details that laid bare all the ambiguity of this accursed couple: Sanza standing barely five foot tall, Monsieur Guillaume towering over him; Sanza in his perennial half-pants, Monsieur Guillaume elegantly dressed; Sanza sporting a mop of hair, Monsieur Guillaume hiding his baldness under a straw hat. They hopped back in the motorcar, direction the Kamalondo district.

The short-time hotel where Franz stayed stood a few stone throws from the municipal stadium. Franziskus lived off this person and that. Djibril, the taximan, drove him all over town for zero zaires. He would eat at the Incubator's one day, at Leandro's another. The bossman of the Mambo de la Fête sold him beer at half price. Magellan subsidized his smokes. He lived for free at the Vaudeville de l'Amour, a third-rate hotel.

In fact he was the sole permanent resident. The other guests stayed only as long as a hookup. Since he lacked the resources necessary to rent an apartment or settle his room bill and had nowhere else to crash in the event of defenestration, Ya Bavon, the manager and owner of the joint, had proposed that he occupy a room for as long as he wanted.

"Frant," (he couldn't manage to pronounce the z), "You've not paid a penny for over a month."

Franziskus apologized profusely.

"I will, you know, I'm just going through a dry patch."

Ya Bavon had a scenario worked out pat. He began to cajole.

"Frant, I'm told you're working on a novel. Is that right?"

"Yes, sir. I've only just begun."

"Middle, beginning, epilogue, it's no matter. You know, Frant, you can stay as many days and nights as you wish. I trust you. But on one condition!"

"What's that?"

"That I become a character in your novel."

Franz was not at all surprised by the proposition. Djibril, Mimi the Incubator—from their very first night, and while they were hard at it too—Magellan, the Mambo bossman, Mère Antonine, Ya Bavon's wife and their three children, Singa Boumbou and his confederates, Tshiamuena, the receptionist of the Vaudeville de l'Amour: all of them had made the same proposition, each with their own specifics. "Keep my dreads, though," suggested Djibril. Sanza was more insistent: "Don't mention my abscesses." Mère Antonine: "I don't eat meat. So please, don't make me scarf any old vittles."

Ya Bavon's tone of voice suggested that this was no entreaty, but an order:

"You know, Frant, I've a weakness for the cinema in general. But there's something that's always intrigued me—as it has every Zairian, I'm sure—Blacks rarely get to play the juicy roles!"

Suddenly he raised his voice:

"Don't make me play any old fucking role. If I appear as a bit player in your book, Frant, I'll beat the crap out of you."

Ya Bavon was riled up:

"I've got kids, a wonderful wife I've shared my life with for thirty years now, cousins, nieces. Frant, don't make me some damn mason, a digger, or one of those street kids you hang with."

His voice dropped a notch. He was begging almost:

"It's not just a question of my label, Frant—by which I mean the name worn by a whole family tree—but the prestige of the Vaudeville de l'Amour. Don't be so reckless as to uproot me. I am descended from royalty. You figure it out, Frant, but find something really substantial for me in your book."

That is how our friend Franziskus was given his pad on the first floor of the Vaudeville de l'Amour. But a short-time hotel remains a short-time hotel, particularly if its walls are thin. When the guests got it on, day or night, he heard it all: the pleading, the gasping, the moaning, the damning, the laughing, the cursing, and other exclamations of joy. Some nights, it seemed to Franziskus that coupling had turned to brawling, so apparent were what sounded like chisel strikes, hammer blows, the thrumming of metal saws. On occasion, a bed would give way, causing a dull thud as it collapsed. Other times, the occupants of a room, unable to maintain focus, would suspend copulation and shout at those in the neighboring room to keep the noise down:

"We know how to make love too, you know!"

And they, no doubt disturbed by such caprices, would retort:

"This is a hotel! If you're allergic to noise, go bang in a monastery!"

Monsieur Guillaume and his errand boy, that pimply Sanza, that snitch of the first rains—since it was a specialty of his to sell out others for his own ego—parked across the way from the stadium and crept forward like thieves in the night. Sanza to Monsieur Guillaume:

"We'll start by burning all his papers!"

The receptionist (in his nightwear) was deep in conversation with his wife or girlfriend—talking about their vacation, their last trip to Luanda, and the lawn they dreamed of for their house. They were vexed, their pride dented at seeing Monsieur Guillaume and Sanza.

"Franz? What do you want with him? Can't you see you're disturbing people?!"

"But you're a hotel!"

"Yeah, a hotel, at three in the morning! And even though we're a hotel, we need our privacy too! This is Zaire!"

They took the stairs four at a time. Franziskus's room: turned upside down. His suitcase was nowhere to be found. Nor were his half-pants (he too had adopted the fashion). Monsieur Guillaume was apoplectic. The operation had been a week and a half in the planning. Three or four days beforehand, they'd received credible intelligence of his presence on the premises.

"Were you aware of this, Sanza?!"

"Aware of what?"

"That he was going to cut and run?"

"How would I have known about it?"

Monsieur Guillaume, quite beside himself, bolted toward the receptionist.

"Where's Franz?!"

"Did you knock on his door?"

"Yes!"

"And?"

"He's not there!"

"So?"

"Do you know where he's hiding?"

"Our guests are not cattle to be rounded up to go graze . . . This is Zaire, gents, seriously!"

Zairians of that period were wont to remind each other that it was Zaire they were in, as if the country was absent from any official map or belonged to a whole other solar system. Franziskus had been shocked when he landed in Kinshasa. Two beer-jackers were chatting. One said: "I was very nearly misfortunate enough to miss my bus." Only for the other to retort syllabically, as if to convince himself that he was still alive or that only in Zaire could you miss the bus: "BUT THIS IS ZA-IRE, PAL!"

"I don't need to know what your Franz is up to! And by the by, Franz Baumgartner"—the receptionist enunciated Franziskus's surname impeccably but at the same time with considerable scorn as if to prove to Sanza and his mentor that he knew Franz better than the pair combined, that he was a very close colleague and that they even jacked beers together in their downtime when he wasn't busy with his wife or girlfriend discussing career and travel plans—"is my adopted son. Even if I knew where he'd gone to ground, I wouldn't tell you. You got it, gents?"

He turned back to his wife or girlfriend:

"Next year is just two months away. How about we get hold of that sewing machine for mama before then?"

Sanza and Monsieur Guillaume accelerated through the starry night. Pimples was nauseous. Despite the speed, Monsieur Guillaume felt no satisfaction at all. He had never driven so fast. He was dejected. Unable to calm down, he turned on the radio. The piercing voice of Lucie Eyenga, one of the first female rumba singers, crooned in Lingala: "As the singers sing / Those who wish to may dance / Those who wish to may watch / Those who wish to may listen / For the rest of us, at the end of it all / Rumba is all that remains / Rumba, our national rumba."

At Magellan's, the watchman was waiting for them with a bottle of red wine and two glasses: "We can also jack beers if you find wine too tiring. The boss told me that a guy, past fifty, would drop by, replete with a proper pimply scallywag—off his head on glue and with awful eyesight—and he wishes them a pleasant start to the week." The motorcar pulled away like a shot before Sanza could even fasten his seatbelt. Monsieur Guillaume screamed with rage, cursing, yelling. Suddenly he screeched to a halt.

"Get out! I never want to see you again in my life!"

Sanza complied. Monsieur Guillaume zoomed off, racing through the gears. A few minutes later, he reversed. A hesitant Sanza climbed in.

"Only you and me were aware of this operation. Even the Lagoon wasn't told about it!"

Pimples began to cry. A real weeping machine. Even when there was little to lament, he'd start sobbing.

"Did you tell Ngungi?"

"We're not pals no more and you know it. You really think it was me let the cat out the bag?"

44. The diamonds dwelled in the belly before alighting in Antwerp or on the neck of someone somewhere around the world.

The soldier cocked his rifle.

He took aim.

And in a somewhat hazy Lingala:

"You are secret agents. Spies in pay of Mobutu."

Molakisi and his bunch needed little persuading to raise their hands:

"We've never worked for the government you allude to."

"Admit it, quick, or I put a bullet in your cabeza, each of you."

"We're not who you claim."

"Your appearance gives you away. You can only be spies."

The soldier yelled something in Portuguese. Immediately, six other soldiers leaped out of the scrub. They pointed their rifles at the diggers and gabbled a mishmash of Portuguese and lousy Lingala, the better to befuddle Molakisi and his accessories. The frightened bunch could only holler:

"We are not secret agents!"

"On your knees!"

The soldiers stood in a semi-circle around them. The oldest gave a perverse laugh. He had only six teeth left, and his laugh reverberated like the Zairian accordionist Camille Feruzi:

"You're well dressed and your clothes aren't dirty. For diggers, you're looking mighty fine."

Molakisi and his pals on the verge of tears:

"We're diggers. We came to Angola looking for money."

"At long last! Now you admit to being diggers, toss your gains out in front of you. We'll spare your lives but only if you leave without the loot."

"We didn't net a single stone."

"We'll see about that."

The Angolan soldiers demanded that they undress. A perfect striptease scene. They removed their clothes starting from the top and working their way down: shirt, pants, underwear, shoes. The soldiers went through the rags and tatters with a fine-tooth comb. Then got stuck into the backpacks the boys were carrying. They rummaged through every possible nook and cranny, even cutting the packs into several pieces in the hope of seeing a fleck of diamond fall out. As it became obvious that the Zairians weren't toting a single diamond on them or that they had squirreled them away in some strategic place, the soldiers flew into a rage. They threatened to execute one of them to make them talk:

"You're not going to tell us you didn't bag anything."

The guy who'd pronounced this phrase angled his rifle at the foot of one of the diamond panners. The man was missing a toe. Reinvigorated by this unexpected discovery, the other soldiers pressed in around their colleague with cries of joy.

It was an open secret that Zairian diggers, congenitally jinxed, would sacrifice a body part, be it a toe, an eye, a tooth, a finger, even their sperm, that is to say their fertility through certain codified sexual acts, in order to boost their chances of unearthing a diamond. The diamond world has its own laws. And a bonanza counts.

"We've not bagged a single gem," the bunch wailed.

The soldiers ordered the boys to follow them. They headed into the bush, walking for an hour until they reached their base comprising several thrown-together shacks. Here they handed the diamond panners back their clothes. Even handcuffed, in a position of weakness, and with weapons aimed at them, Molakisi and his pals held out. Rather croak than relinquish their diamond carats. Molakisi seized his courage with both hands and begged for mercy:

"Are you married? Do you have children? I've got three, including a little girl of two."

The soldier dodged:

"You're never satisfied! In Zaire, you can just stumble upon diamonds, the Kasai region's chock-full of them. What's bitten you that you come sticking your cabeza into our mines then act all startled when we want to take our stones back? A real textbook case, you Zairians. It's the first time in the history of the world that people rush into a war-torn country. Usually it's the opposite! Nothing scares you Zairians, not antipersonnel mines, not grenades . . . "

Molakisi:

"Don't hold it against us."

The soldier went on:

"You all get rich off the back of us and have no shame in continually entering Angola as if it were a chicken coop. Do you know how many of your brethren have built villas with Angolan dough?"

The Angolan Civil War had been a proper business for many Zairians. It's usually money that reviles and flees human beings, but when it came to the Angolan Civil War, the Zairians had got so stinking rich off other people's diamonds that they began to revile and flee their own wealth. Nicknamed the Bana Lunda, or Children of Lunda, thousands of them descended on Angola, particularly the province of Lunda Norte where war was raging. Some would never return home. Shot dead. Swallowed up by the earth. Drowned hunting the stone in the rough waters of the Kwango River (the case of many kasabuleurs and other divers). Blown up by antipersonnel mines. Some got back to Kinshasa and Bandundu either rich, choked in debt, or as broke as when they'd set out. Everyone knew when they had entered Angola, but no one could tell the day or the hour when they would leave. Both the government forces and the UNITA rebellion employed strong-arm tactics to discourage those besotted with the stone. On the Zairian side, the army grimly awaited the reentrants in the hope of profiteering off them. To get around such hassles, the Children of Lunda came up with an array of gimmicks to befriend Angolans, notably village chiefs and soldiers, and enjoy the smokescreen they afforded.

Many women such as Tshiamuena practiced the "Angolan marriage." Officially wed in Zaire, they searched desperately for an Angolan partner or husband—preferably a senior officer—as soon as they crossed the border. Such a man had carte blanche in the mining quarries and influence over the workers, from whom he obtained—and pinched—diamonds. Soldiers willingly gave diamonds to these women of their dreams. It was said at the time that the Angolans did not take the value of these diamonds seriously. With Angola cut off from the world, the Bana Lunda sometimes bartered clothes, food, and other staples for stones. When Tshiamuena sent for her Congolese husband to come to Cafunfo, she passed him off as her brother to her Angolan spouse, a lieutenant-colonel. Moved to tears, the officer gave his fictitious brother-in-law diamond carats as well as one thousand dollars in pocket money.

Molakisi and his cronies refused to cooperate. After two days, the Angolan soldiers ramped things up a gear. To escape Angola with their loot, the Bana Lunda would swallow the stone, or hide it in their anal cavity. For as long as the stone lay in their belly, they nibbled nothing, consuming just water and beer, defecating only once they'd returned to Zaire. Having looked everywhere for the stones without success, the soldiers forced Molakisi and his friends to eat a huge quantity of rice. The diggers dug in their heels. But with the barrel of a gun to their head, they swallowed the food. Molakisi's two colleagues battled with their stomachs to shield their companion in misery. After three days, they ended up relieving themselves. The soldiers threw themselves on the shit, spreading it about, yet they failed to find the slightest stone. So they improvised an enema by means of a beverage. The two lads produced an even softer stool. No diamond. One of the soldiers again put a gun to Molakisi's temple and compelled him to eat and drink. Molakisi complied, but a week later had still not relieved himself. The soldiers freed his two colleagues to avoid having to feed them for nothing. Molakisi stayed there on his own with his diamonds in his belly. Defecation was out of the question as far as he was concerned. Years spent living on the roofs of trains. Years spent living on the streets of Kinshasa. The mistreatments he'd suffered. Long periods of doubt. Before, finally, hope.

"Defecate and we'll let you go," begged the toothless soldier.

Spasms wracked Molakisi's belly. His guts churned. He was at the end of his tether, almost fit to empty himself, but when he thought of all he intended to do if he succeeded in crossing back over with his swag, his resolve hardened and the desire to defecate receded. He envisaged humiliating people with his money everywhere that he'd been called a lout and a son of a bitch; he'd show them that the lout (and son of a whore) was no hollow shell, that the lout was not some tinpot fellow, that the lout was savvy enough to hunt down diamonds and dollars despite his roughly hewn French and his studies halted halfway through. He imagined plying with food and drink his detractors of yesteryear and those of the last rains until they puked and recognized that they'd misjudged him. He envisioned himself playing with money in the streets of Kinshasa, humiliating money, spending money, domesticating money, discrediting money, dirtying it, minimizing it, squandering it, demonetizing it, disdaining it, laundering it, bribing it, disgracing it, throwing it out the window and the door, ruining it in drink and sex, injecting it into an even more lucrative business, then jumping aboard the first Air Zaire flight to Katanga and descending on the Mambo de la Fête, lording it over the patrons (of the male sex) and the onlookers, lording it over the always grouching barman and his children, lording it over the waitresses, lording it over the bouncers, lording it over the musicians spaced out on glue, lording it over the formerly well-to-do and the currently wealthy, lording it over the Whites, lording it mercilessly over the busgirls, the young and the not so young, and that same week undertake a punitive raid on Italian Gianni's, ordering platters of food and bottles of champagne for the patrons of both the female and male sexes.

Alas, lost as he was in his reveries, his body yielded. The Angolan soldiers swarmed over his excrements, consumed with the most frightful joy.

## 45. Do you like it in Zaire, Herr Baumgartner?

Out front of the Mambo, sheer rapture. The patrons (of both the male and female sexes) in fur coats, suits and ties, wedding dresses, half-pants, and frock coats. Inside the building, a population whipped into a frenzy screamed out for Tabu Ley's "Sacramento" for a second time. Which happened only very rarely. The Mambo fauna tended to be hot for novelty, the transient, the ephemeral. The beer jackers had got accustomed to my presence from my second night in the establishment. I was now part of the décor. Nobody talked to me anymore. Still, newcomers appeared disconcerted to come across a White with his ever-present suitcase in this godforsaken hole, until they in turn acclimatized to me. New patrons of the Mambo de la Fête slaughtered their beers while eyeing me with a suspicious air, prattled on about me in Swahili and Lingala, then roared with laughter. More than once, I probed Magellan and Leandro about what was being said behind my back. They shrugged their shoulders:

"They say you remind them of someone."

I was sure they were taking the piss. The majority of them bought me beers, without even asking—as in Angola for that matter—even when I declined the invitation: "No thanks, I've already drunk my fill." Sometimes they even competed as to who could buy me the most. Some of them, after considerable hesitation, took my picture without my permission, and when

I sulked, they ran complaining to Magellan or to Leandro or to the barman's son—even to the more venerable beer jackers of the Mambo de la Fête—"Why's he like that? Just one little photo and he throws a hissy fit!" One evening, deep in conclave at my pad in the Vaudeville de l'Amour, the Incubator lifted a corner of the veil:

"You're putting us off, you know? You never go to the hairdresser, and just look at your outfit! You're the only European who hangs out at the Mambo, the rest isolate themselves together Downtown, nice and cozy."

"Evening, friends!"

Exiting the bathrooms, in the antechamber where, between sets or during a break, the musicians slaked their thirst, ate their beefsteak, or tuned their instruments, I spied Magellan, Whitey, Monsieur Guillaume's wife, the crazy with the wig, Ngungi, Mimi the Incubator in a long silk dress, three individuals whom I didn't know from Adam, and, beneath the table, Monster lying stretched out chewing on a huge plush toy bone. Whenever folks who have nothing in common—except maybe glue, beer, and cigarettes—get together, it's 'cos they're hatching a plan. I joined them without inhibition. They seemed put out by my sudden appearance and switched language the moment I sat down at the end of a bench.

"You looking for someone?" Ngungi squawked.

Whitey scrutinized me and sniggered, despite being ten years my junior:

"When adults are in discussion, little kids should go play."

As for Monsieur Guillaume's wife, I couldn't tell you how

she'd got hold of my surname, even though we had never met, nor where she'd learned to articulate with such grace:

"Do you like it in Zaire, Herr Baumgartner?"

The bossman put on "Youyou aleli Veka" by Wendo, one of the most melancholic rumba tracks there is. The musician's shrill, broken voice echoed off the walls.

Whitey wouldn't let it drop:

"The adults are chatting, Franziskus!"

I turned a deaf ear. Ngungi came to his flunky's aid:

"Didn't you get what he said?"

Whitey made to finish me off:

"We would like a little privacy. You're an irritation to us, can't you see? You're pathetic."

I wasn't going to give in:

"Watch your language!"

Whitey was enraged:

"That there is Ngungi, the most powerful man in the province. He could feed and clothe you for centuries!"

Magellan intervened to put an end to the dust-up:

"How's about dancing for a bit, Franziskus? We won't be long."

As I got up, my eyes met Ngungi's. He flipped me the finger.

"You should have let him sit with us, he can't understand a word of Swahili anyway," lamented Monsieur Guillaume's wife when I took my leave of them.

Magellan kept on going, in a somewhat sad tone—I never would have thought him capable of laying on such nonsense, he and Mimi the Incubator being the two people at this table who knew me the best:

"I'm really quite worried about that boy. It wouldn't surprise me if he were depressive, if you want my opinion. He's been working on that novel of his for years! One moment he says he's writing about Tshiamuena—a two-hundred-year-old woman he supposedly met in Angola—next he leads me to understand that he's actually working on something about the Katangese gendarmes. It's a taxing task indeed for a white writer like him to have to write about Africa, or, more precisely, to sustain not just one black character in his novel but several. That's simply writing in a pool of clichés, I think. What takes the cake is that he's not a writer like Handke or Musil—whose writing journey was a progressive one, starting out with poetry. Franz became a writer by chance; and for his first novel he's already having to marshal a set of characters who elude him."

Magellan's comment triggered a bout of prodigious inspiration. Which is quite normal. When folks jack beers together, with rumba all around, and people knocking it back right, left, and center, it's common to let it all spill out. Each piped up in their own way.

"He seems a nice boy, but he's playing with fire. Do you have the right to juggle characters who don't share the same collective memory as you? Slavery, colonization . . . "

"He's a writer, he writes fiction."

"This is Zaire!"

"As long as he buys me beers, he can write about anything he likes."

"He's only in Zaire to jack beers, don't ascribe such idiocies to him."

"Oh, come on, Mimi, he could be jacking beers in his own country!"

"You're juggling the wolf, the goat, and the cabbage for nothing. Franz is a writer."

"This story of the two-hundred-year-old woman is straight out of his imagination!"

"It's hard enough for African writers to write texts about Africa that are less than admirable without being accused of perpetuating the image of a moribund continent. How much tougher must it be for a White, and one who's writing about the gendarmes too?"

"No, the two-hundred-year-old woman!"

"You contradict yourself. He's European, he can write about whatever he pleases."

"But about what kind of person? You lot with your criminal records, you carry more weight than characters from some novel. I can't imagine the extent to which it's all bubbling away in his head."

"A first novel, with African characters—Zairian no less."

"He's always been a depressive, this guy. Have you seen his face, Mimi?"

"You're all jealous!"

Something I would understand later is that Zairians drop everything and lend an ear at the first mention of Zaire. "Conrad stuff?" admonished Magellan when I first told him about my project. Meanwhile, Mimi the Incubator gave me a tour of the whole city, intent on showing me the nice spots in the province so that I wouldn't, as she put it, "give a flawed image of Lubumbashi." So, pell-mell, we went to eat at Italian Gianni's, took strolls beside the lake, and visited the zoological gardens to see the monkeys, the crocodiles, and a lion.

The Incubator tried to prevent my crucifixion for the nth time:

"What's the point of this gang bang? We're not going to spend ten years of our lives talking about this boy! If it exasperates you so much that he's mustering these African characters in his novel, you've only to write your own with Europeans as protagonists!"

MAGELLAN (not letting anything go as usual): "Seriously, Incubator, you're not going to start encouraging us to write books when we have no desire to!"

MONSIEUR GUILLAUME'S WIFE: "The Incubator's right, you're overdoing it a bit!"

THE MAMBO BOSSMAN: "This is Zaire, we can talk about any subject, can't we?! Yet according to the Incubator, Franzkiskus is now verboten."

Monster started barking over his plush toy.

MONSIEUR GUILLAUME'S WIFE: "They won't be long!"

Ngungi made no comment. Whenever he retreated into silence, it meant he was planning something. Mechanically, he placed several used syringes on the table.

NGUNGI: "I shall sting Monsieur Guillaume like a bee."

MONSIEUR GUILLAUME'S WIFE: "He's always got a pistol on him and you know it. Let Magellan, the Incubator, and the others take care of it."

WHITEY (backing up his leader, as per usual): "It's a bullfight, everyone's got something to gain, we're not going to leave you all on your own."

MAGELLAN: "I hope Sanza won't give us the slip again. Treachery's in his blood."

NGUNGI: "If he dares to dribble round us, he'll have to skip town."

THE MAMBO BOSSMAN: "I'm going to take my place. As soon as they come in, I'll turn off the lights. You all know what you need to do."

Sanza was crying. Crocodile tears.

"Monsieur Guillaume, we've got to do something, it's simply not on. I just know they're all at the Mambo right now jacking beers. Not going there means accepting defeat."

Monsieur Guillaume accelerated through the half-lit streets of Lubumbashi. The singer Wendo's broken voice leapt and pranced inside the car.

"We wouldn't get anywhere just sticking our noses in there. It's Intelligence 101: never undertake an operation in haste."

They drove around for a good twenty minutes until he decided (on the spur of the moment) to drop Sanza off at the Post Office.

"Shall we drop by the République?" muttered the young man as a last resort.

Monsieur Guillaume looked him straight in the eye with disdain before closing the door.

Sanza was short on ideas. He didn't know where he stood. Should he stay out front of the Post Office or hotfoot it to La Cité and witness the murder of Monsieur Guillaume. After a few moments of hesitation, he set off toward the Mambo de la Fête. He didn't even have the wherewithal for a taxi. He began to run. Out front of the establishment, the same patrons in the same outfits jacked the same beers while taking photos of themselves. He barreled into the joint with all the verve and sincerity of a professional drunk demanding his fifteenth beer and who persistently waves his banknotes and threatens to make a scandal if the bossman doesn't sell him this foul liquid then vilifies the patrons (of both sexes) and utters discourteous remarks to draw attention. Sanza, with something very like a yell:

"Did you get him? Did you get that fucker Monsieur Guillaume?"

He gloated, barely able to contain himself. Ngungi was in no doubt that the guy had outwitted everyone yet again. Having failed to snare Franziskus and Magellan, not to mention Singa Boumbou, the Mambo was the only place remaining where Monsieur Guillaume could get his hands on this fine lot, or at the very least collar a bunch of other folk by way of reprisals. Ngungi knew his man very well indeed, after several years of good and loyal service. When an operation went wrong or when he couldn't get to sleep at night, Monsieur Guillaume was wont to let off steam elsewhere.

"You take us for your parents?!"

Whitey threw himself at Sanza, armed with a clothes iron. Sanza made a dash for the exit. Everyone, Ngungi included, rebuked him for having flown off the handle too quick.

## 46. A reunion with Ngungi, Ngungi the oilman.

The street kids dressed like clowns. They covered themselves with anything they could collect, whatever the size, footwear fit, or state of the fabric, as long as it was something they could put on. Sanza was sound asleep, wearing a priest's shirt (with dog collar), his little hands stuffed into a pair of boxing gloves, when Ngungi woke him:

"Hey, my man. Monsieur Guillaume. Ask me what's happened to him!"

Sanza looked up at him, perplexed. This was the first time since his return that Nguni had spoken to him so nicely.

"I've no idea."

"They found the guy's body last night. It seems he killed himself, but I'm not buying it. How could a guy as conceited as Monsieur Guillaume take his own life?"

"You doing anything tonight?"

"You can see yourself that the city's empty. That's why I prefer to sleep. There's nothing to pinch."

For the past two or three months, the city had been slipping into a kind of indescribable melancholy. As the rebels of the Alliance of Democratic Forces for the Liberation of Congo advanced on Lubumbashi, savvy traders restricted the sale of their products. Cornstarch, the staple, was imported from Zambia, which had closed its borders. Mobutu's army, in a series of untimely bulletins on the radio and television, swore to defend the city to the death. There were dark mutterings along Boulevard Lumumba, Chaussée de la Révolution, and even within the Mambo de la Fête, that the soldiers had received their full pay plus a motivational bonus. If this was the case, chances were they'd fight until the supreme sacrifice. Mobutu's troops patrolled the streets on armored vehicles to reassure the populace. The Whites had left the city. Followed by the bigwigs of the regime. Which led the inhabitants to believe that the fighting would last several days and that it would be prudent to lay up stores of food. There was something like a wave of general panic as the sound of marching boots drew closer. The memories of previous wars, climaxing with the landing of the French Foreign Legion at Kolwezi, and the widespread looting of the early '90s, played on everyone's minds. It was at this very moment that the storekeepers and lovers of easy money moved into action, raising the prices of their products regardless. And people, like automatons, delirious, bought up anything at any price, and not just staple foodstuffs but also furniture, household appliances, strollers, books, table lamps . . . How we laughed when we saw the populace running around like headless chickens, loaded up with victuals and assorted curios.

"Come on, let's go check out the Central Market!"

"And here's me thinking you'd stopped dropping by there," replied Sanza with a vacant gaze, conked out of his skull on glue no doubt.

They started chatting about anything and everything, as if there'd never been any animosity between them. Whitey was heartbroken to see the two fools in touch again. He considered it nothing less than a betrayal on Ngungi's part. That very morning, Ngungi had insulted Sanza down to the sixth generation and talked tripe about him to anyone willing to listen; now he was making fast friends again with the one he'd accused of giving up his brother. Whitey tried to hide his disgruntlement:

"I'm coming with you!"

"No you're not!" they replied as one before pissing themselves laughing.

Whitey followed them anyway. Ngungi slipped his gloves on and warned him of the risk he was running if he didn't stay put.

The rebels finally made it to the outskirts of Lubumbashi. We could hear the sound of heavy weapons. Downtown went to ground and even Kamalondo too, which throngs eternally. You could have walked around naked without it really being an issue. An increasing traffic of tanks and military vehicles (to the exclusion of anything else) came and went between the battlefield and the city. Time had almost stopped. We were so afraid, we decided to hunker down in the cemetery. It was the ideal spot to avoid abduction, just as it was in the past when the President of the Republic was visiting the province and the city had to be cleared of all its trash.

There was no real battle to speak of. A few hours of shelling, and the rebels shattered the locks. A scene of jubilation such as I'd never seen before. Residents left their hidey holes and congratulated each other as if it were them who'd sent Mobutu's army packing. At the Mambo de la Fête, they danced the Villain's Dance for seven days straight: a step to the left, a step to the right, rolling your behind all the while, a grimace on your face, arms outstretched with open palms as if throwing money. Everyone rejoiced and shared their happiness with no restraint. On the Post Office forecourt, nitwits who'd never given us so much as a glance or a word, smiled at us. They ran up in greeting, proffered embraces, then rushed off to stand and cheer the liberators.

The rebellion was in part composed of child soldiers, who gave us much to be jealous about! These kids were in the process of ejecting a thirty-two-year-old dictatorship while we spent our days chilling, smoking glue, and extorting the populace by foul means or fair. These baby-faced rebels, affectionately nick-named "kadogo" or "little darlings," were of my generation, and some of them younger still. They paced the avenues in single file, sagging under the weight of their rifles; fatigues too big for their puny bodies; plastic boots on their feet; blissed out—like someone who's smoked glue without eating. The residents blew whistles as they passed, gave cries of glee, sang songs, honked car horns, and uttered prayers. They offered them cigarettes, beverages, and grub, but the rebels politely declined. They were quite unconcerned with what the populace were up to. Their discipline was staggering. They wouldn't imbibe so much as a drop of alcohol, so intent were they on demonstrating how different their behavior was from that of the previous army, known for its harassment. Youngsters from La Cité, brought up on action films, rushed the abandoned police stations and army camps—everywhere that Mobutu's soldiers had been sta-tioned—looted uniforms and munitions, and fired into the air with automatic weapons. Over the following days, in La Cité, people took special care not to provoke each other and trig-ger a guerilla war. Scold someone, and they'd dive into their house and reappear with a revolver. Grenades were traded for rocket launchers. Uzis and Kalashnikovs were already flooding the petty-crime world. People stashed their weaponry under the bed. Those who'd helped themselves more generously dug gaping holes in their living rooms, bedrooms, and gardens, and buried the munitions, packed carefully in trunks. Those in-between days were good for the most ballsy among us, the contraband champs and lovers of easy dough. Each time the army of liberation besieged a town, the penal institutions emptied. It became impossible to tell who was a prisoner and who was not, since the courts and police stations were often vandalized. The criminals disappeared into thin air. And immediately got back to work. The way the scene was now set, nobody and nothing was safe. Guns were selling like hotcakes, while the new, still embryonic administration was barely ticking over. So to get the henhouse in order, the new army took the liberty of acting off the cuff. Delinquents and their like received a whipping with the chicote. Sometimes for peccadilloes. Young soldiers barely out of puberty could be seen with their chicotes laying into a big fella in his mid-forties on Central Square for having forgotten to settle the bill. For a few months, cases of theft and other aggressions plummeted. But residents, including marauders of the first rains, already held arms and ammunition, and they lost little time in picking up their favorite sport again. Meanwhile, the child soldiers, some of whom came from the remotest parts of the country and were clueless what to do with their monthly wage, discovered sex, glue, and beer in the course of their duties. They called us thugs and layabouts and would shoot at the drop of a hat. Drunk on cash and power, they went from door to door looking for girls to marry. Nothing escaped them. They were everywhere. At the Mambo de la Fête, they romped onto the dance floor, guns slung across their backs, and performed the Villain's Dance. Yet the child-soldiers also competed fiercely at hula-hooping, indulged in impromptu kickabouts, and flew kites of their own construction, having forgotten that they'd ceased to be children a long time ago. We, however, the so-called street kids, didn't mix with other children. We would only stick our noses into other people's business if it involved a sizable amount of money.

What we feared would happen, happened. Orders were issued for us to gather all our stuff and clear off the Post Office forecourt. A provocation, pure and simple. The Post Office was my due. It was Ngungi's due. It was our private property! And now some dolts dispatched from the back of beyond were ordering us back to our families.

We were no longer children, much as they might have thought so. Children have no experience of the outdoor life. Of glue, of brawls, of rainy nights. Children live with their parents. They spend their nights at home. Do this, they do this; do that, they do that. Go draw some water, they run draw some water. But we had to depend on ourselves. We ate and we jacked our mango juice by the sweat of our brows. We fed ourselves through larceny, begging, grifting, the hawking of plastic carrier bags and cigarettes, shoe polishing, and odd jobs of renovation and gardening for Mr. or Mrs. Whoever. We existed from day to day. And had been fighting and resisting the demons of the night for a long time. The soldiers, on the pretext of tidying up the place, swiped away our meager income, while the occultists and other possessors of cash-spewing creatures pursued us whenever their animals demanded fresh blood for their sacrifices. They all dreamed of doing dealings with Whitey because of his albinism. We were adults in our own right. We were masters, our own masters. Our own prophets of misfortune.

"Don't make that face, Sanza, we could always enlist," suggested Ngungi, with a glue-frazzled gaze.

The discourse that the new regime brought with it aroused an enthusiasm among the hoi polloi. Students, schoolkids, bureaucrats, the unemployed, vagabonds: the entire populace of the male sex enlisted to swell the ranks of the army—Mobutu's having melted away or gone into exile. The grounds of the Provincial Parliament, the Bâtiment du 30 Juin, were rammed from morning till night. Once registered, new recruits were expedited to the military base at Kamina or elsewhere, where they found themselves dressed in green and shouldering weapons after no more than a few months. An enticing prospect. Particularly for those who hadn't much else to do.

"No, Ngungi."

"We'll get guns too."

"No."

"Please, Sanza, close your eyes."

"Why?"

"First close your eyes."

"OK, closed."

Ngungi, in a husky voice:

"Imagine you're wearing fatigues, green ones. And boots. A red beret. Yeah, a red beret. With a rifle. Doesn't that tempt you? And the cash of course, dollars . . . "

## 47. Pimples Sanza made it all too plain when he didn't like something.

Burials back then had the benefit of being long. Nobody was buried on the fly, especially when there was cash to spare. A slow, dignified sendoff was preferred, whatever derelictions of conduct the deceased had committed. Attendees at the ceremonies in Molakisi's memory regularly numbered sixty-odd. People came at the end of the day. Refreshments were provided, and coffee, along with flaming braziers to get through the night. A tent was erected in the yard under which they could shelter when it rained. Men slept outdoors, the women inside the house, which had been entirely emptied to make space. In the morning, they returned home to take their showers and head off to work in town.

Tata Mobokoli was unable to pull out all the stops to put on a deluxe funeral for his late lamented son, having received his final paycheck a month before. Molakisi's father had struggled all his life to become what my father had never wanted to be: head warehouseman. My father drudged away at the Union Minière for twenty years. In that time, he climbed all the rungs until he became head warehouseman, a post he resigned from three weeks later, much to his colleagues' chagrin. He was so attached to the foundry, he couldn't do anything else.

"Copper makes me happy. It heals me. Watching copper being turned into bars is the most beautiful thing in the world," the man sighed.

Molakisi's mourning period was extended by two weeks. The family were intent on burying their child according to proper custom at any price. This proved to be a difficult operation without a body. According to the rumors that reached Lubumbashi, Molakisi had met his death in the vicinity of a cave-in and his corpse had been interred the same day. The Angolan mining quarries of the time were thirsty for manpower. Cash too. In the event of a death, the deceased was put in the ground as quickly as possible. The hunt for diamonds had to continue. Transporting Molakisi's remains would have been problematic, what with Angola in full-blown civil war. The boy's dad gave up on repatriating the corpse when he found out that Molakisi had already been buried. He made a stirring appeal to the deceased's friends to disinter the body and send his son's nails and hair to the family. Which should have been sufficient to ensure that the child would repose in the earth of his ancestors. Days and nights we waited for the guy's remains. In the end, we buried an empty coffin.

I swung by the Post Office forecourt. The building still stood. As hideous as ever. What had been going through the mind of that seemingly jovial architect—and in good health too, not a germ on him—to churn out such a calamity slap bang in the center of our city? The building seemed to be getting even uglier. You come to appreciate certain things with age, but in the case of the Post Office, it was quite the opposite. I even began to wonder how I'd managed to put up with such vileness all this time. My heart sank. The forecourt had been swept clean and the building painted in the colors of the new Republic. Which only increased its ghastliness. They'd replaced the inscription *Poste Nationale du Zaire* by *Poste Nationale Congolaise* in yellow and dark blue, just horrific! All the street children I used to know had left for (temporary) pastures new. Half had joined the army, the rest had gone back to live with a distant relation or were on the trains. In the streets, there reigned the atmosphere of a dying reign. The city as a whole had gotten cleaner. Which annoyed me even more. The city I'd once known seemed like it belonged to another world. I was used to the sprawl of garbage cans here, there, and everywhere. Now I had become a tourist in my own city.

I went to blow off some steam on Boulevard Lumumba. This busy thoroughfare was where I liked to lazily loiter whenever I had the time. There was always something unbelievable happening. Street brawls. Car breakdowns. Scenes of panic caused by God knows who or what: people would be calmly going about their affairs when suddenly they'd start running in all directions; the boulevard would then remain empty for a quarter of an hour before abruptly filling as if nothing had happened, to the extent that one wondered if these folk who suddenly scrammed took us for dum-dums. But it was just tipsy soldiers firing into the air. Insinuating ourselves into the stampede, we'd gather cash and other trinkets people had dropped in their haste.

As I crossed the boulevard, I spotted a funeral procession returning from a burial. The young and the less young trailing behind the hearse dripped sweat as they sang and danced in memory of the departed. I liked the feel of it all. Among the many dances they executed was the Villain's Dance. I missed the Villain's Dance, even if I didn't always dance it at the Mambo so as to come across as more bourgeois. I'd not performed a single dance step for a small eternity, so I ran over and blended into the crowd. Nobody asked me who I was. The grieving family was of some standing. Who knows what goings-on are hatched in those huge houses? Perhaps they had a money mill or even a snake. When we reached the home of the deceased, we found huge pots of rice, goat meat, and vegetables bubbling away. There were beers in abundance. Three times in the course of the night we were served tea, coffee, and cookies. The next day, half the crowd had gone. I had no business at hand, so I hung around kicking my heels. The deceased's son approached me:

"Do I know you?"

"Me? Sure! My father worked at the Union Minière too. He knew your pa."

Everybody in Lubumbashi was related to the Union Minière one way or another. If it wasn't an uncle, a cousin, or a nephew who worked there, then you yourself had studied at one of the company's schools or been treated in one of their hospitals.

I picked up all of the bottles and swept a large part of the yard. The adults were amazed at my sense of responsibility, whereas the other young and less young—street kids and assorted interlopers who'd joined the mourning all claiming to have known the departed—were loafing about in the sun or sniffing glue. But I knew what I was doing. They pressed money on me. I worked there every day—washing up, sweeping the yard—until the end of the mourning period. And the money kept coming.

I took a taxi: Djibril. His locks now reached all the way down to his butt.

"Where you going?"

"To the cemetery."

"My condolences."

"Thanks." I replied.

"Who died?"

"You want to resuscitate them?"

"Hey, can no one ask anything in this country?"

"Hey, can no one take a taxi in this country without feeling like they stepped inside a police station?"

Djibril got miffed:

"Sure, goof around, but it was kids your age who liberated this country."

"When Lumumba was your age, he was Prime Minister, and you're still driving cabs."

"I'm in no hurry, *one love*."

At the cemetery, at least ten families had come to inter one of their nearest and dearest. I did a little prospecting and appended myself to the one who seemed to possess a money mill or a snake. Later on, we ate like at a wedding. The next day, I did the drudgery, picking up all the bottles and sticking them in a corner. Another cascade of cash.

## 48. An explorer in a cemetery.

Sanza was savoring a most excellently squeezed fruit juice.

His sixth or seventh since daybreak.

They'd dug thirty more graves the previous day.

A collision between a bus and a tanker truck.

Much loss of human life by all accounts.

A characteristic December, the month for sacrifices.

People drive stressed.

Accidents increase.

The phone rang, and kept on ringing. Pimples eventually picked up. It was Dodo, a pal of Sanza's:

"Where you at?"

"Talk, kid."

"It's urgent. A guy says he absolutely must see you."

"Can't it wait till tomorrow?"

"Can't wait, no. He's in a hell of a state. Crying and all. He's offering money," Dodo purred, "it's worth making time for."

"I'm in the café. Bring him along."

This, you won't believe. A half hour later, my pal Dodo walked into the place followed by Magellan. His belly was even more bloated. For someone so well placed in Katangese high society, it was clear the guy was in serious hardship. He was completely filthy. Clothes. Shoes. Shirt half hanging off him. Chin devoured by an equally indecent beard. It had its own story, that beard. A vestige of the First and Second Shaba Wars in which the former primary school teacher had taken part. Barely twenty years old, high-school diploma in hand, he'd left Kolwezi, the town where he was born, in the country's southeast, to join the Katangese rebels of the Congolese National Liberation Front, who operated from Angola and were commanded by a Zairian general. Zaire, which supported the Angolan rebels of the FNLA and the UNITA, was the focus of reprisal attacks by the Katangese secessionist rebellion backed by the Angolan government. The conflict spread. Everyone was fighting everyone else. This was during the Cold War. The Zairians enjoyed the support of France, Belgium, China, the United States, Sudan, Morocco et al. The Katangese of the FLNC were supplied by Angola, Cuba, and the Soviet Union, as well as East Germany. When Magellan and his comrades attacked Katanga and seized Kolwezi, it didn't take long for the French Foreign Legion to parachute in. The death toll was high. At least eighty Whites and two hundred Africans were executed in the city. Magellan fell into the hands of the French troops. Upon being freed, he jumped aboard the first train to Lubumbashi and retrained as a teacher, yet without cutting a single hair of his generous beard.

Utter bewilderment on Magellan's face. He wasn't expecting to find Pimples officiating as cemetery watchman.

"You, here?"

"I . . . I work . . ."

Magellan turned on his heels, emotional, and stumbled off.

"What did he want, Dodo?"

"Blood."

"Didn't you tell him we weren't a butcher's?"

"He simply didn't want to know. Then he said he was capable of anything to satisfy this need, and then I thought you'd maybe change your mind."

## 49. *The Open Debate* of April '88.

Theme of the day: the invention of the average Zairian. The guests were debating the possible emergence—in record time—of a middle class in the Republic of Zaire. Talented participants both, they were possessed of the gift of the gab and a keen sense of repartee. Kabuya was a man of a certain age. A former university professor. A distinguished student at universities in the Soviet Union and in East Germany. Holder of doctoral theses in applied economics, conflict management, and sociology of work. Officially married and the father of four children, the youngest of whom was six. A lover of painting and classical singing. His pitch for hauling the mining region of Katanga out of its "pervasive social slump and crisis of identity" (his words) relied upon the anticipated deprivatization of the Union Minière as well as investment in community potential.

The second participant was a man who needs no introduction in Katanga province, Singa Boumbou. His credo: the radical redistribution of people and assets. He looked forty-five. Fifty at most. Swathed in a blue suit. He headed a congregation of two thousand members. His Church of the Deity Nude Advancing (DNA, for short) advocated a total societal overhaul. "Nothing belongs to anyone, everything belongs to everyone" was its leitmotif. His disciples enjoyed a commonwealth of physical and material assets, be they bicycles, cars, or apartments. You might decide, on a whim, to borrow a fellow church member's shirt without telling them or spend the night in their bed with their husband or wife. The DNA faithful shared everything. They kept no secrets. They considered themselves a chosen people. On Sundays, the religious service was expressly open to the non-faithful. Access to the hall of worship was via the cloakroom. You arrived, left your clothes, and went off to pray with the other adherents.

*The Open Debate* was the most popular show in the province. Participants forever marked their names in the annals of the glorious History of Katanga. Their lives changed following the broadcast. They were idolized. Invited to drink round after round in bars. Received priority service in restaurants. At the Mambo de la Fête, they were welcomed with the Villain's Dance. Brewing companies congratulated them with cars and cases of beer on the occasion of the end-of-year festivities. If they stuck their nose outside, a horde would descend clamoring for pictures and autographs. Audacious, extravagant groupies paraded proudly alongside them.

According to a credible survey carried out by *Le Grand Katanga,* a prominent Katanga daily, out of all the souls who comprised the population of the province, half were on the show's waiting list, 80% were prepared to agree to give their son or daughter to a former participant of the show in marriage, 78% wouldn't exclude the possibility of heading off on honeymoon with a man or woman who had appeared on the show, 69% claimed to have had at least two serious crushes on participants, 96% thought it unfair that the show was not included on UNESCO's List of the Intangible Cultural Heritage of Humanity, 74% were disposed to spending the rest of their days with a new participant in *The Open Debate*, while 47% strongly disagreed with foreign television stations imitating our show.

Water, fruit, a case of beer, bread, and a hunk of cheese were laid out on a coffee table. The participants in The Open Debate were entitled to get up to go relieve themselves. But with the sanitary facilities deliberately situated far from the room where the show took place, the operation took at least a quarter of an hour. The participant who was left on their own in the studio always took advantage of their colleague's absence to develop their thesis, win over the viewers, and so increase their popularity. Leaving the studio before the end of the show was therefore considered cowardice. Despite the urge to unload, guests would go on scrapping at the risk of pissing their pants.

THE PROPHET: "I've let you go on talking for half an hour. We must preach by example. You've mentioned the term communism twenty times, you should learn to practice what you preach."

THE PROFESSOR EMERITUS *(an alumnus of German and Russian universities, as he would mention at the start of each sentence)*: "You should learn to temper your remarks. I am surely old enough to be your father."

THE PROPHET: "You make me laugh."

THE PROFESSOR EMERITUS: "You are African, Katangese. According to African wisdom, the father must always finish his plate before the son can clear the table."

THE PROPHET: "The same African wisdom says that parents must not eat alone when their children are in the vicinity. Let me express myself too."

THE PROFESSOR EMERITUS: "I have been fully immersed in academia for nearly half a century. Something which . . . "

THE PROPHET: "I am not your student. You seem to forget that we are having a debate as part of a broadcast by Katangese Radio Television, a show that accepts anyone whatever their religious affiliation, sexual orientation, age, or race. You would do better not to trade on your status. I look after two thousand souls. Put a little water in your red wine, comrade."

THE PROFESSOR EMERITUS: "Oh, thank you for the lesson in manners!"

The professor and alumnus of German and Russian universities was unable to hold out until the end of the broadcast. He had committed the error of putting away a whole jug of water since the start of the Debate and could no longer sit still. The prophet remained alone on stage.

"My heart bleeds when I stroll down the backstreets of Katanga. Everyone festering in their own little bubble. Festering for themselves and for their families. We fail to share enough. We are proud to be drowning in gold, copper, diamonds, and malachite, but we can barely manage to make all ends meet. Just walk through town and you'll agree with the prophet and pastor of the Deity Nude Advancing that barriers have got the upper hand." He took a deep breath. "What was I saying, again? We don't mix like we used to. It's a pity what's happening to this province. We leave the poor and the needy to their own miserable fates. Whereas a world based exclusively on complete but non-violent sharing would lift us out of years of loneliness and gloom. What's more, people are skimming cash off the state because they're scared what tomorrow will bring. Scared of dying in poverty. Of leaving their children dangling. If what's good for the individual is good for the province, and vice-versa, I cannot understand how a minister of the province can dip into the state's coffers. We, my Church and I, have opted for a collective future. Everything we do, we do as one. We live without getting hung up about things. No one is above anyone else." The pastor rose, jovial in his sincerity. "Speaking of which, the clothes and shoes I wear were lent to me by my congregants. It works out well for everyone. Even when it comes to intimacy. Practicing neither polygamy nor monogamy, our sex life is respectful of those human values dependent on the tastes and aspirations of each and every one. The immediate consequences have been the cessation of jealousy, hypocrisy, and related unpleasantness. Katanga . . .

> I am become a new man
> now, from this day forth
> my house is yours
> my jacket is yours
> my shoes are yours
> come, my door is open
> come, dance with us
> and taste without restraint
> the simple pleasures of a fruitful life."

The professor never returned and the broadcast lurched to a precipitous end.

## 50. The death of the Portuguese explorer.

The cemetery is a city's true barometer. If you had lost touch with a childhood friend, the easiest way to pick up his trace would be to wander the streets in the vicinity of Central Square. You'd wait around for a day, then two, then three, and after a week, you'd spot the guy crossing the road, or else people who knew him would show you which street he was living on. If the guy didn't show, the last chance of nabbing him was in the cemetery. People headed there not only when a member of their own family had just passed away, but also for the relations of friends and acquaintances.

Since starting work at the cemetery of the Union Minière, such meetings were part of my day-to-day. I ran into folk I'd not bumped into for many years. Caught between tears and amazement, they always had time for me, as well as a coin fished from their pocket.

One December day, a number of shiny new motors parked up at the entrance to the concession. Some familiar faces. Classmates from high school. Nearly all of them sported a paunch. The excessive privatization of the Union Minière had seen people accede to strategic posts in the little factories that were sprouting like mushrooms all across the province. Nobody spoke to me. I figured out that a former classmate or teacher had recently gone the way of all flesh and that they'd come to pay him a final homage.

"Sanza!"

I turned my head: Whitey.

His face looked as young as it always had.

"Tell me it's not you, Sanza!"

"Anything's possible, Whitey," I replied, displaying not an ounce of euphoria.

"What you been up to?"

"Earning my crust how I can."

"You can say that again."

"Who died?"

"Magellan."

"I saw him last month."

"You didn't know?"

"How would I?"

"So, then."

"I work here."

Whitey, visibly shocked:

"You work in a cemetery now? Seriously, Sanza, you can't have stooped that low."

"I'm in charge of logistics. I run the gravedigging," I said, trying to inject some value into my trade.

"You bring shame on your parents. Your place is elsewhere."

He mentioned my parents as if he knew them. There was no disdain in his gaze, but rather a kind of pity. I tried to relativize:

"To each his fate."

"No, Sanza," he said decisively. "You had an edge over the rest of us. Every door in the whole wide world was open to you."

"Listen . . . "

"No, Sanza, this is no life, this."

Perhaps Whitey wasn't wrong. I was born under a lucky star. Unlike him, who grew up in La Cité (before his father defenestrated him), I'd had access to the inherent privileges of the town. I could make use of the libraries without performing too many gymnastics. My future was more assured than his. We had a comfortable life. I was sure to be hired by the Union Minière after my studies. Indeed my father planned on enrolling me at the faculty of geology in the hope I'd leave there an engineer. But thanks to hanging around with Molakisi, my own aspirations had gone up in smoke.

Whitey eyed me up and down, astonished at my penury:

"You simply disappeared, and I told myself that you must be living in Europe or in Kinshasa employed in a minister's private office."

"No, my friend. I bury the dead. I'll bury you," I shot back with a grin. "How did you become . . . ?"

"Luck, kid, just luck."

I changed the subject:

"So, Magellan?"

"Such a sad death . . . Don't you watch TV?"

"Have you got any change?"

Whitey rummaged in his pockets and whipped out a twenty-zaire note—we were already the Congo but we still used the currency of the former Republic.

His miserly generosity did not surprise me. The more affluent the man, the more grasping he was. Generosity was something a man like that developed only when he kept a snake or a mermaid in a room at home. Dirty money forces largesse upon its owner. You had to be quite insistent if you hoped to wangle another note. They'd give you a dud phone number, cancel meetings at the last minute, and make you tramp across town just to palm you off with peanuts. They'd take you to Mamou Nationale's or Italian Gianni's, invite you to taste all kinds of wines and eat your fill, then wave you off without a penny.

Whitey told me what had happened to Magellan. He'd resigned suddenly from the high school for no clear reason. And had straightaway fallen into the lap of luxury. The most suitable moments to stuff your pockets are shortly before or right after a war, and during it of course. Arms dealers see their turnover double, or even increase tenfold. Foreign mercenaries come out of retirement. And the broke—at least those who know how to jump on an opportunity—come into wealth. Postwar, it's the same rationale. People cheat, scheme, and haggle amidst the chaos. It seems that Magellan couldn't handle the latest parvenus swishing across the Mambo's dancefloor any longer. He'd consulted Singa Boumbou. Pointing at him, the féticheur said:

"You want to become rich? Or is this still about making City Hall vanish?"

"Yeah, become rich, that's what I want."

"Well, you're rich then."

Magellan forked out some cash and bought the man a bottle of champagne.

The féticheur looked him up and down:

"Just one little thing, though. Whoever gave you my address must surely have informed you of the terms and conditions."

"They told me that I must . . . "

"What's your favorite dish?"

"Salt fish."

"You'll eat no more salt fish until my say so. The second prohibition is more restrictive. You teach in a school, is that correct?"

"I do."

"You'll manage fine if that's the case. Just a little organization on your part."

"Yes, I'm listening, Singa Boumbou?"

"You must avoid sleeping on Sundays."

"That's doable what you're telling me. I'll spend the day resting. It's worth it to live like George Soros."

"He's not a client of ours."

"You know him?"

Singa Boumbou shrugged. He handed Magellan a bottle. Inside was a thin little root:

"If you've got an empty room, or in the worst case an attic, place this receptacle there. With a little water inside. After three weeks, come back to the room. What you'll see there will freak you out. But for the love of God, keep a cool head. Filling the room will be a body. For instead of a snake, which is not necessarily the most romantic of animals—at least in my opinion—I preferred to deliver you a mermaid."

Magellan was sweating.

The féticheur, his eyes roaming the surface of a mirror the size of a clothes iron:

"Red hair?"

"Pardon?"

"I am in possession of three mermaids. One of which is a redhead, a White to be precise. You like Whites?"

MAGELLAN *(sighing, baffled)*: "Well I've never really been with one."

SINGA BOUMBOU *(ignoring his reply)*: "No Congolese woman has red hair. The second one has the advantage of a generous bosom. The third is as sublime as Miss World 1982."

MAGELLAN: "I see."

SINGA BOUMBOU: "What's your choice?"

MAGELLAN: "The one with a generous bosom."

SINGA BOUMBOU: "The African one?"

MAGELLAN: "Yeah, the African one, or the redhead, as long as my life improves."

SINGA BOUMBOU: "Don't rush. After all, you don't want to live with a woman who bores you to death."

MAGELLAN: "Can I take the first one instead?"

SINGA BOUMBOU: "Are you sure?"

MAGELLAN: "The African one."

SINGA BOUMBOU: "There are two. Which is it?"

MAGELLAN: "The one with a bosom . . . no, the White, rather."

A month later, Magellan was one of the wealthiest in Katanga province. As is the way with irrational money, Magellan began making donations to churches, schools, universities, and so on. His mermaid was obedient at first. After a few months, she slowly sank into jealousy.

"Why do you leave me at home all alone? Aren't I sufficiently stunning to accompany you on your outings?"

Magellan brought her to task.

"You know very well that's not possible."

"But my darling," she scolded, "is it embarrassment you feel?"

Her words had the effect of a flood in Magellan's head. He shook with rage.

"Listen, dear, I am not your boyfriend!"

A single tear rolled from the mermaid's left eye.

"So in spite of everything I've given you, I'm still just some low-class girl?"

Magellan, who'd got a grip on himself:

"It's not what I meant."

The mermaid:

"You could spend some evenings with me, at least, couldn't you? Even just once a week."

Magellan, bashful:

"Yes, I'll try, my princess, princess of my heart."

But as is usual when one's pockets are fat and full, one is often out and about. Particularly in Katanga. You go to jack beers with friends. Take a little trip to South Africa for a nephew's birthday. Or you're a godfather and have to attend all of the associated ceremonies. There are rumba and salsa gigs. Spontaneous parties at the Mambo de la Fête. Extended stays in Kinshasa. Inopportune jaunts in the blueish, uncensored Kamalondo nights.

Magellan did his best to make room for his mermaid. But time had made itself scarce. Think about it: if you had ten thousand dollars a day, what would you do stuck at home, in the Africa of glue and the Villain's Dance? Magellan's mermaid vomited twenty thousand dollars a day, and sometimes even more unimaginable sums. Amounts greater than the entire revenue of the Union Minière. Indeed, Magellan had moved to the heart of Downtown, not far from the forbidding Post Office, where he had acquired a building which he'd had demolished to build a house with an upstairs. He needed it anyhow—the mermaid having forbidden him (from the very first remittance) from depositing his moolah in the former Banque Nationale du Zaire.

Months passed. Magellan purchased concessions. He even married and divorced after two days. None of that pleased his princess. She complained more and more.

THE MERMAID: "We agreed that you'd devote a little time to me."

MAGELLAN: "I'm sorry, my darling, wonderful woman of mine."

THE MERMAID: "That wonderful woman you refuse to show off in public?"

MAGELLAN *(diplomatically)*: "You know very well that I can't."

THE MERMAID: "Spend some time with me then." *(A beat. Then.)* "We could even arrange some trips out, in secret."

*(Months later)* THE MERMAID: "I'm thirsty, Magellan. And you have become the richest man in Katanga. I'd like you to bring me back five bottles of beer every day."

Magellan laughed out loud.

"That it? Nothing simpler!"

Every day, he brought back five bottles of beer for his sweetheart.

THE MERMAID: "Five bottles aren't cutting it. I want ten."

MAGELLAN *(guffawing)*: "You can have fifty bottles a day, you wonderful woman, you."

THE MERMAID *(upping the ante)*: "Without wishing to offend you, Magellan, thing is, much as I like beer, it's red wine that really takes me someplace. Beer gets me constipated and makes me antsy. But with red wine, I can evaporate into thin air, become spirit, and reappear on the beach; I'm a water girl, that much you must admit."

MAGELLAN *(wearing the expression of a Mambo waiter arguing with patrons of the male sex)*: "No problem, dear heart."

THE MERMAID: "Twenty bottles of red wine."

Magellan satisfied her wishes.

"Magellan," she wheedled, "some blood please, and not sheep blood or from any sort of insect. After all, what I offer you's worth more than the world itself. And weren't you saying that you'd do anything for me, given how I've transformed your life?"

So Magellan made arrangements to procure blood from the local hospitals.

THE MERMAID: "Magellan, this blood I'm drinking has no taste or smell. But the blood of someone who has died within the past two months, that will do nicely."

MAGELLAN: "You know that's not possible."

THE MERMAID: "If it's not possible then you'd best start thinking about your own funeral. You men take mermaids for fools. When you make a pact with a mermaid, it's always she who wins!"

Magellan tried to get by as best he could. He grew thin. He drank without restraint. He barely ate. He even stopped going to the Mambo. And he was no longer to be seen at the parties held by the Whites and the Katangese mining bourgeoisie.

Nobody had any news of him. His absence from the city's nightspots was put down to him simply being away on a trip. Then, one day, they found his body in the swimming pool. Magellan had drowned himself. At least that was the official version.

What happened to the mermaid? Nobody really knew. Last was heard, a police inspector had leveraged his contacts and succeeded in spiriting the woman-creature away.

## 51. The man who talked to chairs, walls, and his own eyeglasses: pointless chit-chat or serenade of madness?

"I've come on behalf of your father."

"I beg your pardon?"

"He's not well."

"There's nothing I can do."

There are nights when you dream of someone and the next day you bump into them as you go about your business. I dreamt I was accompanying the Incubator and Franziskus to the airport. The next day, around one PM, there was a knock at my door. I was even more surprised because I wasn't expecting anyone. Standing there before me was the Incubator, dressed as only she knew how, dripping with jewelry like a Christmas tree. The shock of it annihilated my ability to react. If I'd known she was going to show up, I'd have thought over the welcome I'd reserve her a thousand times. I'd have made ready a stick, boiling water, a knife, even a long, vitriolic monologue. Or perhaps quite simply a bouquet of flowers. War changes people. Particularly when you've sniffed glue for years and known the splendors of the street. There's a mean toad squats in your head, makes you see the world differently, all the people, animals, and plants that populate it. Who knows? Perhaps I would have welcomed her like a princess. A heaping dish of rice. A bottle of red.

The cemetery had compromised my masculinity. My hut had been constructed right next to the entrance, from where

I had an expansive view over the graves. The scars of the Post Office persisted, even a month after my hiring. I experienced an uncontrollable anger against the world. Strolling among the crosses was the only way to cool my rage. As I meandered randomly between the tombs, I would compare them sometimes and draw conclusions. Two neighboring crosses revealed that one of the people had passed on aged just eighteen months, and the other, at ninety-eight. On the basis of what criteria might one die so young? Without even having lived, smoked glue, jacked beer, enjoyed money, or shaken their stuff to the Villain's Dance? On what basis do some grow as old as Noah and others not? On occasion, as I wandered the paths, I'd cite the causes of death, or better still imagine them. What's more, although some graves were always clean and decorated with garlands, others lay abandoned, swallowed by the high grass. Some families would leave it five years, even ten or fifteen, before visiting their loved ones. That's what drove me to take things in hand, I think. City Hall sold plots without bothering about any sort of layout whatsoever. People buried their kin in cacophonous disorder, quite forgetting the location of their loved one's grave upon returning several months later. I got hold of some notebooks and made an inventory of the tombstones by age of the deceased, alphabetically, period of their birth (before or after colonization), even by special features. On some graves, the family had placed knickknacks relating to the profession of the departed, such as a soldier's helmet or a hammer. Those who couldn't find their relative's grave would run after me, and I'd always know where and how to facilitate the task for them.

The day the Incubator knocked at my door, I had just listed the hundred thousandth grave.

"As I was saying, I have come on behalf of your father."

"You know my father, do you?"

"This is Zaire!"

"What does he want with me?"

"He'd like to speak to you."

"He knows where to find me."

"The state of his health won't allow it. He woke up one morning and began talking to the walls, the chairs, the plants, the television. He talks and he writes a lot."

"And if I refuse? He spent years collecting curiosities and now he starts . . ."

"You can't refuse!"

"Why not?"

"Because this is Zaire!"

"You never change. The ideas you have."

The Incubator looked down at her feet. I felt pity for her. I nodded by way of assent.

"Where d'ya park ya wheels?"

She stammered something.

"What color?"

"Red."

Throughout my body, the remnants of my alpha maleness willed themselves, against my will, to lead the way. She caught up with me and opened the car door. We didn't speak for the entire ride. I was lost in my thoughts. She in hers, probably. Just some superficial phrases to fill the silence.

"It's hot."

"This infernal dust."

"Is *The Open Debate* still on TV?"

"Don't you have a TV?"

"Idiot box . . . "

"Yet, you . . . "

Driving past the Post Office, I wanted to puke. The building had got ten thousand time uglier. And that's putting it mildly. The colors of the Democratic Republic of the Congo, the blue and the yellow, faded by sun and downpour, made the thing hazardous to the eye. Stare at the edifice for an hour, and you'd leave with ocular inflammation. As I looked at it, whole slabs of my life loomed out of my memory: Ngungi, Magellan, Monsieur Guillaume.

We left the car across the way from the Lubumbashi Psychiatric Center. The yard was in total disarray. My father recognized me.

"You came to see me."

"I did, father."

He rose with difficulty from his rocking chair, gathered, with a jittery hand, the many papers riddled with his penmanship that covered the walls of his room, and passed them to me. Then he sat down again. And started to doze. He had already forgotten me.

"Papa?"

"What's your name?"

I rushed out of the room and began running any which way.

## 52. Money, a revelation: where we learn the importance of money in the wake of a war.

Pimples raced down to Kamalondo, his clothes billowing in the breeze of eventide. Vast shapeless clouds drifted as far as the eye could see, desperately stalking each other before coupling in an instant, filling the sky with a phosphorescent liquid. It was a Friday. People were coming from the mosque. An indescribable hubbub.

Arriving at Molakisi's door, he knocked twice, thrice, four times. A lady of a certain age appeared, framed in the doorway.

"Tata Mobokoli?"

"You're after . . . ?"

"I'm looking for Tata Mobokoli."

"I'm the new tenant."

"Since when?"

"What is this interrogation? This is my house you've come to and you start questioning me?!"

"How long's it been?"

"What are you talking about?"

"Mama Mobokoli?"

"Two years. Are you disappointed that we're new tenants?"

"Screw you!"

Sanza was as conceited as they come. The guy had zero respect for his fellow man. Beneath his sweet persona was a mighty little dictator. For weeks after he'd joined the gang, he did his utmost to play his cards close to his chest, until he simply cracked.

She slammed the door in his face.

Sanza walked over to the house abutting Molakisi's. Seven dwellings had been erected on the plot, leaving everybody very little room. Kids were running around in all directions.

He needed to find someone very fast indeed to whom he could unburden the secrets of his tormented soul. He just couldn't understand what was happening to him. His cabeza was about to explode.

"Tata Mobokoli?"

"What do you want with him?"

"I'm a friend of Molakisi."

"You were at his funeral, weren't you?"

"I came to see his parents."

"Ah! The Bolivians!"

"I don't follow you."

"They're living in La Paz now."

"Quit joking."

"You don't have to believe me."

The man was sincere. He didn't have the face of a glue fiend or an excessive imbiber of those cassava-based homebrews that were peddled all over the province.

Sanza was flabbergasted:

"How's that? Rascals don't just wake up one morning and leave to go live in Latin America!"

He felt as if he'd boarded the wrong train. What he'd lost sight of, chiefly because of his temporary death in the cemetery of the Union Minière, was that during or just after a war, countries such as Zaire, the Congo, or Congo-Zaire (it depends), Angola, and many others, become countries where luck, lupemba, lucre flow. You can crawl into bed of an evening a rogue, the vilest villain on earth, and awake the next day minister or inspector in the national police, or even, for the luckiest, plenipotentiary ambassador of the Republic of Zaire to North Korea or the Kingdom of Belgium. It was the only way this country had of giving all its children their chance—even those who took the roads less traveled—of opening the money gates to one and all, including those who didn't come from wealthy families or whom long years of truanting predestined for corruption. In this country of luck, this country of money both dirty and clean, this country of the Villain's Dance, everything was still possible as long as there was breath in your body. From the moment that the Union Minière, the state, the church, and the family unit began to languish, from the moment that all of these things got a fat toad squatting their heads, the way was open for the most courageous to make a fast buck; for money requires courage, as well as luck, both to acquire and to keep, whatever the means of enrichment, be it war, a snake, a mermaid, mines, work, or good fortune.

Sanza ambled slowly back Downtown. The Kamalondo district was in full ferment. The open-air bars a succession of rowdy exuberance. After a day spent slogging away in the mine or some other drudgery, the inhabitants toasted life by getting sloshed on Simba and Tembo, the two most popular beers in the province, in a headlong defenestration into joy come what may, while awaiting their chance, their lupemba, their turn to leave this wretched world of villainy behind. Huge speakers stood in ranks before each bar discharging the same rumba notes into a nocturnal landscape peppered with gawkers, honking horns, and car and motorcycle headlights. As he stepped over the rails to plunge into the ghastly solitude of Downtown, he could still hear a song: "Mbongo," or "Money," masterfully performed by Djo Mpoyi. Sanza felt an urge to return to the Post Office. But he took stock of himself and realized that he was too much a veteran of the street to be taking it up again. Quite apart from the fact that the mere sight of the grim structure might very well give him a stroke. A thousand thoughts in his head, a thousand thoughts in his cabeza . . .

He decided to head back to Kamalondo, to the Mambo de la Fête. Ways of life are changed by war. Meters are reset to zero and records set straight. War smashes or replaces one chaos by another, even more lamentatious. The Mambo had kept the same name, but entry was no longer reserved for any old patron. Bouncers armed with clubs discouraged the riffraff from daring to set foot inside. Flash cars, and even a limousine, rolled down the avenue. Nouveau-riche army generals wearing fur coats in the suffocating heat—to remind the passing indigent and their friends that it was their turn to reign—slaked their thirst out front of the frontage, laughing very loudly.

Money is a serious thing, especially in a province where the double whammy of a war and the collapse of the Union Minière had seen the gap between the wastrels and the rich of the last rains widen considerably. Sanza no longer recognized his town; his beautiful city had given him the slip. For the first time since he was born, he experienced a demented desire to line his pockets.

## 53. The fabulous destiny of Franz Baumgartner, or how to become a Zairian writer.

Luck is what counts in life.

As the rebels approached, we witnessed a stampede (in all but name) throughout the entire Republic. Half-empty cargo planes landed in the major conurbations and departed with people on board. At Ngobila port, whole families waited to cross the river and take refuge in Brazzaville, in the Congo next door. A long procession of cars idled at Kasumbalesa, on the border between Zaire and Zambia. Everyone was trying to save their skin. Embassies made a flurry of calls to their citizens to evacuate the country—those of France, Belgium, and the United States were particularly quick off the mark. Only the riffraff, that is to say those who were unable to procure themselves a ticket, stayed and stocked up on water and food to await the rebels. When it came to Franziskus, the Austrian Embassy took a personal interest.

"You must leave the country."

"I've got Zairian citizenship now."

"It doesn't matter. You're Austrian by birth."

"All the same, I'm not fleeing."

"You must go home."

Franz refused to get on the plane. He was the only White not to up and vanish. More than one resident of Lubumbashi was astonished at his behavior. People would applaud and congratulate him as they strolled down the street, moved by this act of solidarity; they would invite him on binges or to a card game at the Mambo, whereas only a few months before, his appearance in public was met with total indifference.

One postwar day, he was accosted by the new army, not very far from the Mambo. The soldier was one-third his age.

"Papers?"

He handed over his passport.

"This a joke?"

"No, that's my passport."

The young soldier was visibly perturbed; his expression that of someone who'd just missed his train and had a plane to catch:

"But you're white!"

"I know."

The soldier turned the document this way and that, attempted to decipher the name, scrutinized the photograph:

"You're white, with a White's name, and a passport of this country."

"Quick, kid, I've got to go."

The child soldiers were allergic. Most couldn't stand being taken for kids. They became irascible if you raised your voice, huffed, or boycotted their sometimes-excessive intrusions into your private life. Their trigger fingers were itchy indeed.

"Hey, are you really talking to me like that? We freed you from the Mobutu dictatorship and now you dare blackmail me!"

"Be quick, I'm in a hurry. You can see very well that . . . "

Back then, when a policeman or a soldier wanted to collar

you, he always found the knack. The young soldier continued to heft the passport wrathfully. He was thinking about how to nab Franz, who was shifting impatiently from foot to foot. The young man's face brightened:

"I'm arresting you! You have no authorization to stay in this country."

"You can see very well that this passport is in my name."

The soldier, taking his tenacity down a tad:

"And you can see very well that it was issued by the Republic of Zaire."

"So?"

"Zaire no longer exists. Mobutu's been gone for two months now and the country's already changed its name, if you didn't know."

"But you know very well that they haven't created the new passport yet."

"That's not my problem. I'm just a humble agent of enforcement. This is the Congo and you're wandering about with a Zairian passport."

"What nonsense is this? The Zairian currency is still in use. You refuse a Zairian passport, yet you take Zairian money!"

The child soldier, in a soft voice, content to see his trap close on Franziskus:

"Correction, sir. Money's not something one refuses."

Franz was detained in a cell Downtown that very evening.

Franz fair lost his temper with the prison guards.

"I want a bed, clean sheets, and a TV set. And a cell all to myself, while we're about it."

His fellow inmates, as well as the guards, burst into such fits of laughter they rolled around on the floor.

"This is not some fancy four-star joint."

"Even a hotel room has its price."

"Sir's got some cheek!"

He even refused to eat the traditional prison dish of rice and beans cooked all together in a pot, with no sugar, no salt, and certainly no palm oil. A week later, without them having buttered him up the ass, he slept on the bare stone floor like all of his companions in misery. Eventually he broke his silence.

"Some paper and a pen," he called out to one of the screws.

"Paper and a pen?" replied the latter, surprised.

"That's what I just told you."

"Have you become a writer?" he asked, amused, not believing that Franz was being quite sincere.

"Yeah, that's what I am."

"Well fancy that! Yesterday you were demanding a pallet, today paper, and tomorrow? You'll be asking us for a sewing machine at this rate!"

The guard ran to tell his colleagues about Franz's latest caprice. Raucous laughter could be heard from afar. He returned within the hour bearing a sheaf of paper. Franz sat down and began frenziedly scribbling. All of Angola seemed to have slammed back into his brain like a boomerang. Short of breath, sweating, he giggled, and meowed like a cat, as if he had a river in the belly, eyes fixed on the ceiling in the manner of the Madonna when she recounted her first years in Lunda Norte.

54. Archbishop Mukandila, otherwise called by his flock: Prophet to the Nations; Man by Will of the Lord; Special Envoy of the Holy Spirit to the Africans (and the Zairians in particular); Pillar of the Gospel in Central Africa; Descendant of Abraham, Isaac, and Jacob; Consecrated Evangelist; Thirteenth Apostle; Last African Prophet; Sower of the Good News; Destroyer of Night Wives and Husbands (those Libidinous Demons of Dream Time).

After waiting for three-quarters of an hour, a svelte young man, no doubt one of the bodyguards, came out to see Sanza. He beckoned to Pimples. To reach the archbishop's office, they traversed four hallways, the walls of which were covered with posters for evangelization and deliverance campaigns. On each of these placards the churchman had pride of place, attired in a white shirt with rolled up sleeves and a loud red tie, his face beaded with sweat in the manner of someone making a sustained effort. His grasped a mic in his left hand, his right outstretched toward the sky. In the background, serried ranks of believers in an attitude of worship. The photograph must have been taken in a stadium during a service. Stuck between two of the posters were a couple of photographs of a person who was either one of the archbishop's many followers or else the recipient of some miracle cure. The left-hand photo, in black and white, depicted the individual before his healing. His clothes were dirty and he was looking down, the hair on his sorry cabeza unkempt. The man carried a pair of crutches and was either lying on a stretcher or stuck in a wheelchair. The photographer had focused on this believer's disease, his handicap, his plain distress.

The one on the right, in color, showed the same person, likely after a deliverance ceremony. The man stood posed in a state of beatitude, his firm stance calling to mind that of a karateka, as if to prove to the world that the recovery had been most effective. Accompanying the right-hand photograph was a caption giving details of the deliverance. Scanning these images, one learned that Archbishop Mukandila healed sleeping sickness, dispelled family hexes, neutralized night wives and husbands, cast out singleton demons, relieved Alzheimer's, treated leprosy, mended marriages even when couples had been separated for a decade, and wiped out witchcraft.

The young man withdrew most expeditiously after whispering in the archbishop's ear.

"I receive by appointment only. They informed me that you were here. We are trying to ease our visitor policy even though we have our hands full. It won't be news to you that the population is suffering in this country. I refer not to material hardship, which afflicts all societies, but rather to vagaries of a spiritual nature. We strive to be even a little worthy of our mission."

He bade Sanza sit. The words that came out of his mouth were timed to the millisecond. The archbishop weighed every one of them, endeavoring to imbue each of his phrases with meaning. Sanza nearly got up and left. The man before him was the very embodiment of metamorphosis. The French that

Molakisi spoke was not great. His remarks always contained errors of conjugation and grammar. He groped for words when he talked and grew irritable when they failed him. But the man in front of Sanza displayed not a single one of these numerous shortcomings. What's more, he seemed to have aged twenty years. A dazzling baldness stretched right across his head, and a burgeoning paunch had made its appearance. Sanza again realized how important it was to earn a good living. Money fixes ugliness, or at least reduces it. Molakisi had become a handsome man. His nose had flattened. His exaggeratedly wide eyes, which the whole high school reproved, now made him more attractive. His thick arms and his chimpanzee's thorax, balanced by the rounded stomach, contributed serenely to his charm. No excessive virility in his aspect. The Molakisi speaking so sedately was not the one who fought six guys barechested, who never went anywhere without a pocketknife, who used foul language, and who slept on the ground.

Opposite him, Sanza seemed to have descended from another planet. He hadn't washed for three days. He was dusty from head to toe. He realized he was wearing a shirt frayed thin and a creased pair of pants yellowed with age and inordinately large. As if that wasn't enough, Sanza had slimmed right down and retained the scrawny body he had in high school. He looked neither young nor old. You could have stuck any age on him. He felt like a centenarian whereas he hadn't even reached his quarter century.

Molakisi didn't look at him. He trained his face at the ceiling as if reading his friend's past on an invisible screen.

"Brother in the Lord," he addressed him, "I see your pain.

You had a happy childhood. Parents at the Union Minière who broke their backs to get you into higher education. A waste. For a decent life was beyond your attainment, owing to demons embedded in your family tree for centuries. These demons have plugged every channel. Prosperity, health, marriage. No job application can succeed in such conditions. There is no substantial future in sight. What I observe, brother, is a putrid life, one bestrewn with pitfalls. The Lord opens the gates of heaven and bestows his blessing, but it cannot reach you, your family forestall it."

Sanza's face twitched. Memories streamed through his mind. He couldn't help but smile. But the archbishop continued the prophecy session:

"You are innocent, you know? You are reaping what your ancestors sowed, the curse extending, yea, unto the fourth generation. What I propose is a full unblocking session. We must unlock everything: finances, love, health."

He turned the pages of a diary that lay on his desk.

"Friday morning?"

"Friday?"

Molakisi, solemnly:

"Return here on Friday at ten AM for a deliverance prayer session. But we wouldn't wish to starve you; you are in poor enough health as it is. Might you be able to contribute one hundred dollars in order to participate in the Lord's work? Bring this small sum with you on Friday. Such an amount is insignificant compared with the wealth that awaits. We will unpadlock every door and you shall become a great man. Do you understand me?"

"Molakisi?"

Sanza was lost in his recollections and didn't know how the word escaped his mouth.

Molakisi started in his seat; he scrutinized Sanza:

"Does my face remind you of someone?"

"Aren't you Molakisi? From the Kamalondo district?"

He removed his glasses and searched his memories for where he had seen Sanza before. This sobriquet, "Molakisi," floated to the surface of his thoughts like a piece of detritus flung onto the beach by the waves. He was not expecting anyone to trot out his name in this city of Kolwezi, where he maintained no links whatsoever with the denizens of Lubumbashi, where everyone knew him for his deliverance campaigns, where he was respected and feted under the title of archbishop, and where his public appearances caused traffic jams.

"Are you a childhood friend? From high school?"

"Sanza."

Eyes wild, he banged fiercely on the table three times.

In the hallway, someone came running. It was the young man in charge of protocol:

"You wanted me, Archbishop Mukandila?"

Molakisi introduced Sanza to the young man to reassure him:

"This is Sanza, the eldest son of a close friend of mine. I have not seen him for years and I am overcome by his mere presence. These very eyes watched him grow up. He and my son, the one who's in the United States, they came of age together."

Molakisi was a first-class heel. Sanza was now no longer his younger brother; he'd given him the age of his children. Who were fictional, for sure. After the war, people, particularly those who roved from one region to another, doctored their résumés. Most were far from subtle about it, they outright changed their past.

"You may leave."

Once the young man had closed the door, Molakisi stood up, leaning on a crutch. That's when Sanza noticed that his right leg had been amputated just below the knee. He threw himself at Molakisi, who hugged him so tightly he nearly squeezed the breath from him.

"They told me you'd met your death in Lunda Norte."

"They told me you'd met your death on the frontline."

"Angola or the frontline, it's much of a muchness."

"An accident?"

Molakisi pulled himself together. It was not an appropriate question. Among the Zairians who'd stepped on an antipersonnel mine during the Angolan war, the luckiest devils were those who returned minus a limb.

Molakisi, vexed:

"Why did you come to see me? How did you track me down? I am quite dead, after all."

"Listen, Molakisi."

"I am not Molakisi anymore. I'm dead. You buried me, right?"

"Dead or not, this is a business thing."

Molakisi didn't want to hear it, he was adamant:

"When I took the decision to die, to contrive my own death, it was because I wanted to turn the page on Lubumbashi forever. I've gone straight. I earn a good living. So you can take your business . . . "

"You're scared, is that it? Look, it's about a money mill. Reliable guys, dependable. I've tried it myself. I'm busy getting the capital together to fund the project. Just think, a money mill! Dollars!

Molakisi's face lit up as soon as he heard the word. Sanza produced a ten-dollar bill. Molakisi grabbed it, sat back down, rubbed the note between his fingers, turned it over, then back again, sniffed it:

"I won't be involved in your racket, but money is something I never refuse."

## The Tempo

*(a penal poem)*

the Post Office forecourt
a reservoir of shattered
dreams
crumpled kids
kip
scorning the sky
mouths agape
eyelids singed
by the glue
their dreams
an ocean of incandescent images
they dance
until their backbones crack
the villain's dance
the dance of those who disdain cash
fling cash out the door
fling cash out the window
down the latrines
and into the sewers
kids, kids
they dance and they dance
the glorious villain's dance

# Author's Note

The Democratic Republic of the Congo, otherwise known as Congo-Kinshasa or the DRC, has had a series of names since its founding. Zaire is the name most befitting the atmosphere and the life stories of the characters in this text. The years of the Mobutu regime were filled with utopias, dreams, fantasies, and uncontrolled desires for social climbing, the quest for easy enrichment, and the profanation of the places of power. Among these phenomena were the immigration of Zairians to Angola during the civil war (as if their country didn't possess its own diamonds), thus boycotting the inherited borders of colonization; and the occupation of public spaces by street children. I dedicate this novel to each of them.

This is also an opportunity to pay my debts. A nod to my editor, Lise Belperron, for her patience and her eye for detail; to my friends Sayaka Osaki and Filip de Boeck, the numerous discussions with whom nurtured the character of the Madonna; to Ana Lanzas and Didier de Lannoy who believed in this text from its initial draft; to Jean Bofane and Marc de Gouvenain, who know why.

These pages were often written at night, lulled by the South African jazz of Dudu Pukwana, Mongezi Feza, Johnny Dyani,

Pinise Saul, Chris McGregor, and Hugh Masekela, and by the Zairian rumba of Papa Wemba, Tabu Ley, Camille Feruzi, Wendo Kolosoy . . . This novel belongs to them too.

# Translator's Note

I would like to express my gratitude to Nairi Martirosyan for her love and support, to Alex Lais for the fine coffee and intriguing encounters, to Michela Wrong for her wry, incisive writing about the Mobutu years, and to my colleague J. Bret Maney. And when I needed to get into the groove, Abeti Masikini, M'bilia Bel & L'Afrisa International, and Verckys & L'Orchestre Vévé were essential companions.

**Fiston Mwanza Mujila** was born in the Democratic Republic of Congo in 1981 and lives today in Austria. His debut novel, *Tram 83*, published in English in 2015 by Deep Vellum (translation by Roland Glasser), won the Etisalat Prize for Literature and the German International Literature Award, and was longlisted for the International Booker Prize and the Prix littéraire du Monde. In addition to the poetry collection *The River in the Belly* (published by Deep Vellum in 2021, translation by J. Bret Maney), he is the author of the poetry collections *Craquelures* (2011) and *Soleil privé de mazout* (2016), as well as three plays, *Et les moustiques sont des fruits à pépins* (2015), *Te voir dressé sur tes deux pattes ne fait que mettre de l'huile sur le feu* (2015), and *Zu der Zeit der Königinmutter* (2018). His writing responds to political turbulence in his native country and frequently foregrounds its debt to jazz.

**Roland Glasser** grew up in London, studied French and Theatre Studies at Aberystwyth University (Wales) and Film and Dramatic Arts at the University of Caen (Normandy), before spending a decade living in Paris, where he developed a successful career in translation, literary editing, and theater lighting design. His translation of Adéline Dieudonné's bestselling *Real Life* was shortlisted for the Scott-Moncrieff Prize. He has contributed articles and essays to a range of publications and is a co-founder of The Starling Bureau, a London-based collective of literary translators.